In Search of Madness

By

David Owain Hughes

A HellBound Books Publishing LLC Book
Austin TX

David Owain Hughes

**A HellBound Books LLC
Publication**
Copyright © 2021 by HellBound Books Publishing LLC
All Rights Reserved

Cover and art design
By Kevin Enhart
For HellBound Books Publishing LLC

www.hellboundbookspublishing.com

Other David Owain Hughes Titles
<u>Novels, Novellas and Short Story Collections:</u>

All-Wound Up
Wind-Up Toy
Wind-Up Toy: Broken Plaything
Wind-Up Toy: Chaos Rising
White Walls and Straitjackets
Escapees and Fevered Minds
Choice Cuts
Walled In
Man-Eating Fucks
Man-Eating Fuckers
Man-Eating Fucks: The Legacy
The Rack & Cue
Collision Course
Granville
Home Improvements
Psychological Breakdown
Brain Damaged
Puckered
Cold Cocked

<u>Anthologies:</u>

Shadows and Teeth Vol.3
Trapped Within
Hell of a Guy
Unleashing the Voices
Rejected for Content Vol. 4, 5 & 6
Crossroads in the Dark Vol.1 & 2
Fifty Shades of Slay
How to Cook a Baby
Madame Movora's Tales of Terror
Big Book of Bootleg Horror Vol. 1, 2 & 3
Shopping List
Depraved Desires
Easter Eggs and Bunny Boilers
Bah! Humbug!
Slashing Through the Snow
VS Vol. 1 & 2
Black Candy
Into the Abyss

<u>Compiled & Edited Anthologies:</u>

What Goes Around
Man Behind the Mask
Fuck the Rules

David Owain Hughes

Contents:

Foreword

There's no beating about the bush with David Owain Hughes. His character, much like his writing, is unapologetic in its determination and salaciousness. It's all upfront with Hughes — a rarity in this technological age where social media is a prominent unavoidable beast in communicating in personal and professional worlds. Folk are agonisingly image-conscious and fearfully filtered; it can be challenging to differentiate authenticity from a marketing ploy of selectively engineered character. *Where does reality end and fiction begin?*

The social media dilemmas are no different amongst the (at times) dog-eat-dog writing community. It seems the days of the reclusive, introverted writer (no matter how much many of us may long for that) are long gone thanks to the World Wide Web. We must appreciate how remarkable the ease of networking can be digitally. Though it may be easier to connect, finding the right connections can be challenging. And I don't mean for notoriety or being 'discovered'; it's like with any community – finding genuine affinities in this messy world of disconnection and, of course, weeding out those goddam unsolicited dick pics! *Yes, whichever side you're on, and we all have one — you know what I'm talking about.* Apologies, dear reader, for my tangent and to the point; this is how I met Hughes (DP free, thankfully!) — the wonderful World Wide Web. And it's for such happenings that I appreciate the complex nature of social media.

There's no act with Hughes. He puts out much of what the man himself is, wearing all his hats with fierce pride, his appetite for grabbing life (and writing) by the balls is plain in his words and be warned — he uses teeth!

His fiction is gutsy, gritty, littered with seeds of perversion and madness; it's creative and points to stark truths many readers can relate to but would be terrified to utter aloud. Yes, I see you… and the quiet realisation, as your optic nerves, shoot his devilish prose into your pulsing grey matter of, *fuck this guy knows the score,* and he's pouring it all out — salty, bloody, bitter, and sweat all over these pages. An open book that you can't stop reading; *are you consuming it, or is it consuming you?* There's a darkness in his writing that grinds right into the uncomfortable centre of humanity and truths we run from. Hughes bolts screaming — an insatiable mad man — straight at those dark corners (and you, the reader), arms flailing with a fierce determination of the worlds he's going to thrust right into your squirmy, pulsing frontal lobes, so it embeds there, seeds of his horror spindling out of control like an invasive crop.

Maybe you've just run into one of his shorts by chance as I did — *dear innocent reader, hold onto your pants!*

The first piece I read of Hughes was a short story featured in KJK Publishing's 'The Best of Indie Horror', called 'Suicide Shagger'. The skilful weaving of dark subject matter and gallows humour was unforgettable and had me googling him for more.

A few months later, we shared pages in a couple of anthologies and got chatting through mutual writing circles. One thing led to another, and we decided to mess around with some words. Having never co-written anything before, I was a touch reluctant, maybe even insecure, given my admiration for Hughes' style, but he's a persuasive character. A few wicked little drabbles and short stories were born — all of which were accepted into their target publications — a successful collaboration. I've also had the pleasure of editing Hughes. Editing the work of fellow writers can be a strange sort of detached intimacy, an oxymoron in which both are essential to the process. One must be objective and simultaneously connect with the writing, making it more accessible and impactful. Dredging right down into the nitty-gritty of each line of the prose, getting intimate with the very essence of a writer's style comes with that territory. With that in mind, it was my privilege and pleasure to present this collection.

The works contained here span his career; you'll be treated to a novella, short stories and drabbles, some of which have appeared elsewhere and others have never been printed before. You'll discover that no matter the size of the piece, Hughes knows how to pack a punch. This writer has a lot to say. His writing style isn't just witty — it's intelligent and provocative. Each story is more than meets the eye. If you have the mind to read, then revisit — I guarantee you'll find something new each time. This one is after the brains of his audience.

So, whether you're already a fan or this is your first time delving between the raving Welshman's sheets, knuckle down — this guy kicks.

—Natasha Sinclair 09/2021
Author & Editor, ClanWitch.com

David Owain Hughes

In Search of Madness

Bastard Bunny

Same fucking charade, every fucking year! he thought, looking up at the suit that was hanging on the wardrobe. Well, not this fucking Easter. They can all fuck off!

"Henry, do hurry down!" he heard Henrietta call from the dining room. "We're all dying to see you in your pretty getup."

I'm sure you are.

He could hear them chuckling at his misfortune.

"Poor Henry. The chap does it every year!" he overheard John Green say, followed by a horsy laugh from his wife, Charlie.

"Nonsense! Henry loves it," Henrietta said, snorting a laugh.

Bastards! "I'll be down in a moment, dear!" Henry called, trying to remain calm. But it was proving difficult. All week people had asked and ribbed him about Easter: "Will you be dressing as Mr. Winkle Whiskers this year?" or "I can't wait to see your floppy ears and squishy tail, Henry!"

"Ugh! It's enough to make a fucking saint swear," he uttered. A tic had developed at the side of his head on Monday and had gradually worsened as the week wore on. Good Friday, he thought, continuing to look up at the outsized bunny costume his wife made him wear every Easter without fail.

"The children love it, dear!" she'd coo.

Little fucking monsters! I hope they choke on their mini eggs, or whatever it is they eat these days.

Once dressed in the atrocity, she would make him attend the annual church fete and run an Easter egg hunt for the children.

It drove him nuts.

Some of the younger children behaved, but not the older ones. They would often belittle him or throw eggs at him – the chocolate and hardboiled kind.

It was a grown man's worst nightmare.

It was a minefield of snot, taunts, goo-goo-ga-gas, chocolate bunnies and humiliation; a wet dream for a perverted, sadomasochist fuck-sack who has a tendency for young flesh.

Last year, he recalled, some shithead dumped a spoonful of ice cream down the trapdoor of my suit. The dollop of chocolate was wedged against my anus, before making a cold, slippery path towards my ankle. How the people laughed when they saw me shaking my leg like I was having a fucking fit. Then, as if things couldn't get worse, out pops the hard scoop of ice cream.

"Ha-ha, old man Henry's shit himself!" some heinous twerp had bellowed.

"Even Henrietta laughed," he muttered with clenched teeth. His jaw ached. "Well, 'Old Man Henry' has a few surprises of his own this year."

He stared into the rabbit's glassy, hazel eyes. "Mr. Winkle Whiskers, my arse! Bastard Bunny, more like."

The bunny's head looked ridiculous. The ears were pink and white, with one flopped over. The other stood stiff, like a defiant hard-on. The nose was minuscule, with huge, cartoon-like whiskers sprouting from either side. However, one set was longer than the other due to Henry being held down one year by teenagers and having them snipped.

The thought made his blood boil.

Some of those teenagers' parents were currently sat in his dining room, awaiting a feast he was preparing.

"Oh, they're only children, Henry. Don't take it to heart," Tim Nettles had said of the incident. "Boys will be boys!" Emma, his wife, had chirped.

"And nutters will be nutters!" he said. Looking over his shoulder, he saw his bolt-action shotgun lying on his bed. A box of cartridges stood by its side. The gleaming barrel and hypnotic walnut stock were inviting.

Turning back to the suit, he grinned. "This will be the best Easter ever!"

Whooping, he stood and grabbed the costume.

"I might as well give them one last chuckle this Good Friday," he said, a laugh bursting from him.

Throwing the bunny suit onto the bed, he started to undress. He slipped out of his black shoes and trousers before removing his black tunic, clerical collar and white shirt.

Who'd be a fucking vicar anyway?! I've devoted my life to a false god and the worst piece of fiction ever written.

"Hen-ry!" his wife bellowed. "Hurry down, will you?"

"Coming, dear!" he said, before muttering, "Fucking whore."

Naked, he looked at his scrawny arms, legs and body. It disgusted him. Pushing the thoughts aside, he stepped into the Bastard Bunny costume and zipped it up. Before putting the head on, he glanced in the full-length mirror.

I look hideous. On the chest was a giant carrot being munched by a baby rabbit; a small basket of eggs stood by its side. I wouldn't make a child dress like this, let alone a man in his early forties.

Putting the head on, he then picked up the shotgun and shells and walked out of the bedroom door. As he crossed the hallway, he stopped at the room where his girls – Lucy, seven, and Tina, eight – slept. The room also held a Moses basket for Jacob, his baby boy.

Looking into the room, he remembered how the girls had laced his costume with itching powder three Easters ago, which Henrietta had organized. The year before that, they'd put ants and bugs in Bastard Bunny's head, which they had orchestrated themselves.

He was the village idiot, not a man of the cloth, a man who should be respected and somewhat feared.

He gripped the gun fiercely.

Well, that will soon change! A crimson mist rolled over his vision. All he could hear were the screams of the dead and dying. There's only so much pushing a man can take.

Looking away from the Moses basket, he pocketed the shells and hid the weapon down the front of his costume. Filling his lungs, he started downstairs.

"Shh-shh!" he heard Henrietta say. A few titters were stifled. "He's coming. Christine, get the camera ready!"

Poor lambs. They have no idea, do they? Twelve hungry bellies are about to get filled with fish, roast and buckshot!

When he got to the bottom step, he took another deep breath. Just beyond the door to his left, he could hear them whisper and giggle.

Huffing, he bowed his head and shuffled through the door.

A wave of laughter crashed against him.

Beneath his face covering, Henry's cheeks burned. He'd never been good around a lot of people in close quarters, especially when dressed like a fool.

I've always loathed fancy dress, which Henrietta knows. She loves pushing my buttons.

"Do the dance!" Christine encouraged him.

He drank her in. She was a fat, fifty-something slut who wore skirts way too short for her age, leaving her stocking tops visible for all to see.

No wonder that no-good husband of yours left you! Henry thought, trying to avoid the sight of her thick thighs. Even with a gin-soaked brain, he could see through your lies and knew you were screwing every Tom, Dick, and Harry! Well, you're probably not interested in Tom or Harry.

The camera flash partially blinded him as he hopped, bounced and danced the dance of Mr. Winkle Whiskers. Everyone whooped, cheered and laughed as he made a complete spectacle of himself.

That's right… laugh it up!

"Say it!" Catherine Goodson chimed. "I want to hear you say it, Henry!"

"Yes, please do!" her husband added.

"Are you ready, children?" Henry said in a goofy voice, causing a hush to fall over his flock. "I can't hear you!"

Some of his audience members screamed "Yes!"

"Then here comes Mr. Winkle Whiskers with his basket of eggs!" Henry said, hopping around the room in a crazed fashion again. "Follow the rabbit, children! Boing, boing, boing."

"Ha-ha, oh my!" Henrietta laughed. "Look at him, girls!"

"He's silly!" Tina said.

"What a fool," Lucy agreed.

"Mr. Winkle Whiskers has buried his eggs in his cabbage patch. Come and find them, children!" Henry screeched, which was a full-stop to his humiliation, as he bunny-bounced into the kitchen and out of view.

"Ha-ha, what a jester!" Henry heard one of his guests say.

"I know," Henrietta said. "It's nice having a man in his place."

"I need to get my Simon trained," Beth Gibson added.

"Best of luck!" he shot back.

Motherfuckers. All of them!

Taking the head of his costume off, Henry peeked back through the kitchen door and addressed his twelve guests. "Could you take a seat at the table, please?"

His wife perched herself at the head of the impressive dining table, whilst their daughters took up seats on either side of her.

Turning his back, he opened the oven and removed the six large bass from the oven. After seasoning the fish with cyanide, salt and pepper, he whipped the large tray into the dining room and told his guests to dig in.

"The roast and vegetables will follow shortly!" he said, rushing back into the kitchen.

Whilst opening the oven he noticed the radio. "Hmm, why not!" He turned it on, and the room was instantly filled by a band he didn't recognize. They were singing a song about breaking the law. "Catchy!"

Removing the roast, he put it onto a platter, covered it with a lid, and returned to the dining room. He noticed everyone had started eating the fish except his wife and daughters. A smile played across his face as he put the platter down in the center of the table.

"Mm! Smells scrummy!" Charlie said.

"Oh, it sure does!" Henrietta agreed.

"Voila!" Henry said, whisking the lid off the roast.

"Jesus!" Christine said.

"Not quite!" Henry said.

"Jacob!" Henrietta screamed on seeing her son's tiny, smoldering body. It was charcoaled.

When Henry put a butcher knife to it, chunks of flesh fell away, causing a scattering of black dust on the white tablecloth. "Hmm, I may have left it in the oven a tad too long!" Henry said. "Sorry, folks."

To his side, John Green fainted. His face smashed through his plate and slammed against the table. Blood dribbled out of his mouth, along with a few broken teeth and chunks of china.

"Oh, dear!" Henry said.

"You sick bastard!" Simon said, getting up from his seat. But then he started to violently cough blood and vomit.

"Is the bass not agreeing with you, Simple Simon?!"

"You…Ugh!" Simon collapsed to his knees, keeling over. His bowels had discharged in a hostile way, excrement seeping through his trousers and coating the carpet.

The other guests started screaming and crying.

"Don't go, people! What about dessert?" Henry said, removing the bolt-action from inside his costume. Slamming a cartridge in, he cocked the weapon and fired.

The round blasted into Christine's flabby gut; the wide spray of ball bearings tearing through furniture, plates, and picture frames, removing half of Beth Gibson's face.

She hit the deck with an earth-shattering scream and tried to hold what was left of her face together.

Blood splashed across the table and erupted up a wall.

With a fresh cartridge loaded and cocked, he blew a hole through Catherine's neck before unloading a lucky round into her husband's crotch. Mr. Goodson's pulped privates tore through his anus and smeared a nearby wall.

Unloading, Henry slammed another shell into the gun.

Behind him, John was starting to come around. "Argh!" he screamed, picking shards of glass from his face.

Without a moment's hesitation, Henry put the muzzle of the shotgun to the man's head and fired. It blew apart like a ripe pumpkin hitting the floor. Portions of brain and skull matter splattered the table, floor, wall and Henry.

***

When the dust finally settled, Henry made his way around the fallen bodies and clubbed the wounded to death. His kill count numbered nine.

Henrietta and the girls were missing.

Loading a fresh round into his gun, he cocked the weapon fiercely.

He knew they hadn't escaped the house, because he'd made sure every door and window had been locked and bolted.

Entering the hallway, he looked at himself in the mirror. His face and costume were plastered in blood, with chunks of brain clinging to his bald head. Floorboards creaked above him.

"Are you ready, children?" he screamed manically. "Looks like 'Old Man Henry' gets to have his own Easter hunt this year!" He climbed the stairs to the second floor, eager to find the children.

Cadair Idris

"Anyone got a creepy story?" Geraint asked, looking around the campfire. The faces of his friends looked eerie in the shadows that the firelight cast; some of the shadows danced along the trees, creating beautiful, naked squaws in his mind's eye.

Stunning, he thought.

It had taken them less than four-and-a-half hours to travel from Cardiff to Dolgellau, a small town in the north of Wales. Their destination: The National Park of Snowdonia, home to the mountain known as Cadair Idris.

"Ugh, you and your creepy tales, Geraint!" Amy scoffed, rolling her eyes.

"What's the matter? Scared?" he teased, his mind clear of naked American Indian women as he dragged his eyes off the trees. He looked at Amy directly.

"Tut, grow up, dude!" she said, putting her arm around Josh, who was her long-term, rugby-playing boyfriend. He was built like a brick shithouse and could apparently bench press an impressive 235.

"I'm up for a creepy tale!" Josh said, grinning. In the poor light, his glowing teeth looked like polished tombstones.

"Josh!"

"What, baby?" he cooed.

"Don't fucking encourage the weirdo!" Amy said. Across from them, Dylan sniggered. "It's not funny, Dylan!"

"Sorry," he said.

"C'mon on, Amy, it could be fun," Cerys said.

"Yeah, Amy – come on!" John – Cerys' fiancé – joined in.

"What do you think, Emma?" Dylan asked the mousy girl at his side. Although very quiet, and not well liked by certain people within the group, she had been brought along for her excellent navigational and map reading skills.

"Yeah, sounds good," she squeaked, immediately looking down at the floor.

"I can see I'm outnumbered!" Amy said, glaring at Emma.

"No need to be like that, babe."

"Be quiet, Josh. I wasn't talking to you."

"Awesome! So, who's got one?"

"I assumed you had one, Geraint," Dylan said.

"Well, err… Nah, I don't think I do. Sorry!"

"What a genius!" Cerys said, laughing. This caused John to join in, who had opened a can of beer and a pack of jerky.

"Want one, love?" he asked his fiancée.

"Mm, yeah!"

"What about you, Dylan? You're normally a fountain of useless information… Don't you know anything about this mountain we currently have our arses camped on?" Josh asked.

"Will you stop encouraging this nonsense? You know I scare easy!"

"Wasn't that the point of coming here?" Geraint said.

"I thought it was so Dylan could get some inspiration?" Amy asked.

"Well, yeah, there is that…" Dylan said.

"What else is there?"

"There's more to this place than meets the eye," Dylan started, looking at each of his friends in turn. "I told you all that this would be an inspirational trip, but I left out the myths and legends that surround these mountains."

"Oooo, scary!" John said, snorting a laugh.

"Ha-ha!" Emma giggled, giving John a playful thump in his ribs with her elbow.

"I'm being serious. There's been some strange shit said about this mountain," Dylan said, his face taking on a hard edge.

"Such as?" Geraint asked.

"I'll get to that."

"What does 'Cadair Idris' translate to in English?" Josh asked.

"Idris' Chair."

"Who the fuck is Idris when he's at home?"

"My grandmother's next-door neighbor was called Idris. Nice chap, too. He claimed he once died on an operating table when the doctors were working on him," Amy chirped in.

"And?" Josh asked.

"Apparently, he left his body and saw a light… He even claimed to watch the doctors as they worked to resuscitate him."

"Bullshit!" Geraint said.

Cerys and Dylan laughed.

"Why would a sweet old guy lie about something like that?" Amy snapped.

"She's got a point," John said, gobbling down more of his beer and jerky.

More sniggers erupted from around the campfire, which crackled and spat wood chippings. Somewhere in the distance, an owl hooted.

"That reminds me," Geraint said. "Have you heard the one about the two owls playing pool…"

Dylan groaned and rolled his eyes, "Nooooo…" he said.

"Ha-ha! Oh, God, here he goes!" Josh said.

"When one of the owls took his shot and missed, he said to the other, 'Two-hits-to-you!'"

"Ugh!" John groaned, throwing a piece of jerky at his unfunny friend. "Someone pass me a needle and thread!"

"Why?" Cerys asked.

"So, I can sew my sides up from where they have split from laughing!"

"Ha!" Geraint bellowed.

"Can we hear about Idris?" Emma asked.

"For fuck's sake!" Amy exploded. "I'm turning in if you all start talking about ghosts and shit!"

"Don't be a baby," Josh told her. "I want to know about Idris, too. I love hearing shit about urban legends, or whatever they're called."

"Me too," Geraint said.

"Well, if I may proceed, I will tell you all about Idris and his chair," Dylan said.

"That's it, I'm off to bed!" Amy said.

"Sit down, babe. I'll protect you," Josh said, flexing his mighty arms. His rippling biceps would make Sly Stallone blush.

"Fine, but if I get scared, my arse is out of here."

"Wing us a beer, Josh?" Dylan asked.

"Sure," he said, tossing one over the roaring fire.

After taking the top off his beer, he then waited for it to go quiet around the campfire. "Before I tell you about the camping party that went missing around here twenty years ago, I firstly want to tell you about Idris' Chair. From what I remember reading, it's described as an ancient fearsome-looking mountain that looms threateningly over the surrounding landscape. Or something along those lines, anyway. The summit where we're all heading in the morning is dubbed Penygadair…"

"Cut it out with the Welsh, Welshie!" Geraint said, laughing.

"Okay, it's called Top of the Chair, dickhead," Dylan said, grinning.

"What about Idris? I can learn about the frigging mountain from the pamphlet I picked up," Geraint butted in, producing the aforementioned leaflet.

"Shh!" Josh snapped. "Let the man set the scene."

Dylan nodded in appreciation before taking a sip of beer and starting again. "Legend has it, some of the lakes surrounding this mountain are bottomless; that professional divers have tried and failed to find their beds. Some divers have been reported as never coming back from their plunge…"

"That's pretty creepy," John admitted.

"There's more," Dylan said. "Tons of legends surround Idris' Chair, and not just the bottomless lakes. Apparently, anyone who sleeps on the mountain's slopes alone will supposedly awaken either a madman or a poet. The tradition of sleeping on the summit apparently stems from bardic traditions… that poets would sleep on the mountain to help their muse."

"Dylan, you didn't drag us all the way up here to try that, did you?!" Cerys asked.

"No!" he barked. "I know my writing has gone a bit awry of late, but… no…"

"Fuck me, you're like Wikipedia!" Josh said. "Tell us about Idris."

Regaining his composure, Dylan spoke. "So, you all want to know who, or what, Idris is, right?"

"Yeah!" someone called.

"Idris was a giant Welsh warrior. And, in any Welsh historical book you read, it will tell you that he was skilled in poetry and philosophy. That this is his mountain. He protects it."

"I've heard it's supposed to be Arthur's Chair, as in King Arthur?" Cerys said.

"Where did you hear that?" John asked.

"History class, I think," she said, giggling. "Beer, please?"

"Of course," he said, handing her one.

"You're not wrong, Cerys. Somewhere along the line the legend got mixed up, but it's Idris' Chair, not Arthur's."

"So, you're telling us that a poetry-loving giant, who was also a Celtic warrior, used to stalk this mountain?" Geraint said, trying to keep a smile from his face.

"Yeah, why?"

"Well, it's not very fucking creepy, is it?"

"I have to agree," Amy said.

"The part about the bottomless lakes was pretty fucking eerie," Josh said. "You think that's true, especially about the divers?"

"Fairly sure it is. I've seen stories about it online."

"Look!" Geraint yelled at the top of his voice. "Zombie divers!"

"Argh!" Cerys bellowed in mock terror.

"They're coming to get you, Barbara!" John piped up.

Cerys laughed, as did Josh.

Even Emma managed a snigger.

"Yeah, yeah, laugh it up… But I haven't told you about the Wild Hunt yet," Dylan said.

"Oh, great. Now you're going to tell us about a bunch of dickheads who dress up in red coats and hunt foxes with packs of dogs!" Geraint joked.

A few more sniggers burst out around the crackling fire. Thick, black smoke drifted up to the cloudless sky, which was peppered with bright, flickering stars.

The distant owl hooted once more.

A branch snapped.

Leaves crunched.

"Is someone watching us?" Emma asked. "I heard something…"

"Oh, shut up," John said. "If there is, it's probably Jason Voorhees. He's the hockey-masked killer that stalks teens in the woods, right?"

"Yeah, hotshot," Geraint said. "But this is Wales, not Crystal-fucking-Lake!"

"Tell us about the Wild Hunt, Dylan," Josh said.

"The Wild Hunt truly is fascinating, and scary. The Wild Hunt doesn't just take place here, but all over Europe. Once a year, mythical creatures and beings gather with dogs and go chasing through the wintry night skies, hoping to sweep up living souls caught in their hunt. If they do happen to catch some, then they are taken back to the Otherworld."

"All right! This is more like it," Geraint said.

"The Otherworld," Dylan continued, "is said to be a paradise – a Garden of Eden, if you will – but that's a lie. The Otherworld is a sort of Hell, and just like the Hell we all know about, it too, is guarded by hounds, or Hell Dogs. Their bodies and faces are completely white, with specks of red coloring found on the tips of their ears. White and red – these are traditional Celtic colors. The white represents a spiritual entity, whilst the red signals death. These hounds, these dogs, have a more specific name, and that name is Cwn Annwn, which translates to the Hounds of Annwn."

"What's Annwn?" Cerys asked, her eyes transfixed on Dylan.

"Annwn is the Otherworld where living souls get dragged to."

"That's fucking trippy!" Geraint said. "Is there more?"

"Yes. The hounds are usually released from Annwn by Arawn: King of the Otherworld. The hounds' sole purpose in the Wild Hunt is to chase down wrongdoers, but they will take anyone they can find, and they don't give up until their prey is chased into the ground.

"It is said that the Hunt takes place on specific nights of the year, such as Christmas and St David's Day… But I'm sure Arawn can let his hounds free whenever he feels like it," Dylan said, smiling. The group around the fire were silent. Before he lost them, Dylan pushed forward with his story.

"It's also been stated that the hounds are accompanied by Mallt-Y-Nos, which means Matilda of the Night."

Dylan's smile grew wider. Nobody uttered a word – they were captivated. He didn't know if any of what he said was on the money, but it was fun. Most of the stuff he was saying had come from books and sites online. He loved this kind of shit. Hell, he made (or at least tried making) a living from spinning yarns.

Authors – they're just professional liars.

"Mallt, or Matilda, is said to be a fearsome old hag who looks over the hounds as they hunt. It is said that she drives the pack of nine onwards by shrieking and wailing at them. Her cries in the night are supposed to be malicious and immoral, and if she catches a living person, she rips their soul from their body and feasts on it."

Someone gasped.

"Cool!" Geraint uttered.

"Who was this hag?" Josh asked, his curiosity getting the better of him.

"That's right, but this particular story caught my eye, as a party of ten just vanished."

"Ten?" Geraint said, all but shouting.

"That's right. Just like us, they were up here to explore the mountain, but were never seen again. Locals reported hearing the howls of dogs, and that they could have been attacked by wild animals. Also, back then, there used to be a hospital for the criminally insane in Dorgellau, leading others to think a patient may have escaped. But the most interesting theory of all is that Idris snatched them. That he swept them into one of his giant hands and carried them off. Maybe, just maybe, he took them to the Otherworld after a night of hunting!"

"Right, that's it! I'm off to bed," Amy said, getting up and stomping off to her tent, which was less than ten feet away.

"Baby, wait up!" Josh said, going after her.

"I guess the party train has come to the end of the line," Geraint said, also getting up to leave for his tent.

"Great tale, Dylan!" John said.

"Agreed," Cerys said, before turning to John. "Come on, let's go to bed." Yawning, she cuddled into her man's chest.

"Okay, love," he said, rubbing her back.

"Mm, that's nice."

"Yeah, get some rest. We have a long trek ahead of us," Dylan said.

"What about the fire?" Emma asked.

"No harm in letting it burn out," he said. "Besides, I'm going to stay up for a little bit longer. I want to finish my beer."

Before he knew it, John, Cerys, Geraint and Emma had all scuttled off to their respective tents. He could hear sounds of frolicking coming from Josh and Amy's, causing him to smile and shake his head. "Dirty bastards," he muttered. In my voyeuristic days, I probably would have crept up to the tent to get a glimpse of them rocking the Kasbah, he thought, listening to Amy's soft moans of pleasure. Never mind. I'll just store the sounds in my Wank-Bank! If this lot knew how much of a sex-starved perv I am, then they wouldn't want to bother with me ever again. But then again, it's probably not going to matter after tonight…

He turned his attention to Emma's tent. Her camp-light was on inside, which cast her shadow on the thin fabric walls. Asking her along was ingenious, he thought. The girl had come across as surprised when he'd asked her.

She was his friend and his friend alone: Emma didn't really know any of the others, even though she went to university with them. Outside of school, they didn't want to know her, apart from Dylan.

He'd once loved her. A long time ago, but she had rejected his advances on more than one occasion. Somehow, they had managed to remain friends. Or so she thought. He only kept her as a 'friend' as she was a virgin, and her being just that was integral to his plan.

Virgin.

The word made his dick twitch, and his knees go slightly weak.

The beer helped lube his drying lips.

If everything goes to plan, then the virgin bitch will be sacrificed for my greater good.

Movement from within her tent caused him to look with more focus. She was undressing. First her jumper, followed by her bra and trousers. The light sought out every glorious curve her body had to offer.

"You've been hiding one hell of a figure under those dark, hide-me-from-existence clothes, Emma. Wow. I never knew. Had I known, I probably wouldn't…" Yes, you would. Now stop it, he scolded himself, or she's never going to trust you. The thought of what he had planned made his dick shrink.

No, I can't…

The light in Emma's tent went dark.

So did the one in John and Cerys', along with Geraint's.

Josh and Amy's hadn't a light to begin with, but he could still hear their moans and gasps.

"He's not half giving her one!" he whispered, taking another glug of beer. It was still pretty much ice-cold. The bottle was sweating water and thin chunks of ice. When it was empty, he got up and went over to the cooler and grabbed a second and third.

Pointless making another trip, when I can grab a couple now, he thought.

Sitting down again, he let his mind wander.

The night air was chilly, but carried with it a certain amount of warmth, which was a bit odd for the time of year. "Possibly an Indian Summer heading our way," he uttered. "Can't say I'm surprised – we didn't have much of a summer."

With the empty beer bottle by his side, he took the top off the second and started to guzzle it. It tasted fantastic. He wasn't much of a drinker when he was at home or at his desk, but when he was away from that engulfing feeling of creativity, he could relax.

Of late, the writing wasn't going too well – as one of the other members of his party had pointed out. After having great success at being published three times last year, the words had started drying up.

At first, it was just poetry – nothing rhymed. Nothing connected. Ideas wilted.

After turning to fiction in the hope of a creative sanction and some inspiration, it too started to fail him after a handful of short stories and a novella were written.

Dylan couldn't understand it.

Before his pool of imaginative prowess had become a barren wasteland, he'd been turning project after project out. He'd been able to give up a day job and live off his works (plus a gig as a journalist).

Even the journalistic jobs dried up, what with magazines and papers going down in flames to the poor economy.

It was depressing.

All these depressing thoughts were causing a hiatus in his creative impetus. It was also causing a knock-on effect, because without words, he'd have to work full-time in a 'regular' job, which perturbed him.

He didn't want to be like the average Joe.

Dylan, unlike the others, didn't attend university. He dropped out after his writing took off. He also didn't have rich parents or a dead grandmother with an expensive house to sell.

It was him against the world.

If only I had a sugar mamma, he thought. Or a girlfriend to help support me… He again looked over at Emma's tent.

That ship had long sailed.

Besides, that's not the real reason you're here, and you know it. So, stop it.

Could I try and go that route once again?

No, impossible. She rejected me. I know what I have planned for her, he thought, looking down at the knife sheathed at his hip. It's the only way to bring the creativity back…

Possibly.

I have no way of knowing for sure.

Perhaps I should kill them as they sleep? His mind raced, causing him to feel dizzy.

No! I can't, he almost yelled, but managed to keep his temper under control.

Then what the hell am I going to do? I must get Emma away from them somehow. Asking so many of them to tag along was a mistake, he thought.

He took four rapid gulps of beer.

I could just forget the whole fucking thing. I don't need this pressure! Shaking his head, he looked up at the moon. What the fuck have I done? I'm going to have to kill them… unless I can lure her away.

What about witnesses? I'll have to keep someone alive! Fuck!

After swallowing the remainder of his second beer, Dylan threw the bottle into the air. It crashed against the floor in the near distance.

Popping the cap off the third, he started to guzzle.

The beer would help him gain the courage he needed to carry out his plan.

It would seem like madness to others, but not Dylan. He had to get his creative prowess back. Without it, he was nothing, and it was driving him to the brink of insanity.

Putting his beer down, he pricked his ears.

Soft snores were coming from the tents, including John and Amy's.

It was hard keeping a smile off his face.

To be sure, he stood and walked over to the canvas homes.

With all the caution in the world, he raised the zipper on Amy and John's tent. Even in the poor light, he could see they were fast asleep. He then checked on Cerys and John, before looking in on Emma.

They were all out of it.

But before he could get to Geraint, the guy came out and caught Dylan skulking around the camp.

"Hey, what's up, Dylan?"

"Huh?"

"Have you lost something?"

"Oh, err, yeah… You haven't seen my wallet anywhere, have you?"

"Shit, did you drop it out here?"

"Possibly, yeah. What are you doing back up? Can't sleep?"

"Nah, I needed a leak, man. Enjoying the beer?" Geraint asked, smiling.

"Oh, yeah. I'm not ready for sleep."

When Geraint turned his back to lean against a tree, Dylan crept up on him whilst slowly drawing his knife.

The perfect opportunity…

"Oh, fuck… that's so nice!" Geraint cried out when his piss started gushing out in a hot, steamy jet. The sound of it hitting rocks, leaves and bark seemed decibels louder than it should have been.

When Dylan was close enough to punch his knife into the base of Geraint's neck, a sound coming from the distance stopped him.

"What the hell was that?" Geraint asked, zipping up and turning to face Dylan, who had already put his knife back in its leather sheath. "Is someone crying in the woods? It could be a woman… Or worse, a child!" Geraint walked from the tree. "Hello?" he called. "Is anyone out there?"

"Shh!" Dylan said.

"What?"

"Maybe alerting them to our presence isn't the wisest of moves!"

"They could be hurt, man!"

"What if they aren't and decide to hurt us?"

"Don't be a moron! You've watched and read too much shit, Dylan. This isn't one of your stories!"

In that moment, Dylan had never felt such rage. His hand closed tightly around the shaft of his knife. He felt as though he could quite easily kill Geraint in a frenzied stabbing, and not bat an eyelid.

But he didn't.

Through deep breaths, he kept his composure.

The sound came again, but now it was closer.

Then closer still.

"What the hell is it?" Geraint asked.

Branches snapped.

Foliage shook.

"I have no idea, but it sounds like it's coming this way…"

"We should wake the others!" Geraint said.

"No, I… Jesus!" Dylan yelled, feeling a hand touch his shoulder. "Did you have to fucking creep up on us like that, Josh?"

"Ha-ha, you should see your faces!" Josh said. "I wish I had my camera. What are you two benders doing creeping around out here? Not touching dicks, are you?"

"No, we ain't, arsehole," Geraint said. "Can't you hear that?"

All three men stood motionless.

"Nope, I don't hear…" Josh started, but was cut off by intense growling.

"A bit late to be out walking your dog?" Josh said as the sound intensified.

"Is this a shit joke, Dylan? Because if it is, I'm not laughing!" Geraint said.

"What the hell are you going on about?"

"Firstly, you tell us about devil dogs, then the next thing you know, we're hearing shit!"

"Get a grip, twit! The story is an urban legend. Besides, I made half of it up!"

Josh gave Geraint a clip across the back of his head. "Don't be a dozy twat. There's clearly an explanation for this."

More growling came from behind them.

Then from their right.

Then left.

It flanked them.

Circled them, even.

"Fuck, it's all around us!" Geraint said, his voice starting to break.

"Get a hold of yourself. It's one dog… one that happens to be lost out here in the woods."

"What if it's a wildcat, or something that's escaped from the zoo?"

"The fucking zoo?" Josh said, sniggering.

"It's a dog, Geraint. That's all."

"What's all the noise, guys? Can't a girl get her beauty sleep around here?" Cerys said, clambering out of her tent. The sight of her Peppa Pig pyjamas caused the men to giggle. "Hey, I happen to like Peppa!"

"But does John?" Josh asked, trying to keep the smirk off his face.

"It may be a turn-on of his, yes…"

Harsh barking brought them all back to reality. They stood there, rooted to their spots.

"This is not fucking funny!" Geraint said.

"Are you playing some kind of trick on us?" Cerys asked. The colour had drained from her face.

"No, I…" Dylan's words caught in his throat on spotting a pair of red eyes in a bush behind Cerys.

"What?" she asked.

Dylan raised his hand weakly and pointed. "Behind you!" he said, his voice, like his hand, trembling.

Slowly, Cerys turned, along with Josh.

Just over Cerys' shoulder, Dylan could see something push through the bushes and low-hanging branches.

It looked like a rottweiler, but much meaner and savage looking. The dog, if you could call it a dog, looked as though it had been brought up on a diet of steroids and engine oil.

Its pure white body rippled with muscles. Its eyes were ruby-colored, matching the tips of its ears. Saliva clung from it partly opened maw, which revealed more teeth than a normal canine possessed.

The dog's paws were twice the size of any species of dog he'd ever seen. Just by looking at it, Dylan guessed it had to weigh somewhere between the fifteen to twenty stone mark, with a height of 45-50 inches.

Then its second head appeared, which was identical to the first. The sight caused Dylan's knees to go weak.

Both heads had collars, and from those collars hung tags.

Dylan could just about read what was written on them.

"Arawn," he whispered. "No, it can't be," he said, putting a hand to his knife, but he didn't draw it, fearing the dog would attack.

Attached to the dog's collars were chains, which were pulled taut and disappeared into the darkness behind them.

From the woods came a sharp voice. The words it spoke were in Welsh, the translation lost on all bar Dylan: "Eich eneidiau yn perthyn i'r Arallfyd…"

"Your souls belong to the Otherworld," Dylan said, starting to back off from his friends.

The words came again as the dog pulled to get closer to their camp. Along with the hound came its guardian: a bedraggled old hag, whose top half was exposed. Her breasts, along with her skin, looked withered. It reminded Dylan of tree bark. Not a single tooth could be seen inside her mouth. Her chin was soaked in drool. A scarf was wrapped around her head, but it did nothing to keep her wild, grey hair from blowing about her.

She raised a bony finger and pointed at them. "Eich eneidiau yn perthyn i'r Arallfyd…"

From where he stood, Dylan could see Cerys' piss running down the back of her pajama legs to gather at her feet. She started to cry and blubber like a two-year-old as the dog's leash was set free.

It came bounding from the shrubbery like a demented greyhound. Froth sprayed from both of its open mouths; the tongues bobbed and flopped as its body raced along.

Cerys' scream hit its crescendo when the massive dog pounced and latched its first set of jaws onto her face, with the second grabbing her throat.

"Cerys!" John cried, scrambling out of his tent. "What the fuck! Help us!" he screamed to the others as he raced up to the dog and shoulder-barged it. But the hound didn't move, just growled as it ripped through Cerys' flesh like a whirring chainsaw through hot butter.

Her body skipped as though electricity coursed through it. Her blood splashed trees, leaves and bushes. After she'd gargled her last, the dogs didn't stop ripping at her body until they had picked all the skin from her face, neck and shoulders.

When the dog raised its head, bloody saliva clung from its jaws. Its snout was painted red.

John scuttled back on his arse, trying to get clear of the madness before him. "Cerys!" he whimpered.

"What the hell?" Amy shrieked, poking her head out of her tent.

This caused the hound to stop in its tracks and look back at Amy. When their eyes locked, she ducked back inside and zipped the door closed.

"Get out of there!" Josh screamed. As he was about to make a run for the tent, a second dog burst from the bush, followed by a third. The new dogs set upon the tent Amy hid within.

"We have to get the fuck out of here. Now!" Geraint said. Turning, he fled into the woods.

"Emma!" Dylan yelled. Running, he made it over to her tent and dragged the girl out to safety. "Come on! We need to go."

"John, get up!" Josh demanded.

Getting onto his stomach, John tried to get up, but a crushing weight landed on his back, driving him back to ground.

"Argh! Get the fuck off!" he raged, but the fight was taken out of him almost immediately, as the dog sank both sets of jaws into his back. "Ugh!" he cried.

Josh ran over and kicked the dog as hard as he could, before putting one of its heads into a headlock.

"Get the fuck out of there, John!" Josh screamed as he wrestled with the hell hound.

But John couldn't move very fast and was helped to his feet by Emma and Dylan.

Screams came from Amy's tent, diverting everyone's attention. The dogs had torn the canvas to shreds, revealing a naked and terrified Amy.

"Help!" she yelled. Her screams pierced the night, but it was all she could do as both hounds pounced on her.

Rage coursed through Josh, causing him to tighten his grip around the mutt's neck. When he heard bones crunch, he knew he'd snapped the hound's neck so he let it go.

But the second head came at him.

The first head hung limp and lifeless by its side.

"What the…"

Moving backwards, he avoided the snapping jaws and managed to wrap his muscular arms around the dog's body. With his hands locked, Josh bearhugged the hound.

Bones snapped.

A rib protruded.

The hound whimpered, snarled and gnashed its teeth, but Josh didn't allow it to break his hold.

"Fucker!" he spat, then compressed harder still. A loud cracking sound caused the mutt to go limp. He threw the body to one side.

The hag gasped, shook her head, and then muttered something he couldn't make out.

"Josh!" Dylan called. "Watch out!"

Another hound came charging through the brush and pounced. Fortunately, Josh was in a stance that allowed him to catch the dog as it sprang for him.

"No, you don't!" he yelled, carrying the dog over to an exposed tent pole and throwing the hound down onto it.

It shrieked and howled as it wriggled and pulled to free itself, but all that did was cause the pole to do more damage.

***

"Josh, that's enough – let's go!" Dylan said, looking over at the dogs on Amy's tent. They were currently being kept busy by playing tug of war with her intestines "Now, damn it!"

When Josh joined them, all four of them pushed on through the woods, with Dylan looking back now and then to see if the old hag or dogs were giving chase.

"What the fuck is going on?!" Josh asked. "Why is my girl lying dead out there? Torn apart by hounds from fucking hell! Is that what you're going to tell us, Dylan?!"

"I… I… It was just a stupid story. An urban legend. Something children made up hundreds of years ago! You can't—"

"Enough!" John said. He sounded as though he was having difficulty in catching his breath. "We need to get the hell out of here."

"How far away are the cars?" Emma asked.

"A couple of miles back the other way, I think," Dylan said. "My compass is back at the tent."

"Fuck!" Josh bellowed.

"Look, let's just keep going. We might find a spot where we can lay low for the night. We can pick it back up in the morning," John said.

"Sounds like a good idea."

"I agree," Emma said.

"Where did Geraint go?"

"He ran off like a sissy bitch!" Josh told Dylan. "Look, up ahead!" Before them was a clearing. A few large logs lay scattered about for sitting on. "We could make use of that spot."

Close by, a stream bubbled and trickled.

"Yes, I think we should stay here," Dylan said.

I can't believe my fucking luck! he thought. The legend is true? Fuck! Yes! If I'd known this was going to happen, I could have planned things differently.

I could sneak off with Emma now.

No, I can't. The others would notice.

So, what if they did? Would I care? Probably not… But still. I missed my chance when Josh was fighting the dogs.

Damn it!

"Everything okay, Dylan?" John asked.

"Oh, err…yeah. Just pissed off. I'm sorry I got you all into this. I…"

"You didn't get us into anything, mate," Josh said. "I was just blowing off some anger back there. I'm sorry."

"Forget it. Seriously. We're all on edge."

"I can't believe Cerys is dead!" Putting a hand to his face, John started to sob, causing Josh to put his arm around his mate.

On seeing his friends embrace, he gulped. What have I done? Dylan thought, then smiled. Wait. If the legend about the dogs and the hag are true, the part about becoming a poet or finding inspiration must be too! I just need to get to the top of Idris' Chair with Emma. Once there, I can cut the bitch's throat open, allowing her virgin blood to soak into the ground – a sacrifice to please Idris. Once it's done, I'll have poetry in my heart forever. In return, I'll be wealthy and famous. A famous bard and novelist.

The thought brought a smile to his face.

It'll be worth it. All of it.

Snuggling down on the floor, he thought about getting some rest. For now, I'll keep Josh and John around. They'll come in handy for keeping the dogs or hag distracted. With any luck, I'll be able to sneak away with Emma.

When they saw and heard there was no danger approaching, they managed to settle in for a few hours.

***

"Dylan, what time is it?" Josh asked.

Dylan, who had Emma snuggled into him, lifted his right arm slowly to look at his watch. "It's a quarter-past-two. Maybe we should think about circling back to the tents? If I can get my compass, I can lead us all back to the cars."

"John, are you okay to move?"

"I think you guys are going to have to leave me. I can barely stand."

"We can't do that!" Josh said.

"You'll have to. Go and get help!" he insisted. "I'll just slow you down."

What a fucking hero, Dylan thought. Might be a good chance for me and Emma to slip away though. "Look, why don't you stay with John, and I'll take Emma?"

"Sounds like a decent plan," Josh admitted. "We'll be as fast as we can. Besides, you're strong enough to protect John against the dogs, Josh. We all saw you handle them back at the tents."

"Some company would be nice," John admitted.

Josh nodded. "Okay… but be bloody quick!"

"We will. Emma. Emma!" he said, giving the girl a few gentle shakes. "Me and you are going to go for help."

"What about the boys?" she asked sleepily.

"John can't make it, so Josh is going to stay behind with him while we go and get help."

"Okay," she said, stretching.

"Right, we shouldn't…" A loud crunching noise stopped Dylan.

"It's the hag!" John whispered.

"Shh!" Dylan snapped.

There was something much different about this sound to the previous ones. A slight chinking noise could be detected over the crunch and snap of twigs and leaves.

It certainly wasn't a hound making its way towards them, because the footfalls were much heavier than that of the hounds.

This fact probably ruled out the hag, too, as she looked paper thin, and couldn't have weighed more than five or six stone.

No, this was something much bigger.

"Who's there?!" Dylan screamed, his voice breaking. In a flash, he drew his knifc. "We're armed and we're not afraid to hurt anyone!"

"What the hell are you doing?" Josh asked.

"Shut up! Come on, show yourself!"

No response.

The footfalls stopped.

Silence engulfed them.

Drowned them.

Then growling ensued, followed by more heavy, foreboding footfalls.

"Josh, help me up!"

"Come on, Dylan. We need to get the hell out of here," Emma said.

"This is unreal…" Dylan uttered, watching a huge mountain of a man push through the low-hanging branches that surrounded him.

The man, if indeed it was a man, wore a helmet with a vent. Only his eyes, which shone ruby like the dogs at his side, could be seen. His torso and arms were bare. His chest heaved with solid muscle, much like his biceps, traps and forearms.

A mammoth Celtic tattoo graced his left pec, along with one coiled around his left wrist. His breath vented through the holes in his helmet.

His mane, which was raven-colored with streaks of grey, reached halfway down his back. Over his shoulder he carried a great hammer of war. A large sword was sheathed at his right hip, and a dagger hung at his left.

On his back, he carried a quiver of arrows and a bow. Black animal fur covered his groin, the loose ends flapping in the light breeze. The boots he wore were also made from animal skin, along with the straps that were wound around them.

Just like his upper body, his lower body was magnificent. His thighs and calves bulged with muscles.

He stood there, unmoving, like a giant oak tree.

In his right hand, he carried the head of Geraint. Dry, flaking trails of blood could be seen under the boy's nose. Both of his eyes were closed and bruised beyond brutality.

The man mountain uttered a mouthful of words which came out in a gravely, choky tone: "Beth wyt ti'n gwneud yma?!"

"What the fuck does it want?" Josh asked. "Who is he?"

"He's asking us what we're doing here," Dylan said.

Man-Mountain stepped forward, making his knives rattle as he did so. "Beth wyt ti'n gwneud yma?!" His tone sounded more fierce this time. His dogs stayed obediently by his side.

"Let's run!" Emma said.

"I—"

John's words were cut short as the warrior-like figure brought his hammer down on his head. John's skull cracked like a coconut, causing his body to collapse like a house of cards.

Blood splashed Dylan's face.

Withdrawing the hammer, the warrior spoke again: "Beth wyt ti'n gwneud yma?!" He stepped closer to Dylan, who wasn't short himself. "Ni fyddaf yn gofyn eto , crwt..."

"There's no need to ask again!" Dylan said, holding his hands up. "We're here to see the mountain! That's all. We're just here to have fun!"

The man laughed, then switched from Welsh to English. "I know why you are here, Dylan! You can't fool Arawn, the great God of the Otherworld. You've brought your friends here for you own selfish needs. You wanted to see if killing a virgin on the top of Idris' Chair would work for your creativity. Foolish boy!" Arawn barked.

"What the fuck?!" Josh said. "Is that prick telling the truth?!"

"No! He's fucking lying!" Dylan protested.

"You motherfucker!" Emma said, slapping Dylan across the face.

Arawn snapped his fingers, which sent the dogs flying into snarling action.

Josh screamed as the hounds ferociously mauled him. There was nothing Dylan or Emma could do to help as they watched the dogs tear their friend limb from limb. Josh's harsh screams turned to that of wet gargles.

"Please! Don't kill me. Take her!" Dylan said, pushing Emma into Arawn.

"You fucking pig!" she spat. As she tried lashing out at Dylan, Emma was scooped up by Arawn and thrown over his shoulder.

"The virgin is mine, but what you came for shall not be granted, just the curse of madness," Arawn said, laying a huge hand onto Dylan's shoulder. He then uttered words of Welsh that not even Dylan understood, before turning around and stalking off into the woods from where he'd come.

Emma screamed and cried as she disappeared into the green.

"Wait! Come back! What have you done to me?" Dylan cried. Above him, as he looked up, he could see horsemen riding through the star-scattered sky, their hounds howling and chasing after them. "The Great Hunt?" he whispered, watching the psychedelic colours flood the air above him.

***

One month later...

Dorgellau Post:
After a month-long search, Dylan Harding Jones, 22, was found wandering the mountain known to locals as Cadair Idris (Idris' Chair). The young poet, who went missing last month, was supposedly on a trip to the mountain with some friends.

Police have yet to discover the remains of Jones' friends, but are confident they can do so before heavy snow starts to fall. They claim they are dubious about Jones being on a trip with anyone else, as when Jones was picked up, he could hardly utter an intelligible sentence.

"When we found him, it was clear Jones was not sound of mind. What we're unsure of is whether he lost it before or during his trip. We have reason to believe that the lad is local, and that he may have escaped from a nearby hospital," said Sgt Thomas of Dorgellau Police Dpt.

"If that turns out to be the case, then the search for his missing friends will be called off. At this moment in time, Jones is under the care of psychiatrists, who also believe he may have been out there on his own."

When Jones was finally picked up, it was reported that he had carved 'poetry' into the surrounding trees. Even his face, arms, legs and naked body were covered in strange words and phrases.

It was also reported that Jones kept talking about 'The Great Hunt' and a person or place named Arawn. Locals experts have since been looking into this, but so far, research has found nothing on 'The Great Hunt' or 'Arawn'.

One of Jones' doctors had this to add: "After all, Jones is a very creative and imaginative person. He probably has all kinds of tales, creatures and characters locked away in his mind that the madness brought to the surface. And, if he was all alone up there, then God knows what effect the cold nights had on him, and his mind..."

The Patriotic Prowler

Simone scraped the remainder of his latest plaything, Helena (or at least that's what he thought her name was), off the chopping board and into the industrial-sized blender. He then hit the power button. As the last of her blitzed around inside it, he placed the dicing block into the sink and sluiced it free of blood and hair particles.

Not Helena – Henrietta, he thought. *That was her name. Don't you remember the whole thing with her name?* Simone shook his head. *I can't remember a damn thing these days.* He chuckled, drudging up the memory of meeting her.

***

"I've read *all* of your books, Simone. I think you're a wonderful author, and I might just be your number one fan," she told him at a mediocre horror, sci-fi and fantasy convention where he had a stall set up selling his works and other bits and pieces. "Would you be so kind as to sign this for me, please?"

He looked her up and down, took in her revealing attire on the sly, and smiled his best smile. "That's very kind of you, thanks. To whom do I make it out to, please?"

"Henry. Short for Henrietta," she elaborated, mistaking his raised eyebrow for confusion.

"Yes, I thought as much. Beautiful." Before signing her copy of *Wind-Up Toy* – a novel entrenched in filth and violence, which he'd written some ten years ago – he glanced around the near empty auditorium. "Do you know, Henry, you're the first customer I've spoken to all day and the day is almost done."

She blushed. "Maybe your other fans were too shy to say hello . . ."

Simone laughed, signed her book and handed it back to her. "It's a possibility I might have overlooked, but I think it boils down to the fact that I'm a nobody writer who attends events in the armpits of nowhere. However, I do have *some* loyal fans online, mainly Facebook, who are worldwide and homegrown."

"I was too nervous to add you on Facebook," she admitted.

"But you had the bottle to talk to me here, in a . . . not so crowded room?"

They both laughed.

"It was now or never, I guess," she said, looking at Simone's signature and personal scroll. "'I know where you live.' Not yet, you don't," she muttered, winking at him. "So, how 'bout a drink?"

"Once I'm finished here, sure."

Henry cleared her throat and gulped before answering, "Awesome." She clutched the book to her chest. "Shall I come back here at the end of the day, or shall I meet you somewhere?"

"Here is fine. I'll be waiting to escort you to a nearby pub."

"Brill. I'm looking forward to it, Simone," she said and sauntered off.

He smiled as she faded into the distance, lost amongst the hardcore fans, cosplayers, wannabes and those who come to gawk and laugh at the freaks who attended these shows.

I wonder if she'll return for that drink, he thought, going back around to his side of the table to pack away some books along with the various trinkets he'd brought along with him to help sell the horror: fake skulls, candles and sconces, artificial spiders and webbing, severed fingers and detached hands. When he was done, there was hardly anything left to conceal the plain red cloth used to drape the scarred, graffiti-laden table he'd been given by the event's organisers. Before collapsing into the provided chair with an unpleasant back and no padding, he grabbed the pot that acted as his till from off the tabletop.

With the kitty in his lap, he proceeded to count the day's takings. *Barely enough to cover the cost of buying a stall at this convention*, he thought, huffing out a laugh. *Good thing I don't really need the money, mind.*

As the clock ticked off the remaining ten minutes of his shift, Simone decided to pack up the rest of his things and call it a day. *Not like I'll get another customer dropping by now*, he thought, stuffing the last of his books into his carryall as the last of the day's punters drifted towards the exit.

"Had a good one?" someone called, grabbing his attention.

Simone stood straight and glanced at the stall to his left. *Ugh, him*, he thought, his gaze falling on the man dressed as an elf warrior to help promote his new book. *Jackasrse.* Behind the elf stood a woman dressed as a wench (complete with heaving tits) and a man clad in armour. *Fucking gimmicky cunts.*

That they might be, a voice at the back of Simone's mind argued, *but they've drawn the crowds all day.*

"So-so," he lied, glancing down at the meagre amount of profit in his hand.

"That's good, then," the elf continued.

Goddamn putz, he thought, returning the cash to his pot. He went back to clearing the last of his table. *Not sure why the hell I keep fighting on. For my devoted fans online*? "Ha!" Simone snorted, and those around him looked at him as though he'd cracked. "I just . . ." he trailed off, lowering his head.

"Ready for that drink, Mr. Fancy Author Man?" Henry said moments later, standing behind him.

He turned and beamed at her, his eyes unable to avoid tracing the length of her long, exposed legs.

"You're drooling," she whispered, covering the one side of her mouth with the back of her hand.

They laughed.

"Sorry. And yes, I'm desperate for a beer!"

He drained the last of his second beer as she polished off the remainder of their shared bag of fiery hot Monster Munch. As he placed his glass back down, he noticed the edge of a paperback poking out of her bag, a bookmark placed halfway through it.

"You've been reading?"

Henry glanced down. "Oh, yeah!" She pulled *Wind-Up Toy* out of her bag and flipped through it, sniffing at the pages as they fanned her face. "I just love it. I've read it countless times. It's a work of genius. And, dare I say it, gets me a little turned on. Stuff *Fifty Shades*!"

"Huh, you're very kind, but I'm not sure what sort of mind gets turned on by such things," he said, chuckling.

"A naughty one?"

"Ooh, how wicked of you!" He laughed. *The chemistry is undeniable*, he thought. *Well, it looks like the weekend hasn't been a total waste of time, money and effort.* "Another drink?"

"*Wowzah*! It must be true what they say, about authors being alcoholics," she said with a wink. "But yeah, I'd love another, please."

"Half a Goblin, right?" he asked, and she nodded.

Henry invited Simone back to hers for 'coffee' and a further discussion on *Wind-Up Toy*. As he walked her home, he could feel the heat between them.

"One thing I do question about the book, mind . . ."

"Ah, here we go – the honesty. Did you feel the need to ply me with drinks before crushing my feelings?" he asked.

"Shut up, silly! I love the book, and it's nothing about the story, but the author."

He stopped walking, bringing her to a halt. "What do you mean?"

"Why would you name the character after yourself? I just find it a bit . . . odd. Well, not odd – that's the wrong choice of word. I mean, aren't you worried it'll send the wrong messages about you?"

"Ha!" he brayed. "You think I *want* people to think I'm like Simone?"

She smiled, gave a stiff nod. "I mean, I'm not stupid – it's a gimmick, right, and a pretty clever one at that?"

The mere mention of the word *gimmick* helped develop a tick at his temple. "No, not a . . . gimmick, a way of being playful and clever with my readers, as you pointed out. And it works, to a degree. I think."

"Well, I do love it, even it makes me feel a little terrified to be in your company. But also excited at the same time, do you know what I mean?"

He leaned closer to her, their lips almost touching, and said, "*Boo!*"

Her breath hitched in her throat, and he knew at that moment that his half-breed good looks and skin tone had won her over. Not to mention her being at the centre of her favourite author's attention. A glow warmed his gut.

"You're going to have to peel my G-string off," she whispered, biting her lower lip.

His heart lurched and a beat was missed. "I would say 'I bet you say that to all the boys,' but you don't seem the type."

She nodded, continuing to bite her lip, her cheeks colouring. "I only say those kinds of things to dudes I mean to hear them."

"I think I might have to show you my writer's retreat," he said, lacing his fingers with hers.

He fucked her hard, twice, almost erupting on impact the first time. They screwed on his bed, in the kitchen (with her bent over the table) and on the living room floor. Their clothes had exploded off their bodies and they'd gone at each other like wild animals: hair pulling, nails raking.

In the morning, on the cusp of dawn, a virgin sun lit his kitchen, where he made her breakfast: scrambled eggs on toast, complete with a glass of fresh orange juice. After that, they parted company.

Henry gave him her phone number. "You can keep my panties, too," she said, winking.

Simone swore to call, and their au revoir was sealed with a kiss, cementing his aforementioned promise.

Three weeks later, after numerous dates, he invited her to his cabin in the woods.

Nobody lived for miles around and the tall trees helped camouflage his small wooden structure with its soundproofed cellar.

He'd drugged her food and tied her up.

Simone was loath to kill her and spoil her red velvet dress with a split up its side, revealing a slender yet meaty thigh wrapped in silk stockings. So, he decided to keep her, chained to the walls in his playroom below the cabin.

He would use Henry as a sex toy.

Her eyes were permanently covered by an eye mask, her guts fed via a tube, her throat lubed by him when he deemed it fit.

Henry lasted several months.   Much longer than the previous women he'd snared via an online competition – something he was prone to doing these days.

I don't like snatching them off the street anymore, he thought as he cut the dead Henry down and looked into her white eyes. *Oh, Henry. You knew the way to my heart.*

After dragging her upstairs, he wrapped her body in sheets, hauled her outside to his car, threw her body in the boot and took her home for dicing.

***

Ah, the competition, he thought now, switching the blender off to remove its lid. *I'll have to pick a winner soon.*

He poured the minced Henry into a plastic jug and placed it in the fridge. *You'll taste great chilled*, he thought.

Simone closed the fridge, made his way over to the computer desk and sat in the plush swivel chair. He tapped some buttons on his keyboard, waking up the PC. When the screen illuminated, he logged into Facebook and brought up his author's business page.

He navigated to his latest post, which was pinned to the top, and observed the contest. The likes, shares and other interactions had gone up in the hundreds over the past few days. A smile split his face as he scrolled through the comments beneath the competition's rules and the 'Caption This' picture, he'd picked out and posted. His smile grew wider as he realised it was mostly women who had entered thus far, and some had been readers from the outset, each claiming to be his number one fan. A laugh escaped him.

"God, and how long have you been lingering on my page, Emily, hmm? Eight years, nine?" Simone placed the cursor over Emily Whitby's name and clicked on it, which took him to her profile. She'd shared his competition, bragged him up, and told the world how much she loves his books. He often spoke with her in private chat and wondered what her insides would look and taste like. How grand her tits would be cut off and displayed in a jar.

His prick stirred.

"No, it's not Emily's turn yet."

Simone took a deep breath, clicked off Emily's page and went back to his author's site. He continued flicking through the entries, their names (some of which were brand new to him) and profiles. He tended to stay away from fresh meat, wanting them to savour his works, personality, charm and charisma. But there were *so* many lovelies to pick from.

Pre-come soaked through his underwear.

"Well, I'm going to have to choose someone soon," he said, looking at his calendar. St. David's Day was a week away and he needed to get things in order, especially with the prize this year being a tad bigger: not only would the one lucky winner get to spend an unforgettable weekend with him, as usual, but there was also a stack of books and vouchers on offer.

Of course, the latter of the gifts was non-existent. Dead people couldn't read and spend money.

He chuckled, wriggling in his seat, his underwear becoming uncomfortable. *I need a shower. But first, a winner. Someone . . . feisty.* It had to be somebody gutsy. A woman who would fight for survival, but not someone he couldn't handle either. Then again, he had enough weapons and tricks up his sleeve to dupe anyone.

And then a name caught his eye.

Ah, the delicious Neen Long. He'd almost forgotten about her. *Oh, how we've worked and had fun together over the years.* Plus, she didn't live that far away. Not that distance mattered, for Simone had plenty of money stashed away and had boasted he could fly anyone over to see him from anywhere in the world, all expenses covered.

He went to Neen's profile page, started flipping through her photos and rubbed his cock through his trousers. "Your skin is a patchwork of colours and shapes," he whispered, looking at her various tattoos, her tiny tits barely pushing at the fabrics of her jumpers, tees and tops in the pictures he rooted through. "Neen," he said through clenched teeth, his orgasm building. "Aggressive fucking Neen. Ball-buster Neen."

Her images faded into the background as he envisioned tying her up, tearing her clothes off, and teasing her skin with a knife. Once he got bored with the blade, he would take a pair of pliers to her teeth, yank them out one by one, and make a necklace from her ivory. Destroy her winning smile.

His cock exploded.

Simone flopped and juddered in his chair like a fish out of water. When the mini seizure subsided, his body relaxed, and he was unable to move. A warm, fuzzy glow swept through him. His fingertips and toes tingled.

Now that I have my victim – I mean winner *– picked out, I can relax and go take a shower. Once I'm done and I've eaten, I'll message Neen with the good news.* Even though his competition still had a few days left to run, he saw no harm in telling her. Plus, it would give her time to prepare for the journey. "I can tell her to keep it to herself, too," he said, getting up from his chair.

His PC chimed – someone had replied to Neen's comment. It was from Chrissy Sandoval.

"I think we've been his friends for the longest," he read aloud, opening the conversation. As he scanned down it, he saw the ladies' tête-à-tête veered away from the post's topic and towards lesbianism and giving their fave author a sex show, culminating in them agreeing to exchange details via private message.

By the time he'd read to the end of the transcript, he was hard again, his breathing coming in ragged rips. "How did I miss all *this*?" Simone blurted, causing him to rethink his initial plan with Neen. *Do I dare invite . . . both ladies? Two absconders for the price of one?*

A kaleidoscope of butterflies flapped around inside his gut. His hard-on intensified.

I need to think this through . . . Two ladies at once could be troublesome. Nevertheless, the prospect of having both ladies at the cabin to play with was mind-numbing. His body quaked, and a second orgasm filled his boxer shorts.

***

As he showered, all he could think about was Neen and Chrissy, and how they would cavort on the rug by the fireplace inside his secret world.

He wouldn't bushwhack them immediately. No. He would allow time for play. And he would film them.

That final thought was almost too much as he soaped the end of his cock, the purple head throbbing, threatening another release.

As hard as it was, Simone stopped playing with himself, his mind made up. He finished showering and went back to his desk after wrapping his body in an extra-large towel. "Time to deliver the good news," he said, sitting at his PC.

He sent an identical message to both women: *'Congratulations! You have been picked at random as my winner! You are cordially invited to stay with me for one weekend over the course of St. David's Day, my country's national holiday. If you do accept this gift, please let me know as soon as possible so I can arrange for your arrival. All the best, Simone.'*

As he awaited their replies, Simone pulled up a picture of Chrissy and traced her lengthy pins with his pinkie finger. She wore short shorts that ended just above the undersides of her arse cheeks, and her nipples pushed at the fabric of the seemingly thin, second-skin tank top she wore. He licked his dry lips. *Cutting those Daisy Dukes off with a knife, along with her knickers and top, will be something else*, he thought, still skipping through her numerous photos.

His messenger pinged. Simone's face lit up when he noticed it was from Chrissy.

Well, that was fast. It usually takes her a while, a week at times, to reply these days. And to think, we used to converse daily over the phone, he thought. But she had pretty much deserted him over the last year or so. Ignored his messages. He found it hard to swallow the lump of distaste at the back of his throat. *Suits you to talk to me now that you've won something – to be a part of my world for real. It'll be a shame to have to snuff you out*, he thought, beaming, opening her message.

"Fantastic!" he read aloud. "And the trip is completely free?"

'Yes, all expenses paid,' he wrote back. *'In the coming days, I will forward further information to you and the other lucky winner. I decided to up the ante this year. You're in*

for a wild ride, Chrissy. For now, start packing. More details will follow shortly . . .'

When he fired his message off, he saw Chrissy was still online, had picked up his response and started to reply. His smile widened. *She's completely hooked,* he thought, her response delighting him further: *'I'm pulling my suitcase from under the bed as we speak. I can't believe I get to meet my favourite author, and I'll be in the UK next week! We are going to have a blast*!'

"Yes, a *blast*," he sniggered, thinking about the sawn-off he kept in the broom closet in his cabin. *That thing doesn't half make a mess. Remember that woman's face it took apart? Phew.*

Simone decided not to reply. Instead, he went to Neen's profile and spied on her holiday photos. "Excellent." While he waited for her to respond, he busied himself with the pictures of her tanned, slender and semi-naked inked body. *What I wouldn't give to run my hands over that tight, peachy arse.*

Soon, a darker part of his mind answered. *Soon.*

He waited ten more minutes and when she hadn't yet replied, he lay on the small sofa by the side of his desk, imagining the fun to come.

***

Several hours later, the alert of a text pinging through woke him.

Simone grunted, sat bolt upright, and groaned as he pushed himself up and off the sofa. He shuffled over to the computer as he straightened up and rubbed at his eyes, clearing them of sleep and blur as he collapsed into the swivel chair.

He gave the mouse a nudge with his knuckles, moving it across the mat a few inches. The screen before him lit up, exposing Facebook and a message from Neen.

Simone moved the curser and opened her response: *'Sweeeeeet, dude! This is the best news I could have hoped for. Thank you, you're awesome. What do I need to do now? I don't live that far away, so getting to you shouldn't be a problem. Just let me know what's what, and I'll get organised.'*

He wrote back, *'Chrissy is also a winner. After she flies in towards the end of the week, I have arranged a ride for her to yours so you can come to mine together. I hope that's okay?'* he asked, adding a smiley emoji.

A few moments later, Neen replied, *'Yes, I'm fine with that, and she messaged me the good news – OMFG, dude, this is insane! She and I were talking in a thread attached to your competition about how cool it would be to be in your company at the same time.'*

You don't say? he thought, grinning. *'Oh, I must have missed that. Anyway, I'll send you all the details in a while – can you make sure Chrissy gets to you, and that you let me know what's happening?'*

'Yes, of course. This is so exciting! I hope you have grand plans for us ladies – we'll be expecting the full Simone treatment.'

'You can count on it.'

When she messaged back again, he didn't bother responding.

I need to start organising myself, he thought, getting out of his chair. *But first, I need to finish the rest of my sleep.*

***

The day before St. David's Day, which fell on a Sunday, Simone made his way to his cabin where he would wait for

Neen and Chrissy. He hoped they weren't a no-show – he hadn't announced the winners publicly, and they hadn't mentioned anything about it on social media since he'd told them. *Bitches better not stand me up!*

When he arrived at the woods a little after midday, he parked his car in a nearby natural lay-by, got out and locked up. The forest around him was quiet, isolated, the closest neighbour almost four miles away.

Nobody hears you scream out here, he thought.

The echoes of his crunching footfalls rebounded off the trees and stalked him as he walked on. The early afternoon rays of sunlight did nothing to penetrate the thickness of the foliage and hanging branches. He heard the quiet, calming sounds of wildlife: scurrying, chirping and rustles of movement.

When he got closer to his cabin, he could see the solitary chimneystack smoking.

"Excellent, Mary has been," he thought aloud. "Considering I don't pay her well, or that often, she does an outstanding job."

Your wit, charm and good looks keep her in place, the darkness at the back of his mind offered.

Yes. And how I've teased and toyed with her with my snippets of filth, death and danger. The woman seems to eat it up, he thought, slotting the key to the cabin's door into its snug lock. With one swift turn of the Yale, the double locking system unbolted, allowing him access.

Simone pushed the door wide open and was hit by the overpowering stench of carpet cleaner, polishing fluids and disinfectants. And there was another pong in the air, something he couldn't quite put his finger on. It made him heady and unsteady on his feet. His mind swirled. A sneeze ambushed him, driving a single tear down his face.

He giggled against his will, thinking the chemicals were stronger than usual and giving him a quick buzz.

Yes, she keeps the place ship-shape and Bristol fashion, he thought, running a wonky finger across the wood fixtures, fittings and finishes. *Not a dust mote in sight. How long has it been since I was up here? Three or four months? Five maybe? A busy writer finds it hard to keep track of such petty things as time. After all, it awaits no man.*

Four or five months? What the hell am I thinking – I was here last week! a rational part of his mind answered. Bile rose up his throat, his eyes stinging. *What the hell is going on?* His arms and legs felt weak, and his forehead was on fire.

Simone stumbled towards the door, closed and locked it before dumping his scant number of items onto the sofa. His writing didn't make him much, and if it weren't for his wealth, which had been passed on to him from his now dead father, then he wouldn't have been able to maintain such luxuries and living as he'd become accustomed. *All I had to do was beg Daddy for a cheque and he came running. Hell, it was the least he could do, after abandoning me and my mother when I was a child. The fucker had a cheek coming back into my life after he learned of her death. Still, he was easy pickings, what with his shame and guilt. Fucking pathetic.*

"If you want to help, then you can by investing money into my creativity. If I'm going to achieve greatness, then I'll need great things to help me on my way," he had said some five years ago, when he'd approached his newly acquainted father about wanting to secure a secluded place from civilisation. He'd smiled and slapped the man. "You're going to have to buy my affection, shithead. I know you want it."

"Of course, Simone," Dad had said, his bottom lip quivering. "You deserve nice things after the way I've treated you."

When a good enough cabin for Simone couldn't be found, one was built on private property, owned by his great grandfather. Six months after it was erected, Simone had an underground level added (at Daddy's expense). This would be his 'playroom,' where many a woman had succumbed to his torturous ways.

My dad was a fool. A fool whose world spun on a stack of bank notes, he thought giddily, stumbling further into the cabin. *Wait, wasn't I just thinking about Mary? Fuck, my thoughts are all over the damn place . . . Yes, Mary . . .*

Mary, while being interviewed by Simone, had been told never to go near the playroom door. He'd warned her he had CCTV installed within the place and would know her movements, but he'd never needed to check on her: after the first few times she'd come to shape the place up after his weekends of fun and games with a caged canary, he'd been impressed with how the place had sparkled each time.

"You want an older person to look after the place," his dad had advised. "They're reliable and trustworthy."

He'd thought it a little late in the game, his dad giving him advice, but he'd taken it, nonetheless.

Yes, she's also dependable and honest, he thought, another giggling fit escaping him. *She's nothing but a sweet, middle-aged woman who's settled here in the UK after leaving her fiancé in the States almost fifteen years ago.*

A pushover. I have her eating out of my hand.

As he walked around the cabin, scrutinizing the place, his guts flipflopped. A flutter of sorts. He felt drunk. *I think I'm going to throw up!*

A board underfoot creaked as he neared the cellar door.

"Hello?" he called, feeling a presence within the house.

Don't be silly, man, it's just Mary's aromas that's got me spooked! She probably didn't leave that long ago that's why they seem so pungent today . . .

"Mary?" Simone called, edging close to the open-plan kitchen, spotting a few sticks of incense burning. *That's the godawful smell!*

A noise from above caused him to stop dead in his tracks.

He looked up. "Mary, are you up there? If you haven't finished yet, I can always come back?"

No answer.

He scrunched his eyes up, furrowing his forehead as he scratched at the back of his skull. "Is some*one* up there?"

Simone thought his heart was going to explode when the messenger alert on his mobile chimed a handful of times. "*Fuck!*" he laughed, grabbing his chest with both hands. *Why the hell am I so rattled?*

Before checking his phone, Simone inspected all the rooms and every inch of the cabin, making sure there was no sign of Mary or anyone else. The place was clean.

She must have left just as I was pulling up, he thought, collapsing onto the sofa with his mobile in his hand.

The picture message was from Neen: '*Road trip!*' it read, the photo a selfie of Neen and Chrissy in an embrace, their tits crushed together, their tongues hanging out. Neen was winking and Chrissy was punching the air.

"*Mmmm . . .*" Simone growled, a thickness growing in his trousers, his eyelids drooping.

Another message pinged through: '*Hope you don't mind if we're a few hours early? I know we shouldn't really be there until tomorrow . . .*'

This is turning out better than I'd hoped for, he thought, writing, '*Not at all. In fact, I'm at the cabin right now, preparing the place for your arrival. See you soon. X*'

Simone's phone slipped out of his hand.

I'll just grab a couple hours of sleep before the fun begins, he thought, his eyes closing.

***

A whirring, beeping sound disturbed Simone from his sleep.

"Wh-*what*?" he gasped, sitting bolt upright. A cold enveloped his body, which was visibly shaking, chilling his core. Wiping sleep-grit from his eyes, he looked for the source of the draft, but there wasn't one – no open windows or exterior doors.

The beeping/whirring sound happened again. *Sounds like my PC*, he thought, looking upwards. A light shone from the open-plan second floor.

The hairs on his arms and at the back of his neck stood on end. "H-hello?"

Silence.

Simone, keeping a hold on his nerves, stood and walked over to the fireplace, where he removed the poker from its stand next to the decorative coal shovel and handheld sweeping brush. "Who's up there? Answer me, or I'll be forced to come up there and bash your goddamn brains in!"

He put his free hand on the banister to steady himself and took the steps at a snail's pace, his eyes never leaving the area above. When he reached the top, he found the bedroom-cum-workspace empty, his computer lit-up and humming away.

"What the?!" Simone mouthed, moving close to the personal computer.

A Word document was open, a paragraph written on it.

I haven't written a thing . . . Or have I? What's going on?

His eyes skimmed over the words on the screen, his gut dropping. Simone shook his head. "No, it can't be," he said, stepping backwards. His legs connected with the edge of his bed, and he spilled head over heels, slamming onto the floor.

"Who's watching me?!" he demanded, gathering the dropped poker. Simone scrambled to his feet and turned in complete circles, his eyes flicking and darting as he scanned the huge room. The cabin was silent, apart from his thunderous heartbeats, ragged breathing and the working PC.

How do they know about the atrocities I've committed? Why write them on this computer? Was it Mary? Has she somehow hacked my computer and read all my personal files and journal? "Mary? Mary Kiefel? Answer me!"

The sound of rushing blood filled his ears.

Calm down and think, man. How could Mary possibly do that? She doesn't come across as a professional hacker!? Maybe she tampered with my recording equipment? Or viewed me entering passwords into my system? No, never. For starters, she'd never know where I keep the—

A knock at the cabin's door startled him back to reality.

I'm not expecting anyone.

Maybe it's our spy, come to lay their demands down on the table for their silence? the dark voice suggested.

Simone's bladder pinched. Control was lost.

He wanted to shout out, to ask who was there, but he couldn't move.

Another knock was followed by the sound of giggling.

"Women?" he wondered aloud. "Maybe it's Mary and a friend?" The thought that it could be his cleaning lady dissolved the fear somewhat. *The silly thing has probably forgotten her keys or something. Besides, what type of maniac laughs, announcing themselves to their potential victim before carrying out their act?*

Simone shook his head, rushed downstairs, unlocked the door and pulled it open. "What did you forget, Ma—"

"I hope I brought enough booze," the slender blonde girl said, shoving a case of beer into Simone's chest. "I still can't believe I'm here, in your presence! The creator of my most favourite novel of *all* time. You do realise I'm a superfan, right?"

"Nah, I think I'm a bigger fan," the second girl said, giving away her American accent.

Neither of these are Mary. Simone's brain conjured up photos as he clutched the case. He knew these women, but how?

"What's the matter, Simone?" the blonde asked. "Don't you recognise me in the flesh?" She winked, flashing him the devil's grin.

"Aren't we the ones who are supposed to be lost for words? You know, being in the presence of greatness?" the Yankee asked.

"I—I'm not sure what's . . . *Neen*?!" he blurted, realising who the blonde was. *Wasn't she on the cover of Vogue magazine at one time? Fuck, she's hot in real life.* "What are you doing here? What are you *both* doing here, in fact? How did you find me?"

"Huh," the American huffed and laughed. "Are you going all shy on us?"

"Chrissy, right?" he guessed. He hadn't spoken to her on Facebook in a dog's year.

The scantily clad women stepped back and looked at each other, with Chrissy removing her aviators. "He's fucking with us, right?"

Neen looked at him. "Are you?"

Their unexpected arrival had him caught off-kilter. *Did I invite them here? I must have, but I don't remember . . . I'm going to look like a pussy if I don't do—*

"So, when does the three-way party get started, Simone?" Chrissy asked, stepping over the threshold and getting close to his face, the box of beers halting her progress.

"Yeah, Simone, when?" Neen pressed, joining Chrissy's side, lifting her skirt up a little.

"Uh, I—"

Chrissy thrust her tits towards him, her hand interlocking with Neen's. "I think we have him flustered, Neen, babe."

"Maybe he didn't think we'd show up?" Neen giggled, her fingers rubbing against her knickers. "You know, you're kind of cute like this, Simone."

"You're speechless!" Chrissy said, laughing. "You act so, *so* much different online, what with all that flirting and stories of death and danger in your private messages. That's why I was so overjoyed to have won your competition."

"Competition?" he managed. *What the hell are they talking about? And why is my head so fuzzy*?! he thought, staggering backwards due to Neen adding more weight to his chest.

"Yeah, the one you posted on your author page. The one you run *every* year."

The cabin door closed.

"Let's tie him up and take him upstairs," Neen suggested. "That might get him going."

"Ladies, w-wait," he stuttered.

Neen took the beers off him and set them aside. "Come on, big boy – you'll love it!" Her hands roamed his chest and face and raked through his hair. "Such a shy, handsome man."

"I think the coy routine is turning me on more than his perverted persona," Chrissy admitted. "Shit, we'll be the ones doing the dominating this weekend."

Sweat dribbled down Simone's forehead as he allowed his hands to be tied behind his back. *Shit, what am I going to do?* he thought, but his fear gave way to a flutter of excitement.

"Let's get him upstairs!" Chrissy said, smiling.

When the ladies got him to the top of the stairs and into the bedroom, their brows dripping with sweat, they threw him onto the bed. Simone hit the mattress with such force that he sprang back up into a sitting position.

As he tried to get up, Neen stood over him and side kicked him in the chest with one of her booted feet

"*Ugh*!" he bleated, slamming backwards.

Chrissy, yelling like a Native American, jumped onto the bed and collapsed on top of Simone, straddling him.

"*Ooph*!" The wind was knocked out of him. "Christ," he wheezed.

"Let's get his clothes off!" Neen giggled.

Chrissy pushed her arse down on his thighs. "Ooh," she teased, when Neen's hands slipped beneath her cheeks to unbuckle Simone's belt and pop the button on his jeans.

He fought as his trousers and boxers were ripped down his legs.

Neen burst out laughing. "The fuck is that?"

Simone's face heated and he almost cried as Neen flicked his hard, stubby cock.

"It's pathetic! Where's this huge dick we've all read about, Simone?" Neen continued. "We came all the way here for a fucking puny worm?"

"Bitches!" he screamed. "Get. Off. Me!"

The girls broke up laughing.

"Well, we didn't come here just for his cock and some fun," Chrissy said cryptically. "But still, get your phone out."

"No, *please*!"

With every click of the camera, his cock shrivelled until it was almost inside him.

"Post them online!" Chrissy said. Her persona had gone from giggly fangirl to serious bunny boiler.

"Nah, let's have some more fun first," Neen said. "See if we can't wake up that pathetic prick of his and get some truth out of him."

Simone lifted his head from the mattress as Neen approached the bed, her clothes now missing, her nipples standing erect, her pussy shaved. "The truth about what?"

"About Henrietta, or Henry, as she liked to be called," Chrissy said, grinding her teeth.

"Now, are you going to be a good boy?" Neen asked him.

All he could do was nod and think about the name Henrietta. It was familiar to him, but how? Who was she? He dared not ask, in fear of fuelling their escalating anger.

"Chrissy is going to get off you so she can strip and have fun, so don't move, okay? If you do, I'll cut it off and feed it to my dog. Understand?" Neen asked, gripping him by the balls and twisting them.

"*Ugh . . .*" he whimpered, biting his bottom lip, his dick starting to reappear. "I—I'll be good. Promise."

Neen and Chrissy looked at each other, the former nodding. Chrissy let go of his wrists and slammed a knee into his balls "That one's for Henry, you piece of shit! You're not fooling anyone with your 'I don't know what's going on around here' bullshit," she said, getting close to his ear. "We know all about you, Simone."

"*Argh!*" he wailed. "Get off!"

Behind them, a door or board creaked.

Simone clutched his breath. *What the fuck was that?*

"Mary?" Chrissy called.

Mary?!

"You can come out now. We've got him secured. You've got nothing to worry about."

Mary burst from the wardrobe. "Oh, my," she said, covering her mouth, laughing. "I wasn't expecting to see such a pathetic-looking dick!"

Neen and Chrissy doubled with laughter.

"*Mary!*" Simone said, trying to hide his shame by crossing his legs.

"What do you expect, Simone? After all the talking to yourself that I've heard on many occasions and the things I've read that you've written on this very computer, I was expecting a lot . . . *more*," she said, resting her arm on top of the PC's monitor.

"What the fuck is going on here?" he demanded, wriggling, trying to free his hand. "Untie me! And who the hell is this Henry?"

"I think the drugs you used to subdue him have wiped his memory, Mary, unless he's fucking with us?" Neen said.

"Yeah, that special incense is known to confuse the victim," Mary said. "He'll come around." "How—"

"Do we know each other?"

Simone nodded.

"Would you like to answer this one, Mary?" Neen asked.

Mary walked over to the base of the bed and looked down at Simone, their eyes fusing. She smiled. "This was all my idea, Simone. I've had my suspicions about you for some time now, dear. When I moved here from the States, your crimes were all over the news channels and papers, along with your photo. Everyone was looking for you, and when they couldn't find hide nor hair of you, after years of searching, the hype died down. The authorities thought you'd either died or moved away, to which I'm guessing it was the latter.

"Now, I had no real interest in finding you, and it was by chance that you hired me. At first, I thought I was mistaken, but I came to realise that it *was* you – the face I had seen in the local rags and on the TV all those years prior. You haven't changed a bit, not to my eye, anyway. And then I started reading what you had written, and a lot of it rang true to some of the murders that were committed by you, Simone."

He clenched his teeth and narrowed his eyes. *The game's up*, he thought, the clouds of uncertainty lifting. *You want to know where Henry is? I'll fucking show you!* But he kept his mouth shut. After all, there were three of them and he was tied up. *They could jump me all at once. I have to bide my time, see if I can charm my way out of this first, continue to play dumb.*

Fuck, how did this all go so wrong?

Mary, that's how. The old cunt doped me!

"I have no idea what you're talking about, Mary. I'm just a writer who likes to have fun with his readers."

"So, you're telling us you just like stringing women along, is that it, Mr. Author Man?" Neen asked. "But why? So, you can get them out here and scare them half to death? If that's true, and all this is just a fuck-up on Mary's behalf, then you're just as warped, and deserve to be punished."

Simone shook his head. "No, I—"

"But we *know*, Simone," Chrissy said, circling the bed, glaring at him. "Mary has shown us the proof, and it didn't take long to connect the rest of the dots. So, why don't you come clean, yeah? Make things easier on yourself."

"Pft, *proof*. What proof?"

"We thought you'd ask that," Mary said, going over to his PC to wake it up. "Come and read this aloud to him, Chrissy."

Chrissy read from the screen: "Simone scraped the remainder of his latest plaything, Helena (or at least that's what he thought her name was), off the chopping board and into the industrial-sized blender. He then hit the power button. As the last of her blitzed around inside it, he placed the dicing block into the sink and sluiced it free of blood and hair particles."

Oh fuck, oh shit, he thought, looking from Chrissy to Mary, and he was unable to help himself: "You sneaky *bitch*, Mary! You have no right in reading my stuff."

"You killed my baby sister, you fucking animal!" Chrissy said, flying at him.

"Your—Wait, what—Ugh!" he cried as Chrissy landed on him, her knee driving into his balls time and again. Vomit rushed up his throat.

"You killed my sister. My. Fucking. *Sister*!" She dug her thumbs into his eyes, drawing blood, which trickled down his face.

"*Argh*! Get her off, get her off!" His feet drummed the mattress.

Chrissy was hauled off him kicking, biting, spitting and screaming.

After a few rapid blinks, his blurred eyesight cleared. "I can explain everything! I promise." Sweat poured down his face, stinging his eyes. "Henry – or *Henrietta* – is just a character in my book! It's purely coincidental that your sister should share the same—"

"Coincidence," Chrissy scoffed. "You do realise my sister told me she'd been seeing you? That she'd got a place after moving here and found you at a convention a few weeks later? God, how could you have missed the link, dickhead? There are photos of Henry all over my Facebook page!"

That can't be right, he thought. *Surely, I would have noticed? But then again, how much do I actually give a fuck about the people I interact with? They're just words and faces on a screen.*

"Didn't you see the Missing posters, Simone? It was all over social media!" Mary chirped in. "And don't forget, I'm friends with mostly all of your fans – I see all of your interactions and have been admiring you from a distance for some time. When I saw it was Chrissy's sister and she'd gone missing, and then I stumbled on the proof, well, it didn't take much to put two and two together."

"If it hadn't been for Mary putting the pieces of the puzzle together and contacting me," Chrissy said, "then you might have got away with it."

Simone's eyes darted from one woman to the next before resting on Neen.

"You're wondering what my connection is in all of this?" she asked, and he nodded. "Chrissy contacted me after she and Mary had worked it all out. You see, she and I have been friends for many years, thanks to you and your stories. So, when she came to me with what she thought you had done and wanted to exact revenge, how could I possibly say no? And it was so easy to lure you into bringing us both here, together – you didn't think all those saucy comments were coincidence, do you?"

Simone's nostrils flared. Looking back at it now, he should've seen it: they'd used his own methods – and his horn – against him. *Fucking bitch cunts!*

"You know me, Simone," Neen continued. "It makes me hot to see a man squirm, no matter who or what he is to me."

All the women laughed.

Mary went to the wardrobe and retrieved a camera from inside it. "I like a bit of emasculating myself, Neen. Especially since I've seen how he messes with people online and in the streets, giving them the run-around and trolling. He's done other things too, like punishing me for not carrying out certain cleaning duties or being fussy."

Simone's eyes bulged and he shook his head. He had no words as he shrank back against his pillow. *Bide your time,* he thought.

"What, you don't want me to say any more? Tough shit. 'What's that spot on the floor, Mary? Why haven't you cleaned the curtains yet, Mary? Why is there dust on the doorframes, Mary?' And that's not even the half of it!"

Simone shrank further into the mattress, his cock nothing more than a shrivelled peanut.

"Why don't we tell the ladies about the types of punishment you dish out if I do miss or do something wrong? Hmm, shall we? Since you're so *tough* when it comes to pushing older women around, aren't you, boy?"

Simone's mouth formed a perfect *O,* and he shook his head. "Don't do this to me, Mary. Don't give them further cause to—"

"Oh, so I shouldn't mention how you make me stand out in the sun for hours on end when I've made a simple mistake? Or how you like to beat me with a rubber hose if I don't cut your sandwiches right?" Mary smirked. "See, he said he had a rich father who left him a great deal of money and he could make my life a living misery. Hell, I wouldn't have put it past him to get me deported back to the States. I needed this job – I have five kids to feed – and so I bent over backwards for this *little* shit. But he treats me like—" Mary paused as Chrissy whimpered. "Jesus, are you diddling yourself?"

"Uh-huh," Chrissy said, biting her lower lip while touching her bald pussy. "I told you this shit gets me going, even though this fucker killed Henry."

"God, that's hot." Mary bit her lip as she watched Chrissy's diddling fingers. "Girls, I think it's time we get the show rolling. Come here."

"I'm sure we can talk about this, ladies, please," Simone said as Neen and Chrissy turned from him and huddled in a circle with Mary. He pleaded some more as they whispered, but his words fell on deaf ears. *What the fuck am I going to do?* he wondered.

They turned to face him, and he gawped as Mary slowly shed her clothes, revealing stockings, suspenders, garter and no knickers or bra. And, even though he was trapped in a situation he had zero control over and was now fearful for his life, he couldn't stop his prick from stiffening.

Simone looked from one set of tits to the other. *Maybe they'll just humiliate me and go away once they've had their fun*, he thought, trying to settle his nerves, his dick now standing at full attention.

"Is that as big as it gets?" Neen asked. "Good grief."

All the women laughed.

"I'll kill you. All of you! In an agonising way, but not before I have my fun with your bodies," he blurted, his temper lost. "Untie me. Now!"

"Ooh, feisty," Neen said, giggling. "You're a nasty piece of shit, aren't you? You're going to deserve everything you get, *boy*."

Mary set up her camera at the foot of the bed, aiming it at him. "Shall we begin?"

"Not yet," Neen said, picking up one of her socks and advancing on Simone. "We need to make sure we can't be identified. We'll tape the show and post it all over Facebook and social media, making sure we tag our boy here in it."

"No, don't—*ugh*—" he gagged, as Neen rammed her sweat-soaked sock into his flapping mouth. His heart pulled in his chest and his eyes made rapid movements. He wanted to cry, to piss himself.

Simone clenched his arse cheeks. Yet, his hard-on remained.

Chrissy walked over to the steps, her arse moulded into a tight perfection. "I brought plenty of tights for our faces, ladies."

Simone writhed and screamed a muffled scream until he was breathless; until his chest and throat reddened, and the veins in his neck stood on end. But none of the women seemed concerned about his stifled squeals and pleas. *They mean business, all right*, he thought, yanking and tugging against his restraints, but it was no good – they didn't yield.

If I'm not careful, I'm going to be buried with the bodies I've placed in the woods.

Chrissy handed out the tights.

"I think I can smell your pussy on this pair," Neen said, laughing.

"A bonus?" Chrissy said.

"Definitely." Neen winked, licking her lips. She pulled her set of tights down over her chin, and Chrissy and Mary did the same. "Mary, let's get the camera rolling now, please. Oh, and remember don't use our real names! The whole world will see this."

"Oh, no, no, no!" Simone whimpered. *They can't do this to me!*

Mary peered through the lens of her camera. "He's centre stage, guys."

"Good," Neen said. "Let's line up in front of it and get a few words out before we start. Just remember to play it down as a publicity stunt. We don't want some sad act reporting us."

Chrissy handed Mary the whip. "Why don't you have first *crack*? I'll get us going, and then after our words, you can go to town."

"Are you sure? Henry was your sister . . ."

"It's fine, honestly."

Simone watched as Mary put her trembling hand out and grasped a hold of the thin rope. "Mary, please!" he said, his pleas muffled.

"Three . . . Two . . . One . . ." Chrissy said. "And we're a go!"

"Hello there, world of social media," Neen said, "and welcome to something special from your favourite author. The events that are about to unfold may or may not be a publicity stunt. We'll let you make up your own mind on that."

"You are about to see your Lord and Master horror author laid bare and punished like some of your favourite characters of his," Chrissy cut in.

Mary held the whip up. "He needs a good flogging."

The women broke from each other, with Neen and Mary stepping up to the bedside and Chrissy going behind the camera.

"*Nooooo*!" Simone bellowed.

Mary cracked the floor with the whip a few times before swooshing it over her shoulder. She then brought it forwards, aiming for his erection. The thin cord slashed across his toned gut, breaking skin.

"*Argh*!" he screamed, his biceps bulging as he tried to double; piss squirted out of his cock, showering his belly and thighs. When he tried to cross his legs, he farted, and a stream of runny shit spurted across the duvet.

Mary retracted the rope time and again, cutting marks across his abs, chest and face. Blood spewed up the bed's headboard. As she appeared to grow breathless, her final blow caught him on the balls and coiled around his prick. He tried to yell, tears tumbling out of him.

Chrissy spoke directly into the camera while taking the whip off Mary. "You sick fucks enjoying this? We hope so. And we're just getting started."

Mary skipped away from Simone's side, allowing Chrissy to step up to the bed and lash Simone relentlessly, screeching as she did so, until Neen finally stopped her. Her last cracking blow closed one of his eyes and ripped the other open.

"I don't think he can take any more whips," Neen said. She bent over him, her nipple rubbing against his lips. "Are you still with us, Simone?"

"*Ugh* . . ." he groaned, his vision blurring. With all the strength he could muster, he shook his head.

"I think he wants more," Neen said. "Do we have anything to plug up his arse?"

Simone, fighting consciousness, bucked in disagreement.

"I have a few more things in my bag downstairs we could use to mess with him," Chrissy said.

"What about the rolling pin from the kitchen?" Mary said. "Ooh, and there will be plenty of sharp knives and other bits and pieces down there."

"You guys go and scout, and bring back whatever you think we'll need," Neen said.

Mary and Chrissy nodded and giggled as they disappeared from the room.

Simone then felt the straps holding his wrists and ankles loosen, and though he was determined to fight back, he had no energy. All he could do was let Neen manipulate his body. When the gag was ripped from his mouth, his throat bone dry, he tried to bargain with her.

"Please, Neen," Simone rasped, disoriented. "Don't do any more—"

"Don't you dare use my name again. You showed us what you are. We now know the truth, don't we? That you're a killer," she said, getting right in his face, her tiny tits squashed against his body.

"You're so hot . . ." he managed, coughing up blood.

Neen smiled. "You aren't going to charm your way out of this one, boy." She pulled him from his sitting position onto his stomach.

"We have some supplies!" Chrissy said, walking into the room with Mary hot on her heels. "Let's try to stuff a variety of things up his chocolate chute."

"I suggest the rolling pin first," Mary said.

"Followed by the skewers?" Chrissy asked.

Simone screamed.

"Roll pin, please, doctor," Neen said, holding her hand out. "It's nice and heavy. You're going to enjoy this, Simone."

"Lube?" Mary asked, holding up a bottle of baby oil.

"Nah, he can have its entire length dry. But first," Neen said, raising the rolling pin over her shoulder, "I want to test its durability."

She brought the pin down across Simone's backside so hard, the handle broke off in her grip. He bucked, thrashed and yelled.

"Damn, you need to buy better kitchenware, Simone," Chrissy said, giggling.

"Let us know what it feels like up your pipe," Neen said, forcing his arse cheeks apart.

Simone wriggled, trying not to make it easy for her, but it was no use, and the pin slipped inside him, inch by inch, puncturing his anus. Blood spurted across the bridge of Neen's nose.

"Oh, God!" she said. "It's almost *all* in there."

Simone whimpered, his body going limp.

***

A shocking wet coldness enveloped Simone, and he came to with a start and a sputter.

"Buckets of water really do work, just like in the stories," Mary said, chuckling.

Simone licked his wet lips, swallowed, and tried to scream, but his throat burned. "I need a drink. Please. You can't deny me that, surely!"

"I'm sure you denied my sister, you fuck!" Chrissy said. "You get fuck-all. No mercy. You're lucky we like playing and haven't just ended your miserable life already."

Neen kicked him in the ribs, then jumped on him and yanked his head backwards by his hair. "We can do whatever we please," she whispered. "Are you ready for me to unplug you?"

Simone was unsure of what she meant at first, but his twitching anus reminded him of the foreign object invading him. He slowly shook his head, water flicking from the end of his nose as his mouth formed a perfect *O*.

"I need to flick my bean while you do it," Chrissy said.

"Would you like me to help you?" Mary asked.

"You naughty bitch." Chrissy chuckled. "Come on, then." She lay on the floor and spread her legs. "Get down there."

Simone couldn't believe what he was seeing. *Bastards!* he thought, his newfound erection pushing painfully against the mattress.

He felt Neen's hand on the rolling pin and squeezed his eyes shut. "*No!*"

She slipped it out an inch and stopped, much to Simone's begging, whimpering and pleading. "I think we'll stop there for now."

Simone opened his eyes and saw Chrissy pressing Mary's face against her pussy, her head thrown back in ecstasy. "Don't stop!" Chrissy pleaded. "I'll do you next, I promise."

That could've been me, he thought. *These bitches are going to pay*!

What are you going to do, you puny little boy? the dark voice niggled.

I'll . . . I'll—

You'll what? Piss yourself again? You've dug yourself this grave, the voice said.

I should have known my antics would get me into trouble one day . . .

Yes, and now you're paying—

The rolling pin was freed, slowly, another half an inch.

"Take it out!" he screamed, his voice breaking.

Neen appeared before him and rammed the gag back in his mouth. "You're starting to sound stronger. I can't have you blabbing."

"*Argh!*" he bellowed. His eyes flicked from the lesbian show to Neen, who was picking the whip up.

It licked at the back of his thighs, buttocks, calves, back, and shoulders, finally lashing his head, the cord wrapping around his face and catching his nose.

The whip was retracted, the rolling pin eased out another quarter of an inch. Blood trickled and spurted.

"Damn, now I think I need to diddle *my*self," Neen admitted, sitting on the headboard, her feet planted on Simone's shoulders. "Watch me, dog. Or you'll be sorry."

Simone craned his neck the best he could, his muscles pulling and hurting, his eyes falling on her glistening twat and digging, rooting, tattooed fingers. He groaned, his prick leaking.

"I bet you wish you could bury your tongue in there, slave."

Not being able to answer or nod, he blinked his eyes twice.

"I'll take that as a yes." Neen spread her legs wider and peeled her vulva apart, exposing her plump bead. "Can you see it?"

He blinked.

"Oh, she's so sensitive, Simone. Do you think you've been a good enough man-child to lick her? To touch her?"

He blinked numerous times.

"Then maybe I'll let you, just this once, if you promise to be a good boy?"

Simone cast an eye over Chrissy and Mary. They were entangled in a lover's knot, completely oblivious to what was going on around them. *Perfect*, he thought. He blinked at Neen rapidly.

"Okay, being as you've been so obedient." Neen lowered herself from the headboard and stood by his side. "I'm trusting you here," she told him, "So when I take your gag out, I expect you to be on your best behaviour."

He blinked.

We're going to rip your fucking throat out, bitch, the dark voice said.

She pulled Simone's gag free. "Now, I'm going to ram my pussy against your face, so I expect you to lick her until your mouth goes numb. Understand?"

"Yes," he rasped. "But can you untie my hands? I'll need them to brace myself up. Come on, there are three of you, and my body is half dead," he pushed as Neen raised an eyebrow. "I can barely move, let alone do anything else."

"I'll give you *one* hand."

He nodded; pain shot through his stiff, sore neck. "Okay." *That'll be good enough, slut.*

Neen loosened his hand and sat back up on the headboard. "Now, work that tongue! Let's see if you can please me *that* way."

Simone smiled, glanced at the lesbians and went to work on Neen. He lost himself, enjoying her tastes, her moans of pleasure distracting him further. *God, her hands in my hair feel so good.*

Then the pains racking his body spoke up, rallied him, and rage clouded his vision. *Let's see how you fucking like the torture!* he thought, biting down as hard as he could on her clit, determined to tear it from her body.

Blood filled his mouth and spilled down his throat and over his chin.

Simone ragged on the dimple of flesh, ripping his head from side to side, a growl developing in his throat. Neen's piercing scream sent a shiver down his body.

When her tissue tore free and slipped down his throat, Simone wrapped his free hand around the rope binding his other arm and pulled on it. The headboard creaked, splintered and broke, sending him tumbling across the bed.

"The fuck is going on?" Chrissy asked, starting to get up.

Neen, writhing, held her cunt and swore.

"*Neen!*" Chrissy cried.

Simone bounced to his knees, ignoring the aches and pains, and clutched a piece of splintered wood. He clubbed the bucking Neen across the head once, twice, three times. Something cracked. Blood trickled out of her nose, mouth and ears.

Simone licked the blood off his lips and turned to Mary and Chrissy. "Who the fuck's next?"

"*Shit . . .*" Chrissy said backing away.

Mary did the same. "Don't do anything foolish, Simone – you're being filmed. This was only a joke," she said. "We would have stopped."

"Yeah, dude," Chrissy said, shielding herself with Mary.

Simone turned to the camera and lashed out with the hunk of wood, toppling the digital device, which hit the deck and shattered. "I'm not being filmed anymore," he snarled. "What's the matter, Mary? You look as though you're going to shit yourself. You too, Chrissy."

"I think you might have *killed* Neen," Chrissy whispered.

"Bitch got what was coming to her. She got off lightly," he said, "which is more than I can say about you pair."

Chrissy shoved Mary into Simone and ran off.

Mary and Simone tangled, fell and wrestled on the floor, with Simone getting the better of her. He straddled Mary and punched her in the face a handful of times. "Consider this your termination of employment, cunt." He spat in her eyes, got to his feet, and stamped on her tits for good measure. "A shame it had to end like this. I would have enjoyed fucking you on demand. After all, you *belonged* to me. Hell, if you're still breathing after this, maybe I can still have some fun with you."

Simone took a breather, composed himself and checked on Neen. A pool of blood had spread beneath her. "Deader than shit," he said, flying over to the stairs and bounding down them.

The cabin door stood open.

"I'm fucking coming for you, Chrissy!" he raged, standing in the open doorway. He looked left, right and dead centre, his ears pricked. Twigs snapped; foliage rustled. *She's close.* "You're dead! *Dead*! And if it's not by my hand, then it will be by the woods."

And he wasn't lying, either. The area was dense, with a thick covering. It had taken Simone a long time to get used to navigating out here. Walking around aimlessly was deadly and had proven so with the number of walkers, hikers and campers who had gone missing over the years.

Simone walked down the three steps that made up the front porch and jogged into the woods, his floppy cock swinging wild, the dying light at his back. "It won't be long before it's pitch-black out here, Chrissy. I hope you're not scared of the dark."

Ahead, he saw her gloomy shape shifting amongst the bushes, her hair snagging on a low-hanging branch. "I see you!"

"Help! Help me!" Chrissy screamed. She yanked her hair free and set off running again.

Simone slowed to a fast walk, savouring the chase, not wanting it to be over. "Nobody's going to hear you out here, dear. Help! *Help*!" he screamed, proving his point, laughing.

"Please, I'm sorry," she called. "Let me make it up to you, Simone. I'll do *anything*!"

"I just want to fuck and flay your dying, twitching body, Chrissy. There's nothing you can do to help save your life."

"No!"

"I wonder if you'll taste as good as your sister did. I blended that bitch and stuck her in my fridge." He bellowed with laughter and picked up his pace. As he drew closer, he couldn't help but admire her body as she scrambled through the undergrowth: her arse jiggled and her small tits swayed, giving him a shot of side boob.

"Maybe I'll cut those tiny titties of yours off and keep them in a jar. What do you say, Chrissy? Choices, choices."

The snap and rattle of steel brought Simone's laughter to an abrupt halt. Chrissy fell, disappearing out of sight.

"*Argh*!" she screamed. "Oh, Jesus! My leg!"

"What the hell?" he muttered.

"Help me, Simone, please! It's cut through the bone!" she shrieked. "I think I'm going to pass out."

Simone pushed through bushes, shoved some branches aside and discovered Chrissy sprawled across the floor, her one leg caught in a steel snare, its teeth embedded in her calf. Blood squirted out of her. Sinew and bone were on display.

He grinned. "That's not looking too good, Chrissy."

"Call a fucking ambulance, you motherfucker!"

"Is that any way to talk to the person who's about to save your life?"

She looked up at him, tears pouring out of her, and smiled weakly. "You'll h-help me?"

Simone walked up to her, bent over and stared her in the eye. "Nope." His grin hurt his cheeks.

"Get me out! Help! Help! Anyone, please! Help! Help me!"

Simone stood over her and laughed. "I told you, nobody is going to hear you around here. We're on our own. Well, apart from Mary and Neen, but they're not coming to your rescue anytime soon."

Chrissy wept harder, snot bubbling out of her nose, her chin wobbling. "Why did you kill Henry? You piece of shit. She was all I had." Drool dribbled out of her mouth and clung to her chin.

Simone got down on his haunches. "You should be more careful about what you wish for, bitch."

"W-what do you mean?"

"There's nothing fictional about those stories of mine, as you well know. Well, I may have bent the truth or elaborated here and there, but for the most part, it's accurate. And you always told me you wished that Simone was real, that you hoped I was like him, but when you found out I *was*, you couldn't fucking handle it. I'm disappointed in you for letting something like that come between us, even though I killed your sister."

"Fuck you! Get me out of this fucking thing!"

Simone leant on the trap, its teeth digging further into Chrissy's flesh.

"*Ugh . . .*" she gasped, eyes rolling, her body bucking.

"Please pay attention. Do you know how much I've wanted to tell people this shit? About how the books are far from fictitious?"

Chrissy collapsed against the floor and spasmed.

Simone let go of the trap and slapped her across the face. "Don't you fucking pass out on me, fucker! If you listen to everything I have to tell you, I might let you go, okay? But you must be a good girl."

Chrissy nodded.

"I committed the crimes and disappeared a long time before I wrote the stories. Came here, hid, and started out as a writer," he said, narrowing his eyes, his hand tightening around the lump of wood. "Words have always been a passion of mine, so why the hell not, right?"

"I think you need to get to the doctor's, pal," Chrissy sputtered. "You've read one too many of your own stories."

"Cute. Oh well, I did try," he said, standing. "You'll be happy to know that I plan to fuck your dead body. With hope, it'll still be twitching when I do."

"You sick—"

Simone wrapped her hair around his hand and brought the lump of wood down on her face, striking her once, twice, three times. Her nose flattened and her jaw cracked. Bone popped from ruptured skin. Blood splashed nearby trees.

"Look at those neon-pink nipples of yours. Delicious. Denny, the woman I killed years ago, looked a lot like you. It's why I based you off her, Chrissy. Still, she was nowhere near as sexy as you. Your long legs are unbelievable. Would you be against me coming all over them once you're dead?"

"*Help*!" she screamed

"I'll take that as a no, not that you'll have much fucking say in it."

Simone prised the trap's steel jaws open, allowing Chrissy to slip her foot free and to crawl away as he reset it, clicking the teeth back into place.

When he looked up, he saw Chrissy's tail end disappear into a pile of bushes close by. "And where do you think you're going, madam? You call yourself a fan? *Pft,*" he scoffed, rising to his feet to amble after her. "Here piggy, piggy, piggy."

"*Pleeeease!*"

As he walked through the bushes, catching her, she rolled onto her back and stared up at him.

"It's not so great now that the boot is on the other foot, is it, dear?"

Before she could speak, he stamped on her gut and kneed her in the face as hard as he could when she doubled over. Dazed, she hit the deck, the fight knocked out of her.

Simone grabbed her by the hair and dragged her over to the snare. "It was a pleasure knowing you, *babe!*" he said, picking her up and throwing her down onto the trap, making sure her head was dead centre with the trigger.

"*No—*"

The steel teeth closed on her, crushing her head like a ripe pumpkin, her right eye popping free.

"Jesus," he sniggered, giving her trembling body a kick. "You awake down there?" He grinned, his dick hardening to the carnage. He began to stroke it. "I got you good, bitch," he hissed, staring at her obliterated face and chunks of gore that lay scattered about the leaf-cluttered ground. When he got bored of the bloodshed, his gaze travelled the length of her long, blood-mottled legs and didn't stop until it fell upon her tits.

Pre-come bubbled out of his prick, dribbled down and over his fingers, and stringed to the floor.

"Oh!" he gasped, his body bucking. "I'm—*coming!*"

A shot of jism fired from him and landed amongst the pulp that was once Chrissy's pretty face. "*Ugh!*" he grunted, as a second gob of muck exploded from his softening dick and plastered her legs.

Simone collapsed against a tree, his forearm supporting his weight. "*Fuck*! I don't think I've come so hard in my life."

After regaining his breathing, he looked at Chrissy and wondered what he should do with the body. *If I hadn't shot my load all over her, I might have got away with leaving her out here. After all, it could be seen as an accident by the authorities.*

But he knew it would never do.

No, I need to move her. There are plenty of places around here. Either that, or I take her back to the cabin and throw her in my playroom for now.

He liked that idea: *Of course, the playroom!*

It was all coming back to him now, now that Mary's drug had worn off.

Simone grabbed Chrissy by her feet and dragged her towards his cabin.

***

Twenty minutes later, he emerged from the woods. Everything was still. Quiet.

A smile pulled across his face. *I must have killed them, then*, he thought. *Neen was dead for definite, but I was unsure about Mary. Maybe I knocked her out?*

He pulled Chrissy closer to the cabin. "Little pigs, little pigs?" he called, opening the front door. "Chrissy is mashed up and deader than pigeon shit. I made a right mess of her," he declared.

He yanked Chrissy inside and heeled the door closed behind him. Upstairs, he heard either Mary or Neen shuffling around. "Oh, so you *are* still alive, Mary," he guessed, letting go of Chrissy's feet.

Simone crossed to the door leading down to his playroom and opened it. After switching the light on, he peeked inside. Mops, buckets, brushes and cleaning products lined the walls, along with his sawn-off. *Shouldn't need* you *today*, he thought. *Should be easy pickings from here.* He chuckled and pushed a button on the inside wall, activating the floor. It pulled to one side and revealed a staircase leading down into a thick darkness.

"God, I really was out of it, to forget about my underground den."

Simone returned to Chrissy, scooped her off the floor and returned to the door. "I'll be with you later," he told the corpse, planting a kiss on her pulpy face before throwing her down the steps. He laughed as the body rolled and disappeared into the inkiness. "Break a leg!"

"He-help!" Mary said.

"Fuck's sake, can't I have five seconds of fun?" he huffed.

Turning from the door, Simone made his way upstairs to find Mary crawling across the floor, leaving behind a red, slug-like trail. When he looked closer, he saw she was going for a mobile phone that lay close to her.

"Now, now, Mary, you know we can't have that," he told her, walking over to the phone and stamping on it.

"*No . . .*" she whimpered, her fingertips brushing against the shattered screen.

Simone kicked her in the face, sending her sprawling. Teeth pinged off the floor, bed and upturned camera and tripod.

"I bet we have some good footage on this thing," he said, picking up the camera. "Lots of evidence that *could* have be used against me, too, should someone catch on to where you ladies got to this weekend. But seeing as how you dumb bitches didn't tag me in anything and didn't post about your trip – yeah, it's all coming back to me now, Mary – I think it'll all end here."

Mary groaned and wept harder.

Simone laughed, throwing the camera against the wall, watching as bits of it showered the room, bed and unmoving Neen.

"Neen," he mouthed, his eyes lingering on her bare arse. "A shame. You could have been my queen."

"Help!" Mary screamed, jolting Simone.

"Fucking hell, Mary!" he snapped, turning on her. "You scared the shit out of me." Simone crossed the room to where the fire poker had been dropped. "Aye-aye," he said, tossing the weapon into the air and catching it, testing its weight. "This should do the trick."

He strolled over to Mary, whistling, and rolled her onto her back. Simone held the poker up, showing Mary its gleaming tip, and grinned. "I'll miss your expertise around here, Mary. I'll also miss perving on your legs. You really did wear those short skirts and stockings just for me, didn't you?"

"Let-me-ugh-*uch*," she garbled.

Simone rammed the poker through her right eye with such force that he broke through the back of her skull and penetrated the flooring.

"*Oops!*" he said, wiggling and twisting the poker, freeing it.

Mary's heels drummed the floor as her body shook and wobbled. Her lips peeled back in a feral screech of pain.

Simone plunged the poker into her open mouth, relishing the popping and squelching sounds. "*Urgh,*" he raged, forcing the poker deeper and deeper, until Mary stopped moving. "Ha-ha! Fuck you, bitch!"

He left the fireplace implement imbedded in her as he dragged her to the steps and pushed her down them. Bones broke. When Mary hit the bottom, she lay in a twisted heap, her face pointing the wrong way.

"Ouch, that's got to hurt." He turned to Neen, but the bed was empty. "What the holy hell?!"

Simone scuttled around to the other side, but she was gone – only a few drops of blood and some bloody footprints leading to the open window.

"*Fuck*! How—?"

He stormed over to the window and looked outside. She was nowhere to be seen.

"Christ, if she made it deep into the woods, I'll never find her. Also, if she ran in that direction, then she'll soon run into friendly faces. I need to get out there and—*Ugh!*" he cried, as a something hard and heavy crashed over his head.

Particles of annihilated china flew in all directions.

"Bastard!" Neen yelled, bull-charging him, her shoulder slamming into his chest and driving him back towards the stairs.

"Neen!" he yelped, losing his footing.

The pair tumbled down the steps, crash-landing on top of Mary. Neen sprang to her feet before Simone could disentangle himself from the corpse.

"Wait!" he pleaded, holding his hands up in front of his face as he scooted away from the naked, Amazonian-like warrior woman. "Please, I have a proposition for you."

"*Argh!*" she screamed, surging forwards with her hands out in front of her, her talon-like nails going for his eyes. Her claws, missing his orbs, tore bloody tracks down his cheeks and chin.

Simone backhanded her across the face, sending the off-kilter Neen to one side, her head connecting with the chest of drawers. "Stay down if you know what's good for you," he said, getting to his feet. He spied her pert arse again, her tits, and his lust got the better of him. *Maybe . . . Yes – Daddy needs a new dom . . .* "You know, you always told me how much you fancied the *real* Simone, and how much you would love to be the real Chaos, who, as you know, was Simone's mistress and tormentor. Well, you can be her! Think how much fun it would be for us to rule side by side, Neen."

"What the fuck are you talking about?"

"Well, you know I'm the *real* Simone! Chaos was also a real person, until I killed the bitch. Me, Simone; you, Chaos . . ."

"You're fucking deranged!" Neen said, springing to her feet, going for him again. "You killed my friends!"

Simone put his foot out like a lance and Neen ran into it, his heel ploughing into her gut. She cried out and doubled over. "Hardly friends, Neen. They were internet losers.

People who didn't live in the real world. Look, you want proof? That I'm the genuine Simone?"

Neen staggered forward, gripped his shoulders and drove her knee into his bollocks. "Fuck you!" she spat.

"Open. The. Door. By. There," he coughed out, holding his mashed balls.

"A fucking broom cupboard? You think I'm stupid or something?"

"It's not a broom cupboard – that's just a front." His cock throbbed as she moved away from him, her hips sashaying, speckled tits bouncing. "Just look, please," he said, relieved as Neen stepped up to the door and pulled it open. "There's a light switch on the wall to your left."

She hit the lights. "Fucking hell . . ." she whispered. She turned to face him. "Is that Chrissy at the bottom?"

He nodded. "I was going to throw Mary down there too, but you smashed me across the head before I could." He exhaled one good time, gaining control over his breathing again but feeling the ache deep within his sack. "That's *the* playroom, Neen."

"It's real," she whispered, eyes wide. She bent and grabbed something from inside, then spun on him, the barrel of the sawn-off levelled at his chest. Her next words barked out: "Get over here."

Fuck. "Why?"

"I wanna see it," she said, and he didn't miss the curiosity in her voice. "But you're going down first, you fucking maggot."

"Well, you've sure changed your tune," he dared to reply as cold steel glinted at him. "What about vengeance for Chrissy and Mary? What about what I did to your pussy?"

"Meh, they were fuck-all to me, and my cunt is fine. She'll heal. Makes us even for the arse-plugging earlier, I guess?"

Despite the circumstances, he laughed, and she giggled in return. *I've got her, the dirty little bitch*, he thought. *Once she sees the inside of my playroom, she won't be able to resist.*

"All right, maggot." She gestured with the gun. "Give me the guided tour."

"Yes, Mistress," he said and started down the steps until he got to Chrissy's body. "I'm going to have to drag her out of the way."

"Do it, then."

Simone wound Chrissy's hair around his hand and dragged her down the remaining steps and into the shadows of a corner in the room below.

When Neen reached the bottom, she remained out of arm's reach, running a finger along the top of the blunted twin barrels. "What do you plan on doing to me, now that you have me in your little room?"

"Whatever you desire." He held his hand out. "Welcome to my real world and not my imaginary one."

Neen looked away from him to investigate the room. "Oh, *wow*," she whispered, her mouth forming a perfect *O*. "Is that. . . Mr. Tickles?!"

Simone smiled and stared at his favourite stuffed friend, who sat beside his torture table. "Yep." The clown's garish black, purple and violet colours were faded, and his hellish garb was holey and dusty. "He likes it down here in the dark, living with the tortured, trapped screams of those who have fallen to my blade. He tells me how he can still smell their individual blood and piss and excrement apart."

"And is that the table you described in the book? The one—"

"Where all my victims to date have succumbed? Yes," he replied, beaming as Neen stepped to the table, set the shotgun beside it, and caressed its leather ankle and wrists straps.

"Look how used and worn they are," she uttered, biting her lower lip. "God, I'm excited just thinking about all the women you've had locked up down here."

"And I'm happy to lock up one more for fun. Would Mistress like that?"

"Mistress Chaos," she said.

"That's not a name I want to hear. Pick something else."

"You loved her, didn't you?"

"Until she had to go, yes. But that was a long time ago, and now I'm in the market for a special woman. A woman like you, Neen. I've been searching for a long time."

Neen put a hand out and stroked his face. "I really did enjoy beating and humiliating you upstairs earlier. I think I could warm to the idea of continuing to humiliate you and would very much like to take up the role of your mistress – Mistress Long."

"Ooh, I like—"

"Did I give you permission to speak, you sniffling fucking worm?" she asked, rushing to Simone and striking him across the face.

"No, Mistress." Simone dipped his head, his chin resting on his chest.

"From now on, I expect you to love, honour and obey me. Do you under-fucking-stand?" she asked, cracking him across the face with the flat of her hand.

"Yes, Mistress."

"Things are going to change around here, boy. You're my property now, and I will run your social media sites. All your creative properties and monies are also mine. I *may* allow you to continue to write. After all, I do enjoy what you do, and it'll give me a nice little side income."

"Yes, Mistress," he said, getting on his hands and knees.

She snatched up the sawn-off and let it dangle one-handed at her side. "Crawl to me, slave."

Simone moved at a slow pace, his eyes never leaving her. When he got within touching distance, she told him to stop, which he did.

"Now, let's see how well you can behave." Neen placed her foot under his chin and raised his head up, her eyes meeting his. "You'd better obey my every command if you know what's good for you."

"Yes, Mistress."

"Now, clean this shit up," she said, pointing at Chrissy. "And don't forget Mary."

"What would Mistress have me do with them?"

Neen tapped her chin. "Hmm, good question. Cutting them up and burying them in the woods where nobody would find them sounds too easy for my arsehole slave. So too does setting fire to the bodies or weighing them down and dumping them in a lake or river." Neen continued to mull it over. "A tricky one, but I think you should eat both women. And, before you get excited, I don't mean their pussies."

Simone's mouth sagged. "You mean—"

"Uh huh," Neen said, nodding slowly. She smiled and nibbled her bottom lip. "Look at it this way: at least you won't go hungry for a while." She laughed, turning her back on him to walk upstairs, the short shotgun slung over her shoulder. "Now, on with your work while I tidy up. I'll bring you down a good knife and fork when I'm good and ready. In the meantime, you can stay down here, in the dark," she said, flicking the lights off, "and think about things like a good little slave." She laughed.

"B-but—" he muttered, the door's clacking locks shutting him off.

***

With the blood and muck washed clean from her skin, Neen plopped in front of Simone's PC in his room, propping the sawn-off against the desk. Exhausted, aching, and still horny (even with a mutilated clit), she perused his writing. It was good – she could see it fetching a pretty penny, if published.

"Now it's a case of getting my dear old slave to finish this new novel of his," she said, reading over the last few paragraphs of his work in progress. "He'll have plenty of juicy bits to include after this weekend." She smiled, getting out of the computer chair and going into the kitchen to fetch him the promised good knife and fork.

Cutlery in hand, Neen made her way over to the cellar door and called on her slave. "Here you go. Tuck in!" she said and threw the knife and fork into the darkness.

"Thanks," he whispered, bounding up the stairs by twos out of the blackness.

Neen froze, mouth sagging open, as she realized she'd left the shotgun behind. *Son of a—*

He reached her and slashed the knife blade across her throat without hesitating. "Looks like I'll have three bitches to take care of now," he said, his evil grin filling her already darkening sight.

"Ugh! *Uch*!" Neen gargled as hot liquid cascaded down her chest.

"I decided, while 'thinking in the dark,' that I don't want another bitch ruling my life." As she collapsed to the floor, blood gushing, he whispered in her ear, "I'm going to keep your body and fuck it until there's nothing left of it."

"Argh!" she cried, holding out a blood-stained hand.

"And that's all he wrote!" Simone said, laughing, his dick stiffening at the centre of her blurred vision . . .

Clubhouse of the Dead

S ue stood in the beer garden outside his beloved Biker's Bar'n'Grill as a commotion unfolded a hundred feet away on the Old Tampa Bay strip, Florida.

"The fuck?!" Sue muttered, turning his head and pushing himself off the wall he was leant against. He'd been enjoying a joint and beer while listening to the hijinks around him, the sun setting over the sands before him. "Has some kind of brawl started in Murphy's Pool Hall and spilled to the outside?" he mused aloud, craning his neck while blowing smoke free of his nostrils before flicking his spent roach aside.

Objects sailed through the air and people ran in his direction, whipping up a stampede. On the gentle sea breeze, the sound of crying, screaming and snarling reached his ears, replacing the banal noise of laughter, chinks of beer glasses, and the yaps of dogs as they played catch with their masters.

Children shot by on skateboards and scooters, bantering and blowing bubbles with their bubble gum.

Sue's heartrate rose and a sinking feeling dropped his guts like an elevator with cut brakes.

Those around Sue hadn't seemed to notice, or care, about the situation, which worried him further.

Maybe I should get people inside, he thought, looking around at the bikers who were enjoying a cold beer in the dying afternoon sun. Like, right now.

More screaming, louder this time, prompted Sue's attention.

Ahead, the uproar spilled onto the beach. The shrieking and wailing became louder, more frequent, as more and more people were dragged into the escalating situation.

I don't understand what's causing this panic, Sue thought, his palms sweaty; it took a lot to rattle the large, brutish-looking Native American, who people around here had come to fear.

"You have to get out of here, now!" a scantily clad woman on rollerblades said to Sue over her shoulder as she skated past. "They're fucking crazy and chewing people up."

The look of terror on her face and in her eyes was almost enough to stop his heart.

The Boas, the happily named biker gang who treated Sue's bar like their clubhouse, muttered and spoke amongst themselves at his back.

"Yo, ese, what the fuck is going on?" one asked.

"I have no idea," Sue said, his gaze fixed on the people attacking some teenage girls and boys who'd been playing volleyball and tossing a frisbee around on the beach.

"Run!" a man pleaded as he bolted past, his shirt torn, shorts bloody. "You're all going to die if you stay here."

A posse of screeching, sobbing people followed.

"What's happening up there?" Sue asked, but they were all too busy running for what seemed like their lives.

When he faced front again, the volleyballers and frisbee players were lying on the sand.

Dead? he wondered, putting a hand to his mouth.

Their attackers then tore off their skin and ripped out their innards and devoured the gore.

"No…" Sue mouthed, staggering backwards and into a table, knocking over bottles and glasses, which shattered on the ground.

"Jesus fuck, Sue! You spilled our fucking beers, shithead," a female Boa smart-mouthed.

"Spaniard," he called, turning to face the rotund woman who had a Rambo-like tie around her forehead and no teeth to speak of. "Where is he?" he screamed, grabbing her by her vest and drawing her close.

"Get your mitts off me, Sue," she demanded, wriggling in his hands which were the size of bales of hay.

"I'm right here, amigo," Spaniard said, exiting the Bar'n'Grill.

"Get your people indoors, right now," Sue demanded.

Spaniard, the Boas' fearless President, smiled and laughed. "What's got you so spooked, friend? Did you just see the ghost of Custer?"

The Boas around them laughed.

Sue grabbed Spaniard, turned him around, and pointed up the strip. "That!"

"Holy shit," someone said over Sue's shoulder.

"Are they fucking eating people? What are they?" another person gasped.

"Jesus Christ," Spaniard whispered.

"I didn't think you were a religious man, hombre."

"There are ghouls on the strip," a man holding a small child to his chest said as he dashed by.

"A little early for a Halloween prank, don't you think, Sue?" Spaniard said.

"Oh, fuck," Sue said, letting go of Spaniard as the things tearing up the inhabitants of Old Tampa Bay drew closer to him and his bar. "Inside, now!"

As Boas and customers rushed inside the Bar'n'Grill, Sue heard snarling, ripping, gutting, and tearing coming from all around him, almost nipping at his heel.

I have to get in there, he thought, pushing his way through the crowd to avoid being caught up in the bottleneck by the Grill's entrance. If I can get around back, I'll be home free.

But panic ripped through those around him like wildfire, compacting the throng of people and crushing the wind out of Sue's lungs. His eyes bugged.

Tables and chairs were upended, and the sound of breaking glass was near deafening.

With all his might, he dragged himself out of the mob and rushed around the side of his bar, to the rear entrance.

Sue fumbled with his keys as he reached the door.

"Come on, come on," he scolded himself, ripping them out of his pocket but dropping them.

From over the eight-foot fence, topped with barbed wire that encircled his bar's backyard, dropped a couple of men whose bodies were covered in deep cuts, as though they'd been fed through a woodchipper.

"Fuck!" Sue gasped, picking his keys up and placing his back to the Grill's door. "What do you want?" he asked the approaching fellas, whose eyes rolled in the backs of their heads.

"Ugh!" one groaned and drooled, its jaw hanging loose, its left foot mangled and dragging behind him.

The other snarled and sauntered closer to Sue with his arms outstretched, exposing his mutilated fingers, scuffed hands, and the pieces of bone that jutted through the broken, discoloured skin at its elbow and forearm.

They look…dead…Sue thought, drawing the bone-handled Bowie knife sheathed at his hip.

"Stay back," he warned, slashing at the air.

His attackers kept coming, groaning and growling.

"Get the fuck away from—"

Maimed fingers pounced, springing through the air and diving for Sue.

Sue put up his size seventeen booted foot and planted it into the guts of the ghoul, propelling him backwards and into the bins. But he didn't have time to take a breather, as the second one was on him, mouth going for Sue's throat.

"No chance," Sue said, smacking the flat of his huge paw against the thing's face, driving it backwards. He stabbed his knife through its ear and twisted it. The beast crumpled to the floor.

"Oh shit," he gasped, looking at his blood-covered hands and clothes.

"Ugh-uch," his first attacker raged, fighting with the bins and their lids as it tried to get back on its feet.

"Fuck, fuck, fuck," Sue said, getting control over himself and gaining access to the back of his bar. Once he was inside, he closed and locked the door. "Nobody's getting through that, I don't care how many crazies there are."

Sue turned from the door and made his way through the back room, which acted as the storeroom/beer cellar. The area was chilled, and he could see his own breath as he exhaled.

Out in the bar, he could hear a ruckus taking place.

Do I lock myself in here? He looked about – there were enough supplies to last him up to a month, if he was careful. Surely it won't take that long for something like this to blow over?

His eyes then fell on the phone, and he dashed over to it, picking it up.

"Hello? Hello?!"

The line was dead.

"Anyone? Operator?" he asked, tapping the pips. "He—Shit!" he raged, slamming the phone into its cradle.

"Argh!" he heard, and then a noise fell against the back door – someone was pounding on it.

He's not getting in. No way.

Sue walked to the door that would lead him to the bar, opened it and peered around it. His mouth sagged.

Jesus…

Towards the front of the bar, Spaniard and a few other Boas (including the woman with the Rambo tie) tried to close the doors to keep the monsters out. However, some of the ghouls had made it inside via a broken window and were entangled in a fight with Boas, customers and the strippers that worked the Grill's stage.

I need to get out there and help, Sue thought, looking around to see if he could find something to arm himself with. If I can make it to the bar, then I'll have the shotgun at my disposal. But I'll need to get there first, he continued to muse, looking at the monsters that stood in his path.

Sue tried to control his breathing and slow his heartrate down.

Come on, I can do this. He then had second thoughts, closing and locking the door. Let them deal with it. He propped a seat against the door, wedged under the handle. Fuck it, I don't need to be a hero.

If you don't, then your reputation will be worthless, and you'll be the coward everyone thinks you are, a part of his mind argued. And what would your dad think? Do you want to prove him right?

"Fuck!" Sue collapsed against the door and slid down it, hugging his knees to his chest. "What am I going to do?"

You know you have it in you, Sue, he thought, so get out there and kick some ass.

"Five minutes, that's all I need. Just five minutes so I can regroup," he argued with himself.

***

Sue (The Injun) Yazzie, better known as Tomahawk Sue, or Sue for short, got through the tough side of life with a mouthful of stories and a dazzling smile, and not quite the hard fist and unbreakable jaw that was said about him.

It's not to say he wasn't a bruiser, though – he was just the strong, silent type and didn't like to show it. So, he let the grapevine do his talking.

And it worked, for the brutish routine was swallowed even by those who knew him best and entrenched themselves in his bar.

"Maybe it's his Navajo backstory," a barfly once suggested.

"Or his girlie first name," offered another. "I mean, who'd want to fight and fuck with a guy called Sue, right? Folk might figure he's grown up tough as bricks."

"Yeah, and just look at the size of him! Also, it could be that eyepatch he wears," a third chipped in. "I've heard there's nowt wrong with his peeper, that it's all stinkin' lies."

"Aye, and the story about the underlever action he keeps beneath the bar counter helps bolster his tall tales, I'm sure," the first man said. "Anyone ever seen that famous Adler of his?"

The others shook their heads.

Sue smiled, a laugh escaping him, remembering the barfly's words as he cleared empty glasses and bagged spent beer bottles from off the bar counter that morning before the ghouls turned up.

"I can't believe this old joint of mine is ten years old this weekend," he said, shaking his head. "Nobody thought I'd make it work, especially Pa, but I proved them wrong. God, Dad was livid, and jealous, knowing he could never make a go of anything."

"Why do you allow people to spread vicious rumors about you, son? It's insulting to our people," said Sue's dad, who, ironically, had named his son after a country and western song. "Your mother has caught wind of some of it and is mortified, not to mention your grandparents. Give up this glitzy, sinful dream of yours, and come home, Sue, back to Kansas, where our forefathers once ruled."

"Dad, if I show I'm afraid, or any weakness, then folk will walk over me."

"And you won't sell up? Do you think it's right, someone of your heritage behaving in such a manner?" he asked, glancing at the drunks and strippers on stage.

"No, my life is here, in Florida, Dad. With my business."

Speculation regarding Sue was rife on the Old Tamp Bay strip, and not just confined to the ones who frequented the Grill. But that's the way the six-foot-five, two-hundred-and-fifty-pound, long-haired half breed liked it. He'd worked hard at building a nasty reputation and business, which kept him and his bar, free of trouble.

And if it wasn't his infamous status that kept the wolf from the door, then it was his affiliation with the Boa biker gang, who hung out at the Grill daily, having turned Sue's into their clubhouse of sorts.

"I'm going to make your bar my own, gringo," Spaniard told Sue on their first meeting.

Now, even though a lot of wily shit flew around Tampa about Sue, who himself spoke with a folk tongue for reasons above, he wasn't scared to stand his ground and stare danger down from time to time, to help lend credence to the aforementioned guileful BS.

"Is that so, pilgrim?" Sue asked, hunching over the bar's counter, one arm disappearing below, reaching for his well-known Adler. "Do you think it wise, threatening a man who has a shotgun pointed at your balls? Now, how about we cut a deal? A kind of 'you scratch my back, and I'll scratch yours' thing?"

A suffocating silence descended over the rowdy establishment, amplifying the sound of Sue's cocking shotgun and buzzing neon bar lights.

The barman smiled. "What do you say, partner? I don't much fancy plastering your nuts all over my barroom floor."

The three Boas flanking Spaniard stood down, and the four barflies propped against the bar got off their stools and backed away.

"Holy shit," Hank, one of the men playing pool, said, and the three fellas throwing darts stopped to watch the unfolding events.

Spaniard held his hands up and smiled. "Okay, Sue, I guess we can come to some sort of arrangement, since you're showing me how big your cojones really are."

"Excellent, friend."

And then the deal was hashed out there and then, with punters looking on, over two bottles of tequila and three dozen cans of Sol.

"You can do whatever you want to the place, within reason, so long as you help keep trouble, drugs, guns and any other form of illegal activity out of here."

"Sounds fair. Can we decorate it with our colours and bring in some strippers?"

"As long as you don't upset my regulars, you can paint the walls pink with yellow polka dots."

The men agreed and shook hands.

That situation had been perfect for Sue, for it showed all before him how manly he was, and that the grapevine never lied. Still, it didn't stop the odd few from continuing to speculate over him. Whatever the case, it kept the Grill clean, and he was happy for people to think and believe what they wanted to.

It's not like I have to live with them, he thought while re-stocking his bar's fridges with bottles of beers and soft drinks ahead of the day's shift. When he was finished doing that, he prepped the shelves with clean glasses and loaded dirty ones into the dishwasher out back. I got to get this place in order before opening time.

When he looked up at the clock, he saw it was a lick off midday.

Barflies while be here soon, he thought, opening the till to make sure it had a float. Happy, he closed it and turned to face the pool table and huffed out a laugh.

"Paco," Sue called, trying to rouse the sleeping Boa. "You don't look very comfortable on there." He walked over to the sprawled biker. "Aren't those pool balls digging into your back? Paco?" He shook the skinny man by the shoulder.

Paco snorted, farted and rolled onto his back, exposing the cue he was cradling to his chest like a lover.

"What time is it, ese?"

"Time that you got out of my bar and took a shower. And pull your damn jeans up, man – I could park my bicycle between the crack of your ass."

"Maybe, if you had one, Tonto," Paco grumbled, placing the cue aside and struggling into a sitting position. "Ugh, my head." He belched, holding his guts and removing his bandanna with his free hand. "Where is Spaniard and the rest of the crew?"

"The last I saw Hatchet-Face, your astute and charismatic sergeant at arms, he was in the men's toilet – in the urinal trough, trying to get it on with my mop!"

"Ha! Did Bianca give him the brushoff again?"

"You know it, Paco. Now, if you don't mind, could you collect your biker goons and get out of here, please?"

"Okay, okay," Paco said, getting off the table and staggering forward. "Tequila is the devil's invention." He burped again, zigzagging towards the men's room while calling on Hatchet-Face.

Sue shook his head. No way in hell would Bianca touch him, he thought, laughing while staring at the runway where she and the rest of the strippers performed every evening. That reminds me, the girls are coming in early tonight – they're doing their annual Wet'n'Wild show, Sue continued to muse, strolling to the main doors and unlocking them. And who doesn't like a load of lovelies in wet t-shirts? He smiled, opening the doors and clicking them into place, allowing the hot, steamy weather into his dank, stale bar.

"Glorious," he said, breathing in the salty ocean air. Sue put his hands to the small of his back and arched backwards, working the knots out of his joints. "It's a hell of a time to be alive."

Out on the beach, he spotted half naked men and women frolicking on the sand. Some were walking their dogs and others were playing netball and catch, while most sunbathed. On the sea, close to land, were surfers, swimmers and jet skiers.

The sound of laughter and chatter reached his ears.

"Fucking Florida, man," he muttered, turning from the scene to walk back into his bar to grab his mug of coffee from off the counter.

"Come on, brother. Let's get you back on your bike and home," Sue heard Paco say, followed by the toilet door slamming shut.

The bikers shuffled towards him with their arms around each other for support.

"Will you boys be in later for the wet t-shirt competition?"

"We wouldn't miss it for the world, ese," Paco said.

And then Hatchet-Face, who had more tattoos than skin on his face, threw his guts up on the barroom floor. "Sorry, gringo," he managed to say, holding his stomach with his free hand.

"Jesus, just get him out of here!" Sue ordered. "I'll clean it up."

"See you tonight, amigo," Paco said, escorting his friend outside.

Sue huffed, fetched his mop and bucket, and set to work.

Over the course of the next few hours, the barflies, regulars and strippers made their way into the Grill.

***

By six, Sue thought, the Bar'n'Grill was packed and jumping, with Spaniard and his crew of forty dominating the stripper's runway. And then it came to this. Sue laughed, looked up and caught sight of the baseball bat he kept in the storage room. I think it's time to show people what I'm made of. I'll hammer my way through, and use my knife, too.

Sue pushed off the floor and grabbed the bat from the shelving unit that held dried goods, snacks and a variety of soft and alcoholic drinks.

The slugger had Tampa Bay Rays etched into its wood.

I remember buying this thing at the Rays' final game, he thought, smiling at the weight of the weapon. He could almost smell the hotdogs and hear the crowd cheering. It was a great afternoon, and *If I'm going to go down, then I'm going down swinging.*

And then, for the first time, the screaming coming from inside the bar registered with him.

My friends are dying out there.

Sue's hands tightened around his bat as he walked towards the door, removed the chair, and pulled it open. As he charged into the bar, swinging, slashing and shoulder-barging ghouls out of his way, he spotted Spaniard and a few of his biker brothers by the Grill's main entrance, trying to secure it.

Fuck, I need to help them, he thought, mashing his slugger across the face of a rotted ghoul, taking its mouth apart and splashing the bottles behind his bar in blood and gore.

When the ghoul collapsed, Sue spotted his Adler and went for it, but not before gaining the attention of the Boa's leader.

"Spaniard, take this!" he yelled, throwing his bat towards the buffy, six-foot-something biker, who snatched the bat out of the air and began to do some pummelling of his own.

Sue sheathed his blade and grabbed the shotgun, cocking a round into the chamber.

"Come and get it, you rotten bags of shit!" he screamed, blowing the face off a ghoul that crawled onto the bar, its hands outstretched, its fingers going for Sue's groin and eyes.

Brain and bone mattered redecorated the barroom floor.

When Sue cocked the Adler, the spent cartridge flipped out the guns side and tumbled to the floor.

We need to get this bar locked down, he thought.

Most of the windows around the Grill were out, with ghouls pouring in through them.

Over by the stripper's runway, Brandy and the rest of her girls became entangled in a blood-soaked war, which they were losing.

Dead, naked girls rose and attacked.

No…

Some of them used their high-heel shoes to gouge, slice and hack, while others went in with their teeth and fake ceramic nails.

Blood sprayed up the walls.

Impossible… Zombies?!

Sue moved to help Brandy, but his path was blocked by bikers and ghouls as the fight spread over to the bar.

"Quick, barricade the doors!" he heard Spaniard say, and was relieved to find the doors to the Grill had been shut.

Bikers and everyday customers scrambled about the bar, gathering tables and chairs, which they pushed against the entrance.

"We need to cover the windows too," Sue bellowed, blasting the arm and then leg off a zombie closing in on him. "There are hammers and nails in the storeroom, Spaniard."

"Go, Boas," Spaniard told his biker brothers and sisters, whose numbers had thinned considerably. "Gather what we need and start pinning tables over the windows."

With the door secured, Sue, Spaniard and a few others killed off the ghouls inside the bar and helped clear the areas around the windows in readiness to be boarded over.

When the place was fortified, Sue took charge. "Spaniard, you need to kill your dead." He told the biker leader what he had seen with the strippers. "Whatever sickness these ghouls have, it's reanimating the dead."

Sue expected howls of laughter, but a silence fell over the small amount of living left standing within the Grill.

"I saw one of 'em sumbitches get back up," a barfly admitted, adding weight to what Sue had said. "Right after

I'd put the sucker down with one of your pool cues, boy. It came at me crazier than anything I ever damn well saw."

"Someone turn the fucking television on!" Meat-Hook, one of the Boas, said.

"Good idea," Hatchet-Face said, jumping over the bar, his gut jouncing. He walked towards the TV that clung to a wall. When he switched it on, there was nothing but dead air on most of the channels. "Jack shit, boys and girls."

And then he picked something up: an emergency channel.

"Looks like it's only broadcasting rescue stations," Spaniard said.

"Hell, if the strip is full of them damn things, then most of those places on screen might as well be on Mars," a woman to Sue's side said.

"Brandy!" Sue said, throwing his arms around the young black dancer. "I thought you were dead. I saw you one moment, the next…"

"Hell, you can't keep a good stripper down, Sue." She giggled, hugging him back. "I think the rest of the girls are dead," she said, stepping out of his embrace and looking towards the stage.

"We just have to keep it together," he said, rubbing her shoulder. "Why don't you go and get changed, now that things have settled down?"

"Yeah, I kind of look underdressed for a zombie killer, huh."

"Just a bit, kid," he said, looking down at her glitzy bra (which struggled to contain her double E tits) and matching thong, which had a bunch of singles stuffed in the strings.

Brandy laughed and then left.

"So, if we can't get to them places on TV, how are we going to get out of this shit?" someone asked.

"Wait for Uncle Sam to turn up," a barfly replied.

"Hell, that could be days. Weeks, even!" a new person said.

"Calm down, everyone!" Spaniard said. "Why don't you lot do something constructive, like search for weapons, huh? Let us handle this shit, yeah?"

Boas and customers muttered amongst themselves before shuffling off.

"What have you got in mind, Spaniard?" Sue asked.

"Still got that SUV of yours?"

Sue nodded.

"We could bust out of here in that thing, and go for help."

"What about everyone else? It won't take all of us."

"They can hold the fort, gringo," Hatchet-Face said.

"He's right," Paco said, wiping blood from his forehead.

"The SUV will only take seven of us, and I'm not leaving Brandy behind," Sue said, staring Spaniard down.

Spaniard looked away and did a headcount.

"Meat-Hook, if I take Paco, Hatchet-Face and a few others, can you hold the fort here until we get back with help?"

The scar-faced biker fidgeted before gulping and nodding his head. "Yes, I'll do my best to keep everyone safe."

"Good. I'll leave Mudball, Snakes and Patches with you," Spaniard said.

All his high-ranking soldiers, Sue thought, looking around the bar at the Boas that remained. Apart from Hatchet-Face, who's tagging along for the ride.

"Looks like someone's coming on the air to speak," someone said.

Sue looked over at the TV and saw the displayed message. I ain't got the time to sit around and wait, he thought, heading towards the bar. Once there, he rooted around for spare shotgun cartridges and the keys to his SUV.

With everything he needed in hand, he made his way towards the storage room but was stopped in his tracks when a moan sounded over by the stripper's runway.

"What the hell was that?" Spaniard asked, joining Sue's side.

"There, look," Sue said, pointing at one of the dead strippers that started to rise out of a pile of broken chairs and tables, toppling the wood. "Porsche…" he muttered, recognising the short, blonde and buxom woman. One of her nipples was missing, along with an earring, stiletto and a chunk of flesh from around her throat, which exposed sinew and veins.

Porsche tried to growl, letting out a hollow whisper instead.

Sue's ball sack shrivelled at the sound.

"She's dead behind the eyes," Spaniard said.

Sue rose his Adler. "Sorry, babe," he said, pumping a round into her guts.

The blast did little but knock her off-kilter and she kept coming.

"So, it does have to be the head," Sue said, cocking his gun and blasting the top part of Porsche's scalp off.

The body crumpled to the floor.

More strippers rose up.

Some were topless, others completely nude. Dollar bills and blood poured from them, and they banded together like a troupe of Roman soldiers.

"Shit," Paco said, coming up behind Sue holding part of a snapped pool cue. "Hatchet-Face, help me take these bitches down."

"Let us take care of the dead," Spaniard told Sue, "while you get our ride ready."

Sue nodded as Hatchet-Face, armed with a broken beer bottle and a chain belonging to a motorbike, sidled up to Paco and Spaniard. "Okay, I'll leave you guys to it."

As he exited the bar, he heard chain, knife, bat, and bottle go to work on his girls.

Sue swallowed the developing lump in his throat and bit back his tears as he went in search of Brandy.

"Brandy?" he called when he arrived at her changing room. He knocked on the door. "Are you in there, babe?"

"Yeah, come on in, sugar," she said.

Sue opened the door. Brandy stood on the opposite side of the room slipping her bra on, and he caught a glimpse of her tits. "Ready?" he asked.

"One second, sailor," she said, grabbing her denim jacket with the huge Journey patch on its back. "I can't forget my lucky coat."

"Got your lucky knickers on too?"

"Cheeky," she said, giving him a playful shove, her smile dying as fast as it had developed.

"What's wrong?" he asked, putting a hand to her chin and lifting her head up, her eyes meeting his.

"I'm terrified."

"You're with me now, Brandy. I won't let fuck-all happen to you." Sue embraced her and gave her a kiss on the forehead. "Come on, we need to haul ass."

"Where are we going?"

"We're leaving."

"What do you mean?"

"I have an SUV tucked away in the garage, which will take a few of us to safety," he said, and then told her the whole plan.

He led them into the garage and flicked the lights on. The space was bare apart from the SUV, a tool cabinet, and a few other bits and pieces.

"See if you can find anything that might be of use to us out on the road, while I fire it up."

"Okay," Brandy said, and they parted ways.

Sue opened the door to his Ford, got behind the wheel, and then fired up the engine and gave it a few revs. It's been a while, old girl, he thought, for these days he favoured his Harley, which was parked outside. It's probably covered in zombies by now.

Before killing the engine, he popped the hood and checked the machine's oil and water levels. When he dropped the bonnet back into place, he looked over at Brandy, who was rattling some Jerry cans. "We're good to go," he told her. "Are they full?"

"They feel it," she said, handing them to him.

"Yep, these will do us."

"How much gas is in the car?"

"Over half a tank."

"There ain't much in line of weapons, Sue, apart from your tools."

"Hopefully we won't need much – there's a rescue station not that far from here."

"Where?"

"St Petersburg."

"Shit, that's still a pretty good distance, and if those things are all over…"

"Shh," he soothed, taking her in his arms. "We're going to be fine, trust me. We'll have Spaniard and a few of his guys with us."

The door to the garage burst open. "We need to get the fuck out of here, now!" Spaniard said. Behind him, Paco, Hatchet-Face and Meat-Hook poured in.

"I thought—" Sue started to say, when he heard groaning and moaning coming from behind the bikers.

Hatchet-Face slammed the door to the garage closed and shoved the tool chest against it. "We need to go. Now!"

"What's going on?" Brandy asked, close to tears.

"Is that thing running right?" Spaniard asked about the Ford.

"She is, yes. What's happened?"

Spaniard grabbed Sue by the arm and pulled him to the car. "They've broken in, man. Came spilling into the Grill by the hundreds."

"We didn't stand a fucking—" Paco said but was stopped short when the garage door rattled in its frame.

The drawers to the tool chest jiggled open, spilling tools.

"Oh, shit…" Brandy said, opening a door to the Ford and getting in.

Sue, unable to speak, got behind the wheel of the SUV.

Paco and Spaniard also hopped in.

"Come on, Hatchet-Face, Meat-Hook. We need to go!"

The two bikers got in as the door to the garage busted apart and a clown zombie – its red nose crooked and blackened, its colourful costume torn and bloody – stumbled into the garage and crashed against the SUV. Its bright wig was knocked askew.

More followed in behind the Bozo-wannabe and slammed against the Ford.

Arms and fists hammered against the car's windows.

Brandy screamed and the various bikers yelled at Sue to get them clear of the danger zone.

The SUV's back window cracked as Sue stomped the gas pedal, shooting them forward and through the thin aluminium garage door. In the process, the car's front bumper was yanked free and a headlight caved in.

Zombies clung onto the Ford's bodywork to be dragged along behind it like something out of a bad western film.

Sue powered the car though the Grill's backyard fence, snapping and tearing wood free. Planks rebounded off the SUV's frame.

Hordes greeted them out on the roads, but this didn't stop nor rattle Sue, as he ploughed through rotting flesh.

Heads and bodies exploded against his windshield.

Body parts entangled in the Ford's wheels, causing them to spin as traction was lost.

"Keep the pedal to the metal, man," Paco said, "or we're going to get bogged down."

The sound of bone crunching, and shattering was deafening, even over the noise of the growling, snarling zombies as they threw themselves at Sue's ride and pinged back off it.

"Fuck, fuck, fuck," Brandy said, pressing her hands to her chest. "I'm think I'm having a fucking heart attack, Sue."

But the big Native American ignored her even when she placed her hand on his thigh, too intent on getting them to a safer area.

"The road looks clearer up ahead," Meat-Hook said from the back seat.

Sue grunted, clenched his teeth and continued to mash the gas pedal to the floor.

A body rolled over his roof, and something smashed into the SUV's grill.

"If there's much more of this, the car won't be able to take it," Hatchet-Face said.

"She's never let me down before," Sue reassured him, as both the car's wing-mirrors were battered free. "Fuck!"

An ominous smoke started to rise out of the bonnet.

She's overheating with the strenuous work.

Sue took a series of quick lefts and rights, trying to get them out of the back streets and off the little roads.

"There are main roads coming up," Spaniard said, as though reading Sue's mind.

The zombies began to thin out, and the SUV started taking minimal hits and damage.

Sue eased up on the accelerator and, for the first time, took in his surroundings.

"It's a goddamn warzone out here," Spaniard said.

Buildings and vehicles were ablaze, and survivors ran for their lives.

"Let's not hang around, Sue," Brandy said, giving his knee a squeeze.

"How far to the shelter in Petersburg?" Meat-Hook asked.

"Roughly thirty miles," Sue said, steering around a burning bus. Close to the Greyhound, a pack of zombies ripped and chewed at several charred bodies.

Vomit filled Sue's mouth, and his cheeks puffed out. He looked away and swallowed, his throat burning. Jesus, he thought, continuing to drive.

Sue led them farther from the Grill, along the coast, leaving the death and carnage at their backs as he pushed for St Petersburg.

He chipped away at the miles ever so slowly, as the roads were filled with overturned vehicles, zombies, and the dead. It took more than two hours to get ten miles, and the stopping and starting began to eat into their fuel.

Ahead, they spotted an army detail, who'd set up a machine-gun nest complete with mortar units, a tank and six jeeps. The closer they got, the more soldiers they saw – soldiers wearing gasmasks and carrying flamethrowers and M16 Assault Rifles.

Sue stopped the car and eyed the blockade.

"Yo, what the hell are you doing, ese?" Paco wanted to know. "They'll protect us."

Soldiers moved towards them with their guns raised. One of them was yelling something, but it was drowned out by the noise all around.

"He's right, Sue," Spaniard said.

Sue shifted the gearstick into reverse and started to ease his car backwards. "I think we should find another way, people."

"What, why?!" Brandy said, her voice breaking.

"I just don't tru—"

A bullet pinged off the SUV, and Sue slammed on the brakes.

A voice boomed over a megaphone. "Please proceed forward – we mean you no harm."

Sue let the SUV idle while he mulled the situation over.

"What's going on here, man?" Hatchet-Face asked. "We wanted help and we've found it!"

"I would have preferred the police, that's all," Sue said. "I've just never trusted the army – you've all seen how GIs can react in situations like this, guys. They'll haul us in, separate us and do all kinds of tests on us. Hell, we might never see the light of day again."

"You've watched one too many films!" Spaniard said, laughing.

"We've got nothing to lose," Brandy chipped in. "Please, Sue. It's going to be dark soon, and those things are everywhere."

In his mad panic and dash, Sue had forgotten about time. He looked at his watch and saw it was a shade past nine p.m. How did it get so late so fast?

Someone tapped on his window, and when Sue looked up, a soldier stood there, the muzzle of his machinegun pressed to the glass.

"Switch the engine off, sir."

He did as he was instructed, fearing a wrong or fast move would get him killed.

"Okay," he said, raising one hand while the other went for the keys in the ignition.

"Wind you window down, sir. Now."

"What's the problem?" Sue asked, gritting his teeth.

"I'll ask the questions, unless you want my M16 up your nostril, Sitting Bull?" the soldier asked, and Sue shook his head. "How many in your party?"

"Six, including me."

"Anyone injured? Been bitten or scratched?"

"No, not that I'm—"

"Yes or no, civilian?!" The soldier placed the muzzle of his gun to the side of Sue's head.

"No!"

"Then pull the fucking car up to my colleagues. Now!"

Sue didn't need telling twice. He started the SUV and pulled up to another guard, one standing close to the machine gun nest waving his arms for Sue to stop.

"Pull in past the tank. We have a camp set up for survivors: food, water, first aid."

"We were headed to St Petersburg," Sue offered.

The soldier, who was wearing a regular gasmask and no space suit, shook his head. "The south of Tampa is pretty much gone, son."

"But…" Brandy trailed off, closing her mouth.

"Let 'em through!" the soldier called, and a large steel gate, which had clearly been erected by the army, was slowly opened. "You'll be safe here, people. Uncle Sam has this area locked down."

Sue took his foot off the brake, about to put the car into gear, when it stalled. "Shit," he hissed, turning the key in the ignition.

The engine turned over but didn't catch.

"Ease up, fella, or you're going to drown the engine and we'll be stuck here for ages," Meat-Hook said.

"Come on, move along," the soldier told Sue.

"I'm trying."

The engine continued to groan and whine as it tried its best to spark.

"Probably due to the battering it took out on the roads," Spaniard said, and then screamed when the Ford's back window was caved in." Jesus! Get us out of here, Sue."

A back-passenger door was ripped open, and Meat-Hook yelled, "Get it the fuck—Argh!"

Sue looked over his shoulder as a nude female zombie with huge, swinging tits, tucked into the side of the fat biker's neck. Blood sprayed across the seats, passengers, windows and roof.

"Fucker!" Spaniard yelled, driving the fat end of the baseball bat into the woman's rotted skull, which came apart like ripe fruit.

Meat-Hook, dead and defenceless, was ripped from the car by multiple hands.

Sue tried the engine again.

It failed.

A siren started blasting.

"They're all over!" someone yelled.

"You're on your fucking own," the solider said to Sue, and Sue wound his window up.

"Why are the fucking doors unlocked?" Sue asked, his voice hitting fever pitch.

The tank by the side of the SUV loosed a round, and when he looked in the rear-view mirror, Sue saw it impact on the ground somewhere behind, throwing dozens of bodies into the air.

Mortar shells were fired as the soldier manning the fifty-calibre machine gun, which was mounted on sandbags, opened his account. Zombies were torn apart in great big bleeding batches as the gun's robust rounds cut through them.

"Fuck the doors, ese! Get us moving, Sue!" Paco said, and then screamed. "Bitch got my balls!"

Sue tried the engine again as a stray bullet from the fifty-calibre burst through his windshield, ripping Brandy's face.

Her blood tidal-waved against Sue's cheek and drenched her window.

Sue blubbered as he turned the key in the ignition time and again, only for the engine to flood.

A couple of bullets took out one of their tyres and annihilated the SUV's grill.

Paco's scream hit a girlie crescendo, which was followed by the sound of wet ripping and tearing.

"She ate his balls!" Spaniard declared.

"This ride's fucking spent," Hatchet-Face said, opening his door.

"Let's get the fuck out of here," Spaniard said, slapping Sue on the shoulder.

The Native American took a quick glance over at Brandy and wished he hadn't. "Dear God…" he mouthed, and then he was yanked from the car by Spaniard and Hatchet-Face.

"Move!" Hatchet-Face said, giving Sue a shove.

Ahead, Sue saw, the soldiers were pulling back behind the gate.

"Fuckers are closing it," Spaniard said, pointing. "We have to make it."

Shit, Sue thought.

At their backs, hordes of the dead moved after them, the soldiers and any other warm body within the vicinity.

Screams and gunfire tore the early night apart.

"Hold the fucking doors," Hatchet-Face pleaded, pumping his fat arms and legs.

Sue whimpered, feeling brittle, yet there were strong fingers at his shoulders and hot, smelled-like-wet-earth breath on his neck urging him on.

In Sue's peripheral vision, he saw one of the bikers get tackled to the floor.

"Ugh, help!" they cried.

Sue dared to stop, looked back and saw it was Hatchet-Face. He was encircled by a swarm of the dead.

"We can't help him," Spaniard said.

"Go, get out of here," said the defenceless biker.

"Take this!" Spaniard said, throwing the bat to Hatchet-Face, who caught it and began hammering the dead around him.

"Come and get it, bastards!" they heard Hatchet-Face say, his words punctuated by the dense sound of wood smacking flesh.

Ten seconds later, and there was nothing but ripping, tearing, slurping and devouring sounds, followed by low moans and ear-splitting groans.

The tank, along with the soldier manning the fifty-calibre machine gun, had disappeared behind the gate.

Even the mortar unit had given up and retreated.

Sue and Spaniard were within touching distance.

"Hold it open, please," Sue begged, seeing it only had a few more feet until it was shut.

Claws raked his back, shredding his shirt, encouraging him to pick up pace and race through the gate.

Before the first wave of zombies could shuffle near, the metal, ten-foot high gate rattled closed.

"Fuck, fuck, fuck," Sue panted, sprawling across the floor.

"We made it, Sue," Spaniard said, huffing out a laugh.

"My back – check my back," Sue said. "Did they cut me?"

"Nah, just fucked your duds up, dude."

And then Spaniard was off, talking to the military guys, telling them how they had been trapped at the Grill.

Thank God, Sue thought, gathering his thoughts as he caught his breath. It's over. There was no way the dead were making it beyond the gate, into the safe zone.

Blood trickled out from the bottom of his trousers.

"The hell?!" He turned his leg over and found claw marks on his calf. "Shit…" he muttered, feeling a change in his guts as his fingernails grew to razor-sharp points.

A hunger like no other befell him, and before he could get up off the floor, Sue no longer felt like himself.

Horny Dead Fucks
with Natasha Sinclair

Ruby Anya moved from one laminated card of ink designs to the next, scouring the walls of the Glaring Graffiti tattoo parlour, searching for that special piece of work to be ripped into her smooth, syrup-coloured thigh.

She huffed, not finding anything close to what she wanted. *This place is a waste of time. There's nothing of interest,* Ruby thought, about to give up. *Unless they have more—*

"I love your hair," the voluptuous girl working the reception desk said. "It must take you hours to get it to stand up like that."

"Thanks," Ruby said, without taking her eyes off the design sheets. "I've always loved multi-coloured mohawks."

"You're a punk, right?"

You think this is a costume? It's a way of life! Ruby thought, laughing and turning to face the girl, exposing the tight, tits-enhancing Misfits tee she wore beneath her waist-length leather jacket that sported a cacophony of pins and patches. "Punk's dead, right?"

"Not by looking at you, it isn't!"

Girl's bi, Ruby thought, watching the chubby gal undress her with her heavily made-up eyes. *Pretty, mind.* "Goth?"

"When I was younger, yeah."

"Do you have any horror designs? I'm looking for a splash of sick zombie ink, and I can't seem to find anything on the walls."

"Yep. I'm pretty sure we do. Hang on." The receptionist bent, retrieved a large book, and slapped it down on her counter. Dust exploded off its cover and spine. "We should have loads of horror, gothic and creepy stuff in here."

"Do you mind?" Ruby asked, holding a hand out, her green nails looking Krueger-like.

"No, go ahead!" The woman gave Ruby the book. "Have a seat over there. And please, take your time. Coffee?"

Ruby nodded. "Please," she winked before taking the large portfolio over to the plush-looking sofa. With a 'humph', she sat and began to peel through its pages, a 'wow' and 'awesome' escaping her as her eyes fell on the horrific images within. "This is more like it," she said aloud.

"Oh, good," the woman said, causing Ruby to look up, standing with a mug of coffee.

"*Ha!*" Ruby bellowed, laughing at what was written on the porcelain, accepting it into her hands: 'Tattooists Prick You All Year Round.'

"Yeah, it's not mine – it's the boss'!"

"I hope he's as good as his word," Ruby winked, taking a mouthful of lukewarm coffee. *Christ, that's strong enough to wake my ancestors*, she thought, placing the drinking receptacle on a small desk by her side. "Lovely, thanks," she lied, trying not to pull a face as though she'd swallowed her tongue.

"Call if you need anything—"

"Wait!" Ruby jumped out of her seat. "This one!" she said, her mouth beginning to loll, pointing at a large image of a black and white, *Hammer Horror*-esque graveyard scene filled with mist, a new moon and zombies that poured out of the shadows and earth alike. "It's… breath-taking…"

"Aye, that is pretty badass," the girl agreed. Would you like me to book you in for that one?"

"Yes, please," Ruby said, her gaze glued to the image. "Wow…"

"We have next Tuesday available?"

"That works for me."

"All day session?"

"Please," Ruby said.

"Cash or card?"

"Card."

"Great. I'll only take a deposit today – anything over forty pounds."

"Cool."

"And where are you thinking of putting the tattoo?" the girl asked, jotting everything down.

"My thigh," Ruby said, grabbing the hem of her denim skirt and raising it, showing off her stocking-tops, thighs and the underside of her knickers; a jolt of pleasure throbbed through her, stirring her juices.

"I think that's a great idea." After she took the rest of Ruby's details, she handed Ruby an appointment card and smiled. "We'll see you next week, bright and early."

***

When Ruby returned home from Glaring Graffiti the next Tuesday, ignoring her five flatmates, she stormed upstairs and went straight to her bedroom and stripped off in front of her full-length mirror. Beneath her punk band, horror film and undead posters, she eyed the gory, unorthodox bandage hugging her thigh like a fucked-up lover.

I need music, she thought, hitting the play button on her retro tape deck, filling the room with 45 Grave.

"Fuck *yeah*!" Ruby said, stepping before the glass again, slipping her bra off to the sway of her hips and arse wiggling. She loved the way her rear looked in her pink Horror Sleaze Trash knickers; perfectly peachy and tight. She unclasped her spiked collar and let it hit the floor before sliding her favourite panties down her legs, kicking them from her.

She was lost in her music, eyes closed, her hands wandering over her large, golden-coloured tits down her abs and sharp hips.

45 Grave was replaced by The Cramps singing about the Surfin' Dead.

Ruby's hand continued down the valley to her shaved cunt, and she bit down on her pierced bottom lip; a soft moan escaped her as she came upon her perfectly sculptured pussy lips.

It had been a few years since the bottom surgery completed her transition to becoming her true self, the wrapping matching her gloriously feminine interior. She always hated her body before; the thought of touching *it* — *down there* — made her vomit. Now she had finally become whole with her body, and every inch of it couldn't be more perfect.

As the music pumped her eardrums, she thought back to her session on the chair. Getting inked was such a hot rush, the continuous prick of so many needles at once; the gun may as well have been a little fuck machine for her skin. It really was the ultimate foreplay, even if she was going home to fuck herself. Clicking off two of her nail extensions with her teeth and spitting them to the floor, Ruby sucked her fingers, then moved back down, throwing her head back as she dipped two wet digits into her soft cleft… how very far she's come from that depressed little boy of her childhood.

"Can you turn it down a bit in there, Ruby!" someone said, knocking on Ruby's door, which Ruby didn't hear. "Ruby?" came the voice again. Ruby?! Jesus Christ," the person said, opening the door, gasping.

When Ruby opened her eyes, she smiled. "Come to help, Amy?"

Amy laughed. "You're such a bad girl. Why don't you stop fucking yourself and show me your ink?"

"Is she playing with herself again?" a guy yelled from downstairs.

"Okay," Ruby said, stopping what she was doing, her hands going to the bandage. "You know, I thought there would have been a lot more pain at this point, but there's nothing. If anything, it feels numb."

"Odd, considering how long you were there."

"Maybe it has something to do with the Chinese he was mumbling as he rubbed lotion over it helped?" Ruby laughed as she unwrapped her leg before gasping, her thigh black, save a load of running ink, blood and gore. A huge chunk of her flesh thudded to the floor with the bandage, "What the *fuck*?!"

The room began to rumble, followed by an onslaught of groaning, moaning voices. When Ruby looked up, she saw her posters depicting the undead ripple and coming to life – a fog rose from the ground, engulfing her and Amy.

***

Ruby's eyes fluttered open to a haze of eerie smoky darkness; wails surrounded her, and she was no longer in the warm comforts of her flat. She felt her body in motion as her vision bumped up and down; friction cold and hard at her back, she felt her skin shredding. Pulling her hands up to rub her eyes, then her head, she squeezed her lids shut and opened them again, blinking to clear her vision. On top of her, a gruesome, heaving, macabre beast was frantically gnashing its teeth; *a nightmare?* As she further came to, she realised she was being mercilessly fucked by a giant zombie looking fucker; its stink was beyond words. Half its face was gone, teeth glistened like diamonds within its ripped cheek as it furiously chattered and grunted. That's when the bottom half of her body woke up, and she felt the pounding of her life, frantic, animalistic. No human could fuck this fast, closing her eyes away from the horrifying face she submitted to the feeling… "uhhhh, mmmmm, fuck…"

She was in pain, horrified, confused, and at the same time, she knew she was fast heading towards the orgasm of her life. Her pussy was screaming for more, as did she, eyes closed tight, "uhhhh, fuck! Fuck me! Yes! Fuck!" She reached out towards the hips of the beast; its flesh felt firm, highly muscled – evolved for speed and furious fucking. As it continued to hammer into her, she was soaked – a puzzler, considering her inability to produced natural lubricant… maybe it was his…

She ventured to open her eyes again, the sight was ghastly, but the stimulation coming from it was hard not to appreciate; *just go with it,* she thought. She peered down — her tits swinging back and forth like volleyballs. For a second, she worried her implants may burst out. She continued to eye down her body with the stallion zombie-like beast's hulking form raised over her. His monster cock drilled her cunt, like a jackhammer. Her thighs and lower abdomen were blood sodden. It was tearing her apart — after how long it had taken her body to become one with her womanhood; this horny dead fuck was, literally, screwing her out of it. Then, his fevered pace halted, and he looked down from such a height, his eyes full of a cold-dead-fire she'd never seen in the living, he licked the air with his long tongue (one that rivalled Gene Simmons) and laughed — the sound was deep, reverberating through his body, so she felt it within her own. Then he let out an ear-splitting screech; the moans that surrounded her in the dark shifted to other screeches, seemingly, in response.

Pulling out of her and dragging her up by the hair, he threw her onto her knees, narrowly missing smashing her head off a headstone. *How did I get here?!* She wondered. It was then she saw her thigh bone — the flesh where the tattoo had been was gone, yet it was painless. She felt his large bony fingers grasp her hips as he stuffed his meat into her arse. She gasped, letting out an involuntary whimper, eyes watering. She threw back her head in sharp ecstasy as her body let the beast in (not that it had a choice) and finally managed to see where the other noises were coming from; she was surrounded by an orgy. Though most of the participants were deceased, it was like a horror movie set turned porno. Some had a vague semblance of beauty, but most were grotesque; half skeletal monsters banging away, grunting and groaning from decaying throats, skin hung from some, showing raw muscle and dried fat, innards now 'outards'.

Then she saw Amy — screaming as her arm was being ripped from its socket and eaten by the dead thing having its way with her. *Well, I can't exactly do anything to help,* Ruby thought. There was a ghostly faint echo of music, she could just about make out Rob Zombie's infectious gritty vocals over the wail of guitars. And beyond that, the distant chatter of friends in her flat... *a dimension away?* The fog rose, caressing tombstones and the frisky reanimated fiends. Flesh battered into flesh, ghoulish tongues licked, and teeth gnashed and tore into lovers as they cavorted, possessed.

Ruby could feel it too; all she wanted was to be fucked to death. The air was thick with sex and dead things…and she realised she must've been with the real stud of the pack, the king of the horny-fuckin' dead — as they were centre of attention with a harem of zombies touching themselves and groaning desperately as they watched him pummel her. Ruby had never been more turned on; she was his living dead girl. His Trash. She came so hard and so fast, her life flashed before her, in a display of flickering lights. The orgasm rolled through her body, pumping her heart as fast as he did her; she felt the organ explode in her chest, she choked, spluttering blood, unable to breathe and collapsed bleeding out onto the grass...

Milked

with and Natasha Sinclair

Horace stood before the shop, hunched over, eyes darting rat-like, the lapels of his coat standing on end in the hope that they'd conceal him. With his hands buried in the pockets of his jeans, his fingers jangling the loose change found there, he shuffled his feet and pondered his next move as the sun set behind him.

Dare I…? he thought, a giggle almost escaping him as he cast a glance over the building's blanked-out windows, reinforced door and black, almost unsettling, décor.

…Well, I've come this far…

With a deep, shaky breath, sucking in a lungful of atmospheric sin, Horace stepped forward and knocked on the sheet metal entrance three times and winced at the reverberating sounds that travelled the length and breadth of the alley. An old elegant Victorian Dressmaker's sign hung above the doorway, sagging from the sandstone from long ago. A landmark of a history long forgotten. Though, the era's reputation for everyday sadomasochism was not lost on those who knew what hid within this seemingly closed place.

Jesus!

He risked a peep over his shoulder, ballbag and prick shrivelling, and released his balled fists when he saw there was nobody behind him.

What does it matter if I'm seen? It's not like I'm committing a crime! It's a sex shop, for Christ's sake, he thought, his heart pounding at the mere thought of what the establishment was. Could it cost me my teaching job? I wouldn't have thought so… unless a colleague or student spots me. So what? I'm not wrongdoing. No, but a lot of shame would come of it, forcing me to possibly leave my position. Pfft! It's not …

Bolts clattered and chains rattled. "Who is it, please?" someone asked.

Dude sounds like Vincent Price, Horace thought, sniggering, his pent-up anxiety leaving him but returning in an instant.

"Is that you, Mr Parker? Horace Parker."

"How…?"

"Do come in," the man said, pulling the door open, revealing his dapper appearance.

It really is Vincent Price! Horace thought, looking at the tall, moustachioed fella.

"My dear fellow, are you alright?"

Horace shook his head, abandoning his trance-like state, and smiled. He looks like he should be running magic shows or a thespian on stage. "How do you know my name? Has Roger been blabbing? I thought this was a place built on a reputation of utmost discretion."

The man tittered, coughed and apologised. "Excuse my amusement, please, Horace, but Roger did no such thing. Let's just say, I have a way of knowing things. And I know exactly what you need. So please, do come in, Horace, and let's begin to ease your burden."

A crack of thunder broke across the cloudless sky as Horace stepped over the shop's threshold.

"Just in time," the proprietor said.

At his back, Horace heard heavy rain hissing against the asphalt. "Burden?" he asked.

"Come, there's no need for coyness here, Horace! I know all about your needs and how they're manipulating you and causing you much pain and grief. It doesn't have to be like that. You should be free to live a happy life. To do as you please, no matter how taboo your desires."

Horace felt his face flush. "I only wanted a bit of porn – something to help occupy me (he lied) – and I was told…"

"You were told all your fantasies would be fulfilled if you came to me, weren't you?" the man smiled.

"I… how…"

"Shh, Horace. The how's and why's don't matter. The important thing right now is for you to realise that I'm here to help, at a cheap cost which we'll cover later, and that you put your full trust in me."

Horace felt hypnotised. "I'm a bad boy," he confided. "I have awful thoughts and wants, and I'm losing the power to keep them under control."

"I know, Horace," the man said, smiling, clapping a hand to his shoulder. "We'll sort you out, don't worry."

Horace shook his head. "I think it was a mistake coming here," he said, drinking in his surroundings, eyeing the shelves upon shelves of pornographic DVDs, sex toys, dildos, BDSM gear, ball gags, wigs, crops, whips and everything else he could imagine. "You can't sell me what I need! I need professional help, goddamn it!"

"Calm yourself, Horace. Please. There's no need to get your panties into bunches," the man laughed. "Now, come over to my desk – I have something for you."

"Excuse me, Mr DeVile?" A weak voice called from behind.

When Horace turned to look, he saw a short, balding man standing there. What's he clutching?

"Oh, I thought you'd departed, Mr Harpis. My apologies."

"Can I have a word? In private."

"Of course," DeVile said. "What is it?"

"Are you sure I can cruise by schools, and do as I wish without getting in trouble?" Harpis said, his voice low, but Horace could hear all the same. "I've been good for so long now that I don't want to get in trouble for acting on my fantasies. You did say it would be okay!"

DeVile laughed. "Go. Go indulge. Your actions will not land you in hot water. I promise. Just, don't forget my payment, there's a good man."

When the little guy shuffled off, pushing his glasses back up his nose, Horace turned to DeVile. "That man's a paedo—"

DeVile held his hands up. "That he may be. But and I guarantee you this, I've sold him a package that will allow him to release his demons safely. No harm will come of anyone. Just like I've sold packages to those with necrophilia, rape, murder and a whole host of other sexual tendencies."

Briefly, Horace's mind snapped to his own family, his baby son giggling in his swing chair, as his wife stared vacantly out the window, with bleary eyes, blankly waving the oldest off to school. She was so absent these days, especially to him, he didn't understand, this is the life she wanted, not me… then he thought of the only time she seemed alive now, with the child latched on to her big darkened nipples. His cock stirred again, pushing against his jeans, like a trapped animal, "and that's what you plan to do for me?"

DeVile smiled. "Of course. It is, after all, why you came here?"

Horace wanted to back off. This can't be right. What's going on here?

"Come closer, Horace."

When DeVile stooped to retrieve something, Horace turned to run but was stopped when he heard a thud.

"This... is your package, Horace."

Horace turned, his eyes immediately drawing to the black, medium-sized box with a red bow wrapped around it on top of the man's counter. "Take it with you. You won't be disappointed," DeVile said, pushing the parcel towards Horace. "I offer a 30 day no satisfaction policy. So, if you're not happy, just bring it back. No fee required."

"And if I do like it?"

DeVile smiled. "If you do, then I'll want paying. A little something in return for relieving you of such a terrible burden..."

***

Leaving the seedy alley, another snap cracked through the darkening clouds, bringing with it an onslaught of spider-web-like lightning as backdrop to the torrential rain, lashing mercilessly at the street. He made it back to the Volvo and placed his box on the passenger seat. How am I going to get what I need from the contents of this box? Like everything in life, this will be another disappointment... he was almost sure of it. I've been a fool to come here. What a dirty, filthy perv! No woman wants this kind of 'bad boy'. What choice did he have but to try this?

The rain pounded at the windows, rattling the metal roof; he was caught in static contemplation. As the pelting slowed, he checked his phone — the only messages were one from his wife reminding him to pick up milk and oatmeal and a notification that his favourite 'Only Fans' performer was doing a special show soon, for all her 'special babies'. It just wasn't enough… not anymore, if it ever was.

The orange streetlight flickered overhead; a failing engine stuttering to start before it submitted to its failure. He clicked through the camera roll into videos. Biting his lower lip, Horace thumbed up until he saw what he wanted. He drew down his zipper and freed his prick into the near-open air of the family car. He pressed play: The camera view is from the dresser, adjacent to their sensible double divan. Addy is asleep, her heavy breasts free of her open nighty, a damp puddle of milk staining the sheet. Horace naked before her; she looks like an Angel. He peels back the light damask printed sheet revealing the delicious slopes of her body. Kneeling before her, he opens his mouth wide and takes in her breast. Miraculously she barely stirs, only grunts in her sleep. As he watches the replay, Horace fondles and squeezes his balls. His breathing becoming ragged as the memory of the sweet watery fluid coating his tongue, filling his mouth pours through his cerebellum. He pulls his warm palm up, gripping his shaft and pumps, furiously milking himself… if she knew how he wanted her, if anyone knew… he was a very bad boy indeed. He imagined her talking to him, cooing over his head like she did that damned baby… "fuck, yes mummy," he whispered, deep and low as he pumped his fist up and down faster. Slick with pre-cum, he watches himself sucking and wanking in his secret video, his arse clenched and bicep rising and falling. In the car, he stifled his orgasm, turning and biting into his own shoulder, shooting his thick creamy load into his hand.

Flicking his eyes open, Horace jumped back, seeing the long face of DeVile grinning sinisterly back at him through the rain, a wavering shimmer of red outlining his lanky form, what the fuck… Squeezing his eyes shut and opening them again, DeVile was gone. "You're losing it, man, get a grip! Time to get going." With nothing to wipe it on, he sucked down the thick white salty spunk and tucked his prick back into his trousers. *Why couldn't my milk taste as good as hers…* With that, he pulled on his belt and started up the car, eager to get home and unwrap his package.

***

It took him two weeks to work up the courage and have the solitude to actually open the mysterious black box. *How could he even know what I want? How can what I want be inside this box? I don't even know what I want… maybe the impossible.* Unfastening the ribbon, he lifted the deep black lid. Inside, a puff of red dust rose up and pummelled itself into his eyeballs. Horace fell back off the bed where he had been perched, thumping his head off the corner of the dresser.

Pulling himself up to sit, Horace rubbed the back of his head, coming away with a wet smear of crimson across his hand. *Fuck.* He felt dizzy, almost separate from his body; pain swelled at the back of his skull, thumping as thunder boomed within his temple. He used the bed to pull himself up and peer into the box. Using his bloodied hand, he removed a dark crystal skull. It was heavy and carved with intricate mystical symbols and ruins— none of which he was familiar. He peered into the sockets and became mesmerised; inky galactic swirls began to move within this peculiar artefact, hypnotic. The lower jaw dropped open, and a blinding white light emitted from the gaping maw and its cavernous sockets – shooting straight into his eyeballs. His soul burned as if being torn from his body. Within the light, DeVile's sinister face materialised, eyebrows arched in sadistic points over black eyes… "The exchange shall be done." His sardonic laugh boomed around the room as if from a megaphone.

At that, the pain scorched through his entire body, an erupting of magma ran through his core as he collapsed and seized, emptying his bladder and bowels all over the plush cream carpet.

***

Addy was crying, her bleary eyes now pouring. He gazed at her confused, then he saw the body… his body being strapped down and placed upon a stretcher by three men – he recognised one of them, Mr Harpis, what's that paedo doing in my house?! He thought. A low deep voice came from the doorway. "I'm so sorry for your loss Mrs Parker. If you just sign here, we'll take care of everything."

DeVile?! His eyes landed on Horace's, "I can hold him if you like, while you sign and say goodbye."

Goodbye?! What is he talking about, the creepy, lanky bastard? It was then Horace looked down. He could barely control his head as DeVile's arms came into contact with his body. He watched Addy crying, stroking his face as he lay drooling on the stretcher.

"The exchange is complete, Horace. Don't worry about the body on the stretcher. I know just the client that package will be perfect for."

***

As he gazed up, sucking insatiably on his wife's engorged milky tit… he finally felt complete. He felt her nipple elongate as he sucked, it nestled tight against his soft pallet as the warm milky goodness squirted into his throat, he was so excited his whole body felt it may explode, biting down – a reflex, well, maybe it was the first time, now he liked it. She squirted harder when his gums clammed shut, and he liked the way she jumped. She squealed and patted his rump, "Ouch! Naughty boy!"

She was right, he really was… her naughty boy.

The Covert Kinkster and the Embryonic Eunuch:
A Love Story from Beyond the Shadows

Trevor brought his BMW X6 to a crunching halt on the gravelled driveway, killing the engine and relaxing in his seat, arching and stretching his back. "*Ow!*" he giggled and wriggled, a little sore still from the licking he'd taken from his mistress and her trusted assortment of whips, crops, and lashes. "Bitch is worth every penny," he said, gritting his teeth.

When he leaned forward, chest pressing against the steering wheel, he looked out of the windscreen and up at the darkened bedroom windows of his luxury home that loomed over him and his European beauty. *Shelia must be asleep by now,* he thought. *She's always in bed, snoring her fat arse off when I've returned home, no matter what the hour. Lazy fuck.*

He plucked the keys from the ignition, pocketed them, and opened the car door. As he walked up the short, winding path, flanked by ponds, gnomes, pots, plants and other garden trinkets and clutter Sheila deemed necessary to keep up with the Jones', an image of her snoozing in her flowery nightie, eye mask, bed socks and extravagant neck pillow exploded in his mind. *Ugh! Like a beached fucking whale,* he thought, looking down at a fishing elf-gnome wearing bright yellow wellies. He wanted to kick the thing into the pond its fishing line was cast into but decided against it. *If she put as much effort into our sex life and marriage as she does with our garden, then we'd get somewhere.*

Trevor huffed, looked up, and thought he saw a dull, gloomy flicker of light from behind the curtains in a downstairs window. *No, she can't be up watching TV this late,* he thought. *Surely not!* He crept up to the glass, pressed his face to it, and tried to peer through the crack in the curtains. *I can't see anything. It's dark in there. Hmm… Now what? I better have an excuse ready. She might ambush me in there.*

When he reached the front door, he eased his key into the lock and turned it. Trevor winced, pulling his lips back and exposing his gums, as the bolts thundered into place. "Je-*sus,*" he said with clenched teeth. He depressed the handle and stepped into the inky hallway.

"Sheila?" He stood there for a moment, ears pricked, listening to the natural sounds of a home. *All quiet on the western front!* he thought, smiling.

Trevor closed and locked the door with as little noise as possible, before continuing down the hallway to the foot of the stairs. "Sheila, are you up there?" A snort and a fart were his replies. A smile split his face. *Sleeping, sleeping, sleeping,* he thought, listening to the springs of their reinforced bed creak and crunch as she turned over. *Like a pig in a pen.*

With a snigger, he pulled away from the staircase and entered the living space. From within the guts of the room, Fluffy meowed, Trevor jumped. "Fucking moggy," he muttered, turning on a lamp to find the cat curled up on an armchair like a duchess. "Come on, you – come and get some chow." Trevor led the cat into the kitchen and poured some dried food into its bowl. "Once you're done, you can go outside to do your business."

After unlocking the back door and pulling it open for Fluffy, Trevor filled the kettle with water and set it to boil. *I wonder if Sheila left me some supper?* he thought, moving to the fridge for a peep inside. On the middle shelf, tucked behind a bottle of red sauce and a couple of yoghurt pots, was a plate wrapped in tinfoil with a note that read "*Trevor*" attached to it. "Excellent," he said, plucking the china from its chilly depths.

Fluffy meowed, the bell on her collar jingling, as she fled to the outside. Instead of closing the door, Trevor left it ajar. *I'll only have to reopen it when she wants to come back in. Hopefully, by the time I've scoffed this lot, Fluffy'll be indoors*, Trevor thought, setting his food down on the kitchen table. *Did I see my protein shake in there with my grub?* He went back to the fridge, opened it, and fished out his drink. "Sheila's a good 'un in some respects," he said, laughing.

She treats you like a king, a voice at the back of his mind said.

Trevor sat at the table and lowered his head. *I can't deny it, she does, and what I do behind her back is dreadful. I've broken my vows time and again, but it's the only way I can keep our marriage afloat. God, if she ever did find out though... Fuck! I'd lose everything: swanky car, fancy house, money, status...the lot. And it would come out in the papers, too! The media love a good, grubby tale about a dirty politician.* Sweat broke across his brow. *It won't come to that. I'm careful, and the lady I use is discreet.*

He uncovered his food and set to work on the ham and egg salad. "*Mmm*," he said, licking dressing from off his chops. As he devoured the last of his meal, Fluffy made her way inside, darting into the living room.

"Cold out there, puss?" he asked, laughing and setting his cutlery down on the empty plate. "Bloody lovely." With a burp, Trevor got up from the table and placed his dish in the sink. Once he was done, he took his drink into the living room and sat down. "Christ, my back is still killing me! Madam Christine went for it this time. Well, I did ask for it."

When he tried to relax in his chair, wincing, grunting and gurning as he did so, Madam Christine's words came back to him, stealing his wind. *Was she being serious*? he thought. *Sounded it, but she'd slipped out of character.*

"Trevor, are you feeling okay?" she asked. "Your ball sack has been looking increasingly discoloured the last few weeks, and I'm sure your wee man has got smaller?"

Trevor laughed. "Really, Mistress? I have been feeling under the weather, mind. Maybe that has something to do with it?"

"Perhaps. You haven't been taken my punishments like you used to, either. Also, your fantastic physique seems to be slipping. You're sprouting hairy bitch tits!"

"You think?" he said.

Mistress nodded, smiling.

Trevor looked down at himself. *It's true,* he thought. *But how? I've been eating cleanly.*

Yeah, but you haven't been frequenting the gym or running of recent. And it's not like you haven't noticed, is it? You've been ignoring it, thinking it was your tired mind playing tricks on you, the voice at the back of his mind said.

"I've been fatigued a lot of late, and I've caught a number of colds."

"Has work been stressful?"

"Yeah. Well, no, not really."

"Maybe you should see a doctor, Trevor. Get a full check-up."

"I'm sure it's nothing," he smiled.

Trevor hadn't given thought to what she'd said upon leaving her dungeon and driving home; he'd been too occupied by thoughts and feelings of what Madam Christine had done to him. But now, as sat in the dark living room with the effects of tonight's games fading, it bore down on him.

I have *been ignoring it,* he thought, sipping his protein shake. *No, not ignoring, but avoiding. My dick has gone smaller. I noticed it a few weeks ago but choose to circumvent the issue. I thought I was being silly, but then I noticed the discolouration of my nuts, too. It's time to be honest with myself.*

"It's not just my cock and balls, either, or the changing of my physique," he said, putting his drink down on the coffee table. "No, it's bloody not, is it!"

"Trevor?" Sheila called, her voice cracking. "Is that you down there?"

Who fucking else would it be! he thought, wanting to say it, but couldn't muster it. "I'll be up soon."

"Try not to wake me *again*," she said, which was followed by the sound of her retreating footsteps and the slamming of their bedroom door.

"Pig bitch," he muttered with a smile, thinking of going up there and waking her with his hard cock. "That would piss her off, but she'd take, just like she always does. She's a good wifey."

Trevor settled in his seat and went back to his thoughts. *No, my privates and physical appearance are not the only things I've noticed a change in. I'm not as driven as I used to be. I was a right go-getter, and I'd step on anyone who got in my way. I've lost my bite, and I'm knackered all the time. All I seem to want to do when I'm not visiting Madam Christine (which I can barely manage now) or working is sleep. What is going on?*

Ring the doctor tomorrow, the voice said.

With a nod, Trevor drained his drink, got up, and headed towards the hallway.

"Why do you stay with her, Trevor?" Madam Christine asked.

"Because she's a loving woman and she takes good care of me."

"Is that enough, though?"

"What else is there? I have it good."

When he got to the foot of the staircase, he sighed. *Sheila was such an attractive woman when we got together. Smokin' hot! But a ring on her finger ruined it all.*

"I'll shed the pounds," she'd promised, her sex drive dwindling into oblivion.

Still, it didn't stop him, no matter how much she protested.

If it does all come out, he thought, looking up the shadowy staircase, *then the blame will be put at her doorstep. A man has needs, fantasies and desires, damn it!* Trevor huffed. *But they're starting to diminish… I hope there isn't something seriously wrong with me. Don't be silly. Just overworked. Yeah, either that or my libido is starting to slacken with age. Christ, I'm not that old!*

He climbed the steps and entered the bathroom. After brushing his teeth, peeing and washing his hands, Trevor left the room and went into his bedroom. With the curtains open, the moon shining through, he was able to see Sheila's large shape beneath the duvet.

Going to snuggle right up to Sheila and stuff my dick in her, he thought, slipping out of his boxers. His prick twitched, but it didn't come to full life. Trevor looked down at his cock and began to stroke it. "Come on," he hissed, forcing it hard. *That's better*, he smiled. But when he let go of it, it grew lifeless, shrivelling. *Jesus, it looks smaller again! What's happening to my larger-than-life python*?! In his panic, he hadn't heard Sheila's snoring stop, as he tried rubbing it to life. But the more he tried, the less his prick co-operated. "What's wrong with it!"

"My, my, you do look ridiculous," Sheila said, giggling. "Standing there, trousers and boxers around your ankles, trying to coax your ever-growing maggot to its full potential."

Trevor looked up and gasped. Sweat dribbled down his forehead and ran into his eyes and mouth. "Don't laugh!" he said, throwing a hand out and sweeping the photos and trinkets off the tallboy that stood by his side. Glass shattered and pinged off his face, opening a nick across his chin.

"What did you fucking say?!" she said, throwing the duvet off her and getting out of bed, her feet pounding the floor. The timid woman he had grown to know had disappeared.

She looks...fierce, he thought, his bollocks retracting. His guts grew cold. Trevor clenched his arse cheeks and a fart escaped him.

"You're going to clean up that mess, *loser*! Hell, I might make you pick up the shards with your anus!" she giggled, stomping closer to him, her shadow swallowing his scrawny frame.

"Who do you think—?" he tried, puffing his chest out, but he withered when Sheila pressed her massive tits against him, shoving him back against the wall and pinning him in place. "*Argh*! There's something digging in me!" he whined, his bottom lip quivering. *What the fuck is going on here*? his mind screamed.

Sheila struck him across the face with the flat of her hand. "Shut. Up. Or I'll hurt you worse," she said, cupping his wrinkled ball sack. "That's if I can find them."

"What the hell has come over you? *Ugh*!" he gasped, her hand tightening.

"Don't play stupid, Trevor. I know exactly what's been going on."

"*Argh*, my balls!" A tear slid down his cheek.

"I thought you'd be able to take a lot more punishment than this, lover. I've not started yet."

"Wh-what are…*ugh*…are you talking…about?" he gasped, pulling his lips back, exposing his gums. P-p-please, Sheila – you're going to pop 'em!"

"They're not going to be much use to you anyway, Trevor. Shall I remove them? I bet you'd like that, wouldn't you? You'll be my little eunuch bitch."

He started to shake his head, his dick betraying him, as it grew.

Sheila smiled, but the smile wasn't full of warmth and caring as usually, he thought. *No, it's cold and bitter; the smile of a twisted, scorned woman. A woman that's been pushed too far.* It dawned on him, that if she knew *every*thing, then he'd been mentally abusing her. *I'm a bully! But on the other hand, I've opened her—* "Argh!" he blurted, as his nuts were twisted. "Don't rip them off! Not even Mistress Carla is *this* rough. There are safe words!" he forced a smile, thinking he knew her game.

"Safe words? What do you think this is, fucking playtime, cunty?" she spat in his face and ripped downwards on his scrotum, digging and clawing her nails into his flesh. "I've been strengthening my grip, too, working on it, ever since I found out what was going on and came to terms with it. I can squash apples, Trevor, so bursting a couple of raisins like these won't be an issue. Is that what you want? Your dick tells me yes. Well, I think it is, because it's not getting very hard. Is it? No, not these days. It used to stand up so proud, remember? And look, you have titties!"

Jesus, she's being serious. "I like this game…"

"Game? *Game*! We're not playing a game, dickhead! I've already told you that! We're beyond fun, fucker. You're about to live the *real* deal. Kiss goodbye to your freedom, because I'll be running the show from here on out."

"But-but!"

"But nothing. I own you now. And, if you try and wriggle out of it or say no, then I will burn your fucking life down to the ground! I'll make sure *everyone* knows you pay whores for sex, and that you can't get your dick hard at home. I'll even post photos and stories all over the internet! You'll never work around here again. I'll make sure of that. Unless you fold to me and become my pet," she smiled, licking her lips. "Fuck, you don't really have a choice, do you? I just wanted you to know what will happen if you try and fuck with me."

"Jesus," he squealed, as Sheila towed him across the room by his nuts.

"Come with me, bitch." Trevor squeezed his eyes closed, tears spilling, trying to block out the pain. His hands went hers and he tried pulling her fingers loose. "Don't make me crush harder, shit face. You wouldn't want me to rupture something."

"Okay, *okay*!" Trevor removed his hands and allowed himself to be manhandled. When the pressure was gone from his bollocks, he thought he was going to vomit as he collapsed to his knees and held himself. "What have you done to me?"

"Can't you handle a little bit of crushing? God, that *ex-mistress* of yours must have been a right pussy," Sheila giggled. "Here, have a look at this, arsehole – it's going to be your new home," she said, opening the door to their walk-in wardrobe. "I had it made for you, *dog*."

Trevor gawked at the thing before him, which looked like an outsized dog house with a heavy wooden door with bars in its window. "Wh-what *is* that?!"

"I told you. Your new *home*." Sheila put a heavy foot to his shoulder and pressed down on him. "I'm going to keep you in there and bring you out when I see fit," Sheila smiled. "That cock of yours is useless now, and I hope you enjoy watching me getting fucked from in there," she said, hooking a thumb towards the small house.

"Useless?"

"Yes. Totally. Well, it will be, in another couple of weeks or so."

"What do you mean?!"

Sheila grinned. "I've rendered it worthless without you knowing."

"Hang on…"

"Yes?"

"Have you *destroyed* my manhood?"

Sheila tittered, placing a hand to her mouth. "I shouldn't laugh, really, but I can't help it. God, it's made me so horny, emasculating such a powerful man."

"It's limp because of *you*?"

"Losing inches, too, aren't you? At first, I was worried I'd give you a heart attack or kill you, but nope, it worked like a charm. You could have gone blind or started pissing blood, even, because I didn't really know much about what I was giving you."

"*What*?!" Trevor said, the veins in his neck bulging. "The fuck have you done, Sheila?"

"Relax, sissy boy. You're still here, aren't you?"

"I'll fucking—" Trevor started, but Sheila flicking her hand out, her knuckles connecting with his lifeless balls. "*Ooph*! Bitch," he managed from behind clenched teeth.

"Still got a bit of fight coursing through you, 'eh? Well, my little friends will soon knock the last of that out of you, once they're finished closing down your reproductive system."

"No! I won't take anything you give me. You can't make me!"

"I've been lacing your meals and drinks."

"No more!"

Sheila kicked him in the guts. "You fucking will, worm, if you want to live."

"Wh-what do you mean?"

"I'll continue drugging your food. You won't know when it's coming. And, if you want to keep breathing, you'll have to eat and hydrate," she laughed.

"Bitch!"

"*Miss* Bitch to you, fucker." Sheila turned, bent over, and picked up a crop that lay close by. "Now, into your home, boy," she said, whipping Trevor about the face, neck, head and chest.

"Ah, fuck! *Fuck!*" He scrambled backwards on his arse, using his hands and feet, fleeing the torture as he entered the cage. "Please, no more!"

Sheila rushed towards him and slammed the door shut on his prison, locking it in place. Trevor watched as she plucked the key from the lock, the Yale attached to a chain, and it placed around her neck. "It'll stay right there," she said, patting the key that lay between the crevice of her tits. "Now, be a good boy, Trevor, and do as I say to a pleasing standard if you do, you *might* be rewarded."

"Don't do this! You're playing, right?" Trevor said, pressing his face to the door's bars, his hands wrapping them.

"*No!*" she said, whipping his fingertips. "This is for your own good, Trevor."

"Argh! *Fuck!*"

"Carry on like this, and your first meal will be a Sheila shit sandwich washed down with a glass of piss. Now, silence! I need my sleep."

Trevor crawled to the back of his home and sniffled. "Why?" he asked, watching as Sheila picked up a large blanket.

With a smile, she turned to him. "You can't keep quiet, can you, maggot!"

"Please…"

"Okay, but once I've told you, I want peace. Do you understand?"

"Ye-yes."

"Yes, what?"

"Yes, Sheila."

"*No*, you fucking insubordinate mongrel!"

"*Ma'am*! Yes, ma'am!" he whimpered and blubbered.

"I took action against you because I was fed up. I was pissed off with your constant libido, the forced sex, constant hard-ons, your rubbing up against me, feeling my tits – you were like a fucking dog with two dicks! Always excited. And I knew what you wanted – what you desired deep down. At first, I knew I couldn't give it to you, so I was happy for you to pay your whores. It was a relief at first because you gave me little attention, but you soon started again, didn't you? So, I snapped, worm. There's only so much anyone can take. Maybe if you'd stopped pestering me completely, we wouldn't be at this juncture."

"I'll be good! Please!"

"Too late. Besides, I'm enjoying myself too much. You've awoken something in me."

"You could have spoken to me, Sh—Ma'am."

"No, there was no talking to you. You couldn't hear me over your pathetic horniness and erections and panting. You were like an eager fourteen-year-old who'd just seen a pair of tits for the first time."

"So, you hurt me?"

"Still alive, aren't you?"

"You could have divorced me!"

"Nah, I like the lifestyle too much. I knew I had to come up with a better way to sort things out, so I started planning."

"Whore!"

"Now, now, worm. Do I have to punish those raisins of yours?"

"What have you been giving me?"

"It's glorious what you can find on the black market. After I read an interesting article online about chemical castration, I went digging on the dark web and found drugs that had once been used by the Russian military to 'sedate' their troops by suppressing their testosterone."

"Oh, Jesus…"

Sheila snorted. "Yeah. And, as it turns out, the drug worked too well. The Russian hierarchy and scientists discovered their little creation was too powerful. After an ex-number of doses were administrated, it closed down the generative system and shrank everything. This, in turn, however, depressed the troops and left them unable to train and fight. The project was deemed a failure."

Trevor's mouth sagged. "You're joking? Please, tell me you're joking!"

Sheila shook her head and piggy-laughed. "Seeing the drug do its thing on you was amazing. My g-spot's never had it so good."

"I'm sorry," he tried.

"I don't give a shit, faggot." Sheila stepped closer. "Now, it's sleep time. Mistress needs her rest. I'll be along in a few hours with your breakfast. How does dog food and a glass of vomit sound, shithead? I've even bought you your very own dog bowl, slave. Now, thank your Mistress, there's a good boy."

Trevor looked at her, mouth agape. "I can't believe—"

"Don't make me come in there and thrash you!"

He eyed her, detecting the seriousness in her eyes. *This can't be happening*, he thought.

"Well?"

"Thank you, Ma'am."

"That's good. Now, sleep tight," Sheila said, raising the blanket. "Tomorrow, if you're lucky, I'll let you meet my stud. He's a huge black guy, and he's going to enjoy having you suck his prick."

Trevor shrank further into the cage. "N-no…"

"Goodnight," she winked, throwing the blanket over his prison.

"No!" he wailed. "*No!*"

"Oh, what fun we're going to have, dear," she said. "You lucky thing."

"*Noooo!*" Trevor continued, hearing the light switch click off and the door to the walk-in wardrobe close and lock. "Ma'am! Please! *Please!*" he continued, his pleas falling on deaf ears…

Finders Keepers, Perverts Weepers

*W*ank *lines don't cut it anymore, and prossies are far too expensive, especially when you want them to do weird kinky shit*, Bobby thought, tossing his mobile phone onto his bedside table. *Besides, fake, phony play doesn't do shit for me nowadays, even if the whores can act well! My brain knows the difference, and it needs the real* fucking *deal*!

With a huff, raking his moist hands through his damp, shaggy hair, Bobby looked at his naked, glistening form in the mirror above his bed. "So, what am I going to do?" he said, staring himself in the eye, the swirling ceiling fan causing his skin to prickle. "I'm horny as fuck, I have a raging hard-on, and I'm all out of options. *Bollocks*!"

He pounded the mattress with his fists and legs like a toddler in full tantrum. *I need to take shit back to* that *level, that's what, but how?* he thought, calming himself. *No, I can't, it was a dangerous place to be in, and I could have done some serious jail time! I was lucky to have never been caught; it was a good thing I sought help when I did.*

Just wank! a voice at the back of his mind said, which sounded a lot like his ex-therapist's. *When you get like this, fighting your urges and your emotions are going haywire, just wank. Wank it out.*

"Fucking easy for you to say, doc! You have no idea what it's like having urges you can't control. All that 'Write your feelings down,' bullshit. Where did that get me?" Bobby could feel his anger bubbling over, but he managed to keep a lid on it. "Wanking for wanking's sake is boring without the fantasies. Besides, if I did just bash it out, the urges would just come back stronger and stronger until I gave myself what I need."

You can't go exposing yourself and doing other weird shit to women in public, Bobby, his therapist continued.

"I wish you'd get out of my fucking head!"

Don't let your kinks control you, Bobby. They do not *define you!*

"*Ugh!*" Bobby said, getting off his bed and covering his ears with his hands. "Shut up, shut up, shut up!" When he looked up, he was glaring at himself in the mirror on top of the chest of drawers. "We're losing it again, Bobby!" With a swipe of his hand, he brushed the trinkets and paraphernalia off the dresser. "I am *not* losing it! I just need to satisfy my urges!"

You make it sound as though you have a god or demon to appease, Bobby, as if a simple stroke of your cock is turned into some form of sacrificial ceremony. Are you in the hunt for a virgin or goat to slaughter? The doctor sneered.

Just wank.

Wank.

Wank.

Wank...!

Bobby stepped back from the chest of drawers and thrust his fist into the mirror, relishing the sound of smashing, falling, tinkling glass. "How do you like me now, doc?" he said, smiling into the multitude of shards about his feet, a hundred Bobby's staring back at him with bugeyes, laughing. "You don't like my pretty mouth and haunted features? Fucker!"

Get a hold of yourself, Bobby, a new voice interjected.

"Oh, it's *you*," Bobby said, his smile widening.

Miss me?

Bobby nodded. "Have you come to instruct me, as you used to, like the good friend you are?"

Yeah, now you're not taking those stupid little pills anymore. You won't phase me out again, will you, Bobby? I've been good to you.

"I won't. I *promise*! Please, just help me out! I'm fucking clinging on here, old pal."

I want you to settle yourself, Bobby. Kick your heartrate down a few notches.

"The breathing exercises the doctor told me about should help." Bobby started counting, backwards, from twenty. When he reached one, he felt relaxed, his breathing normal.

Lie down on the bed, Bobby. I have something to tell you.

Bobby smiled, stretching out on his king size, the silk sheets cooling his skin. "What is it?"

You're forgetting something, Bobby.

"What?"

Think, Bobby. Think! What day is it? Where are you? You've been given a massive opportunity here… Think.

Bobby, lifting his head up off the pillow, scanned the room. "I'm at my cabin, tying up a few loose ends for work. So what?"

Think!

"Okay, okay… It's Friday, and I don't normally come here until Monday…"

And why is that, Bobby?

"Because… *Fuck!* I'd forgot that!"

There we go! And that's the answer to your situation. Well, for today, at least… Maybe.

"Maybe?"

Yep, because Tilly might turn out to be something you never expected her to be, solving all *your kinky problems moving forward.*

Bobby turned his head and saw his handcuffs hanging off the bed's headboard. His heartrate started to soar, and pre-come pooled at the head of his prick and dribbled down his shaft. *What time does Tilly start?* Bobby thought, snapping his head towards the clock above the bedroom door. *Almost midday… Isn't she late?*

She normally starts at one, remember, because she has her sick mother to see first?

"That's right, of course! She does Fridays at the nursing home as her sister can't."

You better get ready – you don't have long, Bobby.

"I can't believe I'd never thought about doing this before!"

Bobby, you have *thought about doing this before! Don't you remember? That's the reason* why *you got help. Jesus! Those tablets really did fuck your head up! I'm surprised you can still get your pecker hard!*

"Yeah, well, fuck those tablets. And fuck therapy! The only thing that makes me happy, and will again, is immersing myself in filth, fantasies and porn. God, I *love* women, and I want to play with them *all*!"

Stop fucking daydreaming, Bobby! Tilly'll be here soon.

"Okay, okay! I'm excited, that's all." Bobby grabbed the handcuffs and snapped one of the bracelets around his wrist. Then, with expert precision, he put his hands behind his back, fed the loose cuff through the metal slats in the headboard, and clicked it onto his other wrist. *It was a great idea of mine, to drill the bedhead to the wall. Fucker isn't moving*, he thought, giving the handcuffs a tug. *I could pull, yank and rip at them all day, and they'd never budge. Keys? Where did I put them?*

Bobby skimmed the room, his gaze falling on the ceramic bowl on top of the TV, a smile pulled across his face. He settled on the bed, wriggling into a comfy spot, watching the clock tick off the remaining seconds to one P.M. *Soon*, he thought, a giggling escaping him.

When the landline started ringing, crushing the silence within room, Bobby jumped and wrenched on his arms, the cuffs cutting into his wrists and burning. "Oh, *fuck!*" he giggled. "Like miniature Chinese burns."

"Hey Bobby, it's Tilly—"

Bobby's heart sank. "Oh, no…"

"—Sorry," Tilly continued, sobbing, "but I won't be able to work this weekend. I did try your mobile phone, your home one too, and when I couldn't get an answer on either, I thought you might have been there at the cabin... Anyway, my mother died last night, in her sleep, and I'm a wreck. I'm not sure when I'll be back, so I'll contact you in a few days. I hope that's okay? Again, I'm sorry, and I know this is short notice—"

Tilly cut off.

"*No!* No, no, *no!* Oh, fuck! Fuck! Fuck this *shit!*" Bobby ripped and pulled at his arms, trying to dislodge something. *Anything.* "This can't be happening! *Nooo! Aaargh!*" he said, grunting with strain and effort as he tried to tear his hands out of the cuffs, feeling his skin break. Blood trickled. "What the fuck have I done? *Tilly!* Tilly, you *bitch!*"

"*Hello?*" a voice called from downstairs. "Mr Gerald? *Bobby* Gerald?"

"What, *wait! Hello*?! Is someone there?"

"Oh, hi…Bobby?" the voice came again. "My name's Janeen – the agency sent me."

Oh Jesus, thank God! Bobby thought, forgetting about his predicament. "Yes, I'm Bobby!"

"Brilliant. Shall I come up?" Janeen said.

"I—" he started, hearing her footfalls on the stairs, his hard-on wavering. "No, I don't think—" But before he could finish, Janeen talking over him, she burst into the bedroom and gasped.

His cock shrivelled to the size of an acorn when he saw her. *Jesus Christ, she looks about a hundred-and-five years old*! he thought. *Pretty*, though. *And I love her tattoos and short work skirt. Bet she was a right dirty bitch back in her day.*

"Oh dear," she laughed, which sent a bolt of electricity through his prick, stirring it to life.

I'm glad she's taking it lightly, he thought, feeling his cheeks heat.

"Well, well, well, Mr *Gerald*... What a pre*dick*ament you appear to be in."

Bobby laughed, his breathing hard, his dick grown to glory. "I-I wasn't expecting anyone, sorry! Could you just...the keys are over there, behind you, in the ceramic bowl," he said, indicating with a nod of his head.

"There's no need to apologise, Mr Gerald."

"Call me Bobby, please," he said, her searching, accusing eyes bored into him, and he crossed his legs.

"No need to be shy, Bobby, I've seen all sorts, so don't you worry about that," she said, running a digging, scrapping fingernail up his leg, breaking skin. "It's always the rich ones."

"What's always the rich ones?" he winced.

"That are kinky and perverted. You *were* expecting Tilly, weren't you? Come on, spill," she said, narrowing her eyes.

Bobby shook his head and his bladder pinched. *What the hell is going on here? Who is this old crone?! And where's her cleaning gear and uniform?*

"What do you think your bosses at the bank would say?"

"W-wait… This was a total—"

"Yes, yes, you weren't expecting anyone, you told me. That may have worked on young, dumb Tilly, but not me, Bobby. I know a rotten egg when I see one," she said, her grin widening, her back teeth revealed.

She looks insane! What the fuck am I going to do? he thought, hoping the voice inside of him would help him, but it had disappeared.

"Now, I'm sure you'd love me to ridicule you, to take pictures and put them up on social media, to fuck your world up, to whip you, to shame you, to piss and/or shit on you, but I'm not going to. No, sir. Because that would give you what you wanted, wouldn't it? It would make you fire your muck all over the place and give you the most pleasure ever. Heck, maybe just me seeing you naked is enough, Bobby?" When he didn't answer, she kicked on. "No, I don't think it is, because your prick's gone hiding now; this didn't go according to plan, did it?"

"Please…" he whined. "It was only meant as a joke."

Janeen's scratching, flaying fingernail, which looked more like an impish talon to Bobby now, reached his scrotum and stopped. "A joke?" she laughed. "*Really?*"

Bobby whimpered when her aged, wrinkled hand cupped his balls. "Yes, *really!*"

"Would you be saying that if Tilly was here right now? She has great tits, doesn't she? I'm sure you've noticed she doesn't wear a bra."

Bobby remained quiet, and a pressure built on his nuts, as her hand squeezed. "*Yes!*"

"Yes what, Bobby?"

"She has great tits. Don't hurt me!"

"You're not the pain liking type?"

Bobby shook his head.

"You just like showing off?"

"Yes, yes!" Bobby said.

"That's bad news for you."

"Wha-what do you mean?"

"It means you won't like the torment I'm going to dish out, Bobby. So, shall we get started?"

"*No*! Let me out of these cuffs, please. *Please*, and I won't say—"

"You won't say anything? That's rich!"

"You could lose your job if the agency found out about this!" he said, finding the gravel in his guts.

"What agensssssy?"

Bobby gasped, spying her serpent-like tongue. "T-t-the people you w-work for! The ones who sent you here in Tilly's absence! The *cleaning* agency!" he managed, feeling piss splash against his thigh. *I'm seeing things, that's all. Relax!* Bobby closed his eyes and breathed. When he reopened his peepers, staring into the ceiling mirror, he saw Janeen glaring back at him with reptilian-like eyes. "Jesus *Christ*!" Bobby squealed, thinking his voice box was going to shatter, throat aflame, his bladder releasing in full.

"Oh, you mucky boy!" Janeen said. "That's going to cost you extra," she laughed.

"Wh-what *are* you?!"

"Something old; something your filthy, dirty, rubbish-filled mind couldn't comprehend," she said, jabbing a talon into his face, ripping flesh and drawing blood.

"*Bitch*!" he said.

"We've only just started, Bobby, and you'll find, *you're* the bitch!"

"You can't do this! You're my employee, woman! I pay your goddamn agency, for fuck sake!"

"I *can* do it, and I *am*! You're going to learn your lesson, buster! I'm not from the *cleaning* agency," she sniggered. "A *different* agency sent me…"

His mouth formed a perfect O. "*Who*?! I haven't done shit all!" he said, kicking his legs and pulling on the cuffs.

"The people who send me out to clients like you are heinous, Bobby, and they dwell in dark realms you're about to discover."

"Please—"

"Stop saying that, you snivelling toad!" Janeen buried her fingernails in his chest and raked them down to his pubic region.

"*Ugh*!" he gasped, sitting up as far as the handcuffs would allow him to, the agony smothering the words he wanted to yell; tears and blood pissed out of him.

"Shall I bite it off? I'm feeling rather peckish."

Bobby could only shake his head and wheeze.

"You're going to make sure Tilly's set for life, Bobby."

"Wh-what?!" he choked.

"You're going to sign your fortune over to her!"

Bobby shook his head. "What about *me*?!"

"You're not going to need it, so don't worry, and by doing so, you'll make amends, Bobby. If you're lucky, my employees might have mercy on your disgusting soul."

"But I haven't done anything!" he cried.

"Stop! Just stop! We both know the truth, Bobby, of what you had planned, and I'm here to collect."

"This has got to be some kind of joke?"

Janeen shook her head. "I'm afraid not, Bobby, and I'm not just collecting on Tilly's behalf, but for all the other dirty, degrading, and seedy shit you've done in your life, like whipping your cock out in public, upskirting woman and being an all-round sex fiend. You've thrown thousands at females, to shut them up, but not this time. I'm going to fix you and all your problems, Bobby. Something your therapist failed to do."

"You can't do this! You'll never get away with—*Argh*!" he said, as Janeen twisted his balls until he thought they were going to pop. "Get—*Ugh*!" Bobby threw up as she ripped and clawed at them.

"A bit more pressure, and I think this left one will go…"

"You're crazy," he managed between gulps of air.

Janeen sighed, tightening her grip, and crushed his nuts until one ruptured. "How was that, dear? Feel like squirting yet?" she laughed. Bobby bucked and thrashed as though electricity coursed through him. "Shall we try for the second one, Bobby?" When he didn't, or couldn't answer, Janeen ruined his other ball with such force, that his scrotum tore and yellow, pearly-white mucus oozed out of him. "Don't you pass out on me, Bobby!"

"Hospital…"

"What will you do for me?"

"A-anything,"

"Will you give your money to Tilly?"

"Ye-*yes*!"

"Good. Then I might take pity on you after all."

"I-I can't do it yet… Too much pain… Later…" he gasped and blubbered.

"You'll do it now, or I'll take your cock!"

Bobby gargled and nodded. "Okay… Give me… Tilly's bank details…"

Janeen removed an electronic gadget from her pocket of her skirt. "No, you give me *your* bank information, Bobby."

"B-bitch," he muttered, his breathing becoming laboured.

"I suggest you hurry, or I'm going to lose my temper, and there'll be no turning back then." Without further hesitation, Bobby gave her the codes and passwords she needed to access his accounts. "Tilly will be most happy, Bobby!" Janeen said.

"You-you're magic, aren't you?" he rasped.

"Something like that, Bobby."

"Take—take me to the hospital."

Janeen smiled. "No, I can't do that, sorry, but look on the bright side – you've paid for your sins!"

"You, you, *cunt*!" he mustered. "You had no intention— Oh, *Jesus*!" Bobby wanted to seal his eyes shut when her face changed into something beyond his world.

"You have one more price to pay, Bobby, and that price is your ticket to hell," she said, flipping him over, his arms and wrists breaking, his shoulders popping out of their sockets.

"*Urgh!*" he said. "H-h-have mercy," he squealed, feeling her sharp, jagged fingernails clawing and rooting around inside his anus. "*Ugh…*" Bobby started to seizure as her hands went deeper and deeper inside him, crushing his organs to pulp.

"Come for me, Bobby. Come for me!" she roared, laughing and panting.

The last thing Bobby felt, was her hands bursting through his chest…

The Winner Is…?

He started to come around slowly. His head felt heavy. A medium to large lump had formed at the base of his skull. He tried to open his sleep-laden eyes but failed. What the hell am I lying on? he thought. The ground was soft, comfortable, almost. Am I on a beach? "Oh, my fucking head…" he groaned.

Rolling onto his back, he opened his eyes. The sky was clear; a cloudless blue. He placed a hand to his thumping head and tried to massage the pain away. God, what the hell happened? he thought, trying to recall a shred of memory, but his mind only offered a blank canvas. Up, he told himself. Sit up. Let's start there.

Getting into a sitting position, his body screamed. Joints ached. Looking about, he could see he was in a coliseum; the crowd were strong in number. A slight murmur rippled through the audience as they watched him animate. He rubbed at the back of his neck and thought, What the…? Where am I? How did I get to Rome? Fucking Rome! No, it can't be. I was on my way to work last night and…and…I don't remember. His head swirled as he tried to force his thoughts out. *Think damn it, think.*

Nothing. Only a black void of nothingness.

He pushed with his hands and legs. His fingers dug into the blood-spattered flooring. The crowd cheered him on as he got to shaky pins. His shirt was torn. His distressed jeans were even more distressed; blood and muck adorning his thighs, along with cuts and scratches here and there.

His jaw dropped as he looked about him. The terraces were made up of large granite slabs, and there was even a box that looked like a VIP; like those found at a football ground or theatre. People appeared to be in them drinking from goblets and eating meat off the bone.

"Hey!" he yelled at them, waving his arms. The thrashing of his limbs caused pain to race through his head. All they did in the 'VIP box' was tip their cups in his direction.

"What the fuck are you arseholes playing at here?" *Am I in a dream, or what?* he thought. "Hey!" he tried again, rage slowly coursing through him. "Where am I?"

The crowd roared as loud as they could. He felt like a mite under a biology microscope; one that could be crushed at any moment.

"Look, please, I…"

A man dressed in imperial robes stood, sweeping his hand over the crowd. Then they were all brought to a hush inside the great building as his voice boomed around the stone structure.

"You! Down there! You have one chance for survival!" instructed the emperor.

He felt like he had been gut-punched. Winded.

Then, as he was about to protest this fate, his eyes instinctively went to the gates that were directly beneath the stone terraces, as torches were ignited from within. Behind them were tunnels; tunnels filled with God only knew what.

Getting to his hands and knees, he clawed frantically at the sand, searching for a weapon. Sweat broke out across his brow. But there was nothing, just sand.

He gulped as one of the rusty, wrought iron doors opened. He spun around to face it. Out of the gloom came a lone figure; a child, no more than seven or eight. She had a slight frame with a short stature and held a clubbing instrument in her left hand.

Is that thing fucking spiked with nails? he wondered.

Seconds passed, then minutes. She didn't move. Neither did he. He thought about making a run for the fence that circled the front of the structure, but it was barbed at the top, and too high to scale. Probably jumping with electricity too, he thought.

Then, like a jungle warrior screaming a war cry, she ran at him with the timber she carried swinging from side-to-side. He leapt backwards, scared witless by her sudden scream. There was nothing he could do but watch her. Spittle flew from her open mouth.

His job demanded fitness and a no-nonsense attitude. But this was a long way from his work as a riot cop. She was less than thirty feet away…twenty…fifteen…

She was a child…

Ten…

Five…

When she was within reach, he did what he thought would be impossible: he ploughed his fist into her mouth. His knuckles connected with brittle front teeth, sending her from her feet, flying backwards. She landed on the ground, hard. Blood pooled at the back of her head.

Her petite body began to spasm violently. Frothy blood bubbled out of her mouth and ran freely down her cheeks and chin.

The crowd whooped and clapped.

"You sick fucks!" he shouted. "You fucking bloodthirsty freaks…"

A hefty weight fell on his back, almost sending him stumbling. He felt chipped, broken dentures chomping at the side of his neck. Can't be, he thought. She's dead… Then, there was a boy on his back. He was merely a child, no more than ten, his hair long and scraggly; breath stinking of sour milk or meat.

He gripped the youngster by his long fringe and yanked him off his back. The boy tried to get up, but his throat was crushed by the riot cop's heavy boot. The boy gargled on his own blood and vomit, before death took him.

He looked at the boy, then the girl. Neither moved. Fuck, Clayton, mate. You've just killed two kids, he thought. Clayton. At last, his name had come back to him.

He noticed another attacker approaching. This one looked like a teenage girl; fourteen, maybe fifteen. She had a mace. Her clothes were missing, unlike the first two. Mud plastered her body, acting as camouflage.

He made for the spiked club the first girl had dropped and got it in enough time to bludgeon the second girl's skull. The nails made a sickening thwacking noise as they penetrated the side of her head, caving in the cranium. Her whole body lost its rigidness and flopped to the ground. She bucked a few times like a fish out of water before laying still.

He didn't have time to stop and mourn, for two more came at him from different passages. He grabbed the mace from the fallen teen and swung it above his head. "Stay back," he told the closest boy charging him. "Stay fucking back or I will kill you."

Still the boy kept coming… until the mace was brought down on his face. One of the spikes cut across the boy's eyes, causing the left one to pop and splatter across the sandy ground. The child hit the deck and rolled, gurgling like a pig with a torn throat. The red liquid soaked into the flooring as it pissed from the empty socket.

Clayton turned to find the other attacker but was surprised by a diving tackle. He tussled with the tubby teenage boy frantically. Rolling onto his stomach, Clayton tried getting away from his opponent, who had started laying into his kidneys with pounding fists.

"Argh, you little fuck!" he spat between gritted teeth. As his fingers dug into the sand, a glint of light caught his eye. Looking down, Clayton saw a handgun buried in the bloody sand.

Feverishly, he uncovered the gun and soon found the weapon in his hand. In one quick movement, he was on his feet with the firearm cocked and aimed. He hoped to God the weapon hadn't been in the ground that long. If it had, sand would have got into the firing pivot. Hell, the ammunition could be dry and useless. The fucking thing could misfire, or, worse still, blow up in my hand.

The boy head-butted Clayton, dazing him. His gun hand was knocked to one side as the boy dug his fingers into his eye sockets, gouging. The pain was almost unbearable. "Argh!" Clayton screamed. "Get. The. Fuck…"

The crack of gunfire did nothing to silence the crowd but rather heightened their warped sense of pleasure.

A squirt of blood landed in Clayton's mouth as he turned to look at the gaping, gory wound in the middle of the boy's forehead. The boy's mouth sagged open, smoke filtering out, allowing his tongue to flop forth. Buckling, the youth fell to one side and hit the sand so hard that his whole chubby body rebounded and rippled.

Doing a crabwalk, Clayton scooted backwards as he saw three more children spew forth from the gates around him. As they closed in on him, he managed to get to his feet. His legs ached; his arm, too. As he raised the gun, he prayed it had more then one bullet in it.

The first of the three were a mere stone's-throw away as the bullet tore through the six-year-old's face and raced out the back of his tiny head.

Blood and bone matter splashed the sand.

The youngster's body hit the deck and slid slightly backwards.

Bile leapt up Clayton's throat, and hot tears blurred his vision.

He composed himself and released two more rounds. Both bodies dropped within feet of him. "Shit…" he gasped on seeing the bullet-ridden children, but had little time to let it sink in, as he was spun around and punched on the nose.

So powerful was the blow, it took him off his feet.

"Ugh," he yelled, hitting the floor. He could taste blood.

A massive shadow was cast over him as he looked up at the armour-clad warrior. This was no child – this was eighteen stone of man looking down at him. He wore a spiked helmet. His face was not visible, as his helmet was fitted with a metal grill with breathing holes drilled into it.

Half of his chest was covered in gladiator armour. He wore a studded war skirt with sandals. In his left hand he held a double-headed axe. A hunting knife was sheathed at his right hip; a net hanging from his left.

"You've got to be fucking kidding me?!" Clayton spat. Had he not been aching as much, he probably would have burst out laughing. Feeling the gun in his hand, he raised it.

The hammer fell on an empty chamber: click.…

The warrior growled and balled his free hand into a fist, which was gloved and covered in a sort of chain-mail. Rolling, Clayton avoided the punch, which pounded the sand.

Getting to his feet, he threw the gun at the mountain of a man, who rippled with muscle. "You look like Arnie's kid brother!" Clayton said, ducking a few more punches and a swipe of the axe.

Diving, he landed close to the mace, which he grasped. He got back to his feet and swung it above his head. "Yeah, now what are you going to fucking do?!" Clayton yelled as he moved in a circle.

Both men watched each other with squinted eyes.

"Come on, come on!" Clayton said. "Make your—"

Sand was kicked into his face. Some of the golden particles got into his mouth, which he chewed on as he tried spitting them free.

Fearing he'd be caught whilst blinded, he swept the mace about him in a maniacal way. "Dirty bastard!"

"Argh!" his foe cried as a metal spike lodged into his exposed shoulder.

As Clayton tried to pull the weapon free, it was ripped from his hands, just as his vision cleared. "No!" he cried, seeing the bloodied gladiator approach with his axe held across his chest. Bracing himself, Clayton put his hand above his head and threw himself into a roll.

Clayton grabbed the sheathed knife and rammed it into the guy's exposed neck.

Blood spurted.

"Yeah!" Clayton yelled as the granite-like man staggered on shaking legs. "Die, you motherfucker! Die!"

Before the warrior could fall to the floor, Clayton pulled the knife out of the man's neck as violently as he could, before ramming it home again, and again, and again…

He whooped as his foe fell away, defeated and dead.

A horn blared.

The gates to the stadium started closing.

No more children.

No more challengers.

"I fucking win!" he yelled.

His joy was short-lived, as the person who had addressed him at the start of the 'Game' stood again.

"Congratulations. You now have a ten-minute interlude. Use it wisely!"

"But…but…" Clayton started, but his words fell on deaf ears. The emperor had sat back down. "You blood-thirsty fucks!" he spat.

A subconscious clock ticked the seconds down inside his head, booming like claps of thunder. Think, Clayton. Think. There must be a way out of this. There must be. But how? He looked at the fence surrounding the stands again. He could scale it and probably get over the barb.

The million-dollar question was whether it was alive with electricity or not. If it wasn't, and he dropped into the crowd, would they lynch or tear him apart? More than likely. What about the tunnels? They had to lead somewhere.

Yeah, deep into the bowels of this fucking stadium, no doubt. What about the walls? No, too high to climb.

Fuck, I'm shit out of luck.

The horn sounded again.

"Round two," someone called.

Crap, I need to think, and fast! he thought, looking about him. Just beyond the fallen gladiator, Clayton saw more shimmering in the sand. He went to it and saw something buried there.

Getting to his hands and knees, he dug until he unearthed a massive shield. Dragging it free, he held it up. It was heavy, yet perfect. Turning to the dead warrior, he grabbed the axe.

I'm not going down without a fight, he thought, putting his back to a wall.

The horn sounded for a second time.

"Let the round begin!" the emperor bellowed. The stadium erupted into a rapture of applause, whoops and cheers.

"I'm glad they're enjoying themselves," Clayton muttered, crouching behind the shield. He took a few deep breaths. He couldn't believe he was choosing to slaughter children. *I've done some wrong shit in my time as a cop, but this is a new low.* Having been a riot cop for the best part of eight years, he was in fit, physical shape. He wasn't the tallest of men, standing at five-eleven, but his physique made up for it. His stature had earned him the nickname 'The Stone' by his work colleagues. "No time for tears," he uttered, watching the gates roll up.

Three children appeared at the foot of the tunnel in front of him. They were girls – teenage girls at that – and they were nude, much like the rest had been up to this point. Their bare flesh was caked in filth.

"Shit! What the fuck is going on here?" he said between clenched teeth. The muscles in his jaw tensed as he bit back tears. *They could so easily be my girls,* he thought, realising he didn't know what his children looked like these days. Their mother had not sent any recent pictures or letters in months.

He focused as the three girls rushed him. Two had swords, whilst the other wielded a cleaver. "Come on, come on…" he whispered, gripping the axe as tight as he could.

As the first one came in for a swipe of her sword, he ducked lower still and smashed his axe into her ankle, which took her foot clean off. Her body went into a spill and crumpled to the ground. He rushed forward and flattened the second girl with the shield, before thudding the axe into the third one's face.

With sheer grit, he finished the two wounded girls, who snapped and snarled at him as he broke their necks.

Shuffling backwards, he got behind his shield and crouched once again, readying himself for the next wave of attackers. *How long can I keep this up? I'm fit, but not that fit!*

Then something happened that he didn't expect: the horns sounded within the stadium again.

He stood up. Have I won?

The ground rumbled.

He had just enough time to move as a portion of the ground slid away. A tiger leaped out of the gap. Its talons missed Clayton's face by mere inches as he collapsed onto his back. The animal was chained to the ground, only capable of wandering so far.

Getting up, Clayton realised more tigers had been released into the killing zone. "Cunts!" he yelled, making the tiger join in with an ear-shredding roar. "Fuck," Clayton said, moving further out of the cat's path.

This caused the tiger to crouch, then leap – its chain pulling taut, causing some bricks to fall from the wall behind it. Out of the gaps came tumbling whole skeletons, bones, skulls…

Clayton doubled over and retched.

Chunks of spew hit the floor and mixed with the blood and gore.

Wiping his mouth, he regained control of himself, and moved back against the wall. The tigers shouldn't get me this far over, he thought, hiding behind his shield once more.

"Come out from behind there!" a woman yelled from the crowd as she launched a rotten cabbage at him.

Even though it missed, it distracted Clayton enough to fail noticing two large boys rushing him. They shoulder-charged him, one running straight into his shield, knocking it out of Clayton's hand.

The other lad rammed into his guts, lifting him off his feet. But the boy hadn't braced himself correctly, and Clayton's collapsing body pulled the boy with him – and into the path of a tiger.

Clayton turned to see the animal pounce. Claws ripped through his left shoulder, causing him to scream in pain, but he wasn't about to die this way. He slammed the axe into the beast's belly and tore it sideways, causing the massive cat to flop onto its side.

The duel wasn't yet done, as one of the boys jumped on him. He bit and scratched Clayton as the other tried pinning his legs to the floor. Panic raced through his guts as he tried desperately to roll onto his back. With a massive push of effort, he managed to turn over.

With his back once again to the sand, Clayton could see the other children rush him. He grabbed the boy on his upper body, roughly by the hair, pulling his head backwards viciously, which exposed the boy's oesophagus. Clayton drove his knuckles into it and felt the youngster's throat collapse just as another lad leapt on him. This child was heavier. They seemed to be getting bigger. Older, he thought.

The boy was still trying to pin his legs as five more bodies crashed on top of him.

The pressure on his body was almost unbearable.

He felt rough fingers around his neck. Then they were searching for his eyes. He shook his whole body in a vain attempt to dislodge his attackers, but soon there were others on him. He crumbled under the weight. He closed his eyes as tight as he could, as they tried prying his lids open.

One of them grabbed his testicles and squeezed hard, causing Clayton's eyes and mouth to instinctively open, leaving him defenceless. He felt cold steel in his mouth as they started to slice his tongue loose. Hungry fingers gouged at his eyes, tore at his lids. They were soon ripped from his head, along with his eyeballs. The nerves that connected them were severed. He could do nothing as torrid pain racked him.

Their hands were everywhere, tugging, prodding, pulling, hollowing, digging, ripping, drinking…

Before he succumbed, Clayton heard the emperor's voice one last time: "The winner is…"

DRABBLES

The Rich Get Richer

Orchid House, a brooding, security-lacking mansion, was their next target. A peach ripe for the picking, or so the trio of cat burglars thought.

"We'll retire after this one, boys," the gang's leader, Charles, said. "Crowbars up, balaclavas down!"

However, within the manor's walls lay an age-old secret, one that had snared many.

"Don't kill me," Charles cried, offering the aristocrat cannibal-handler his swag bag of goodies.

Close by, in the dark, he heard the nobleman's interbred family slurp on his crooked friends.

"Why go out for steak when you can have hamburglars at home, Charles?!" the lord asked, laughing.

Urination Damnation

Tina swam from the lifeguard and pressed her bikini-clad vagina against the bubbling underwater pipe. She then released her bladder, squirt by squirt, savouring the feel.

"God!"

She knew it was wrong. That people had become sick, the sports centre scrutinised. But she couldn't stop.

The children are worse, I'll bet, she thought, throwing her head back and spotting the sign: **Urinators Will *Now* Be Punished.**

She gasped, the dawn of an orgasm breaking.

Tina then screamed as hot, wriggling beasties invaded her genitals.

Blood bubbled.

"Another one dealt with," she heard someone say, before sinking to the pool's bottom.

Tribal Beard

*B*eards, *a showing of manliness*, Chester thought. *But I can't grow one, so I'll never attract the women.*

However, after seeing an advert for Tribal Beard, a tonic concocted in deepest Congo, he bought and used some.

The next day, he awoke to the sound of drums and a thick, forest-like beard.

"A miracle," he cried, rushing to the mirror to run his hands through it.

Piss trickled down his leg.

Amongst the bush were people planting hairs. When they saw him, they yelled in their native tongue and fired their arrows. His newfound manliness done nothing to protect him.

Knight of the Road

When the S.O.S call came in over his scanner, a female stranded on a dark, lonesome road, her car stalled, Bruce was quick to adorn his suit and helmet.

"No female shall be beached on my watch!" he pledged, getting into his van that was a mobile garage.

After discovering the damsel, who wasn't distressed, terror seized him.

"So, you're the one helping the hapless women?" she asked, advancing with a club. "Let's get him, ladies, and see how big his heart is."

Bruce cowered, as women popped out of bushes and from under the car, each holding a weapon.

Road Rage

Four a.m., and the road was theirs, as they rode it at ninety.

"Fifty?" Leon said, swigging his beer, his Porsche swerving. "I'm not driving like a tard."

Mike, Leon's intoxicated passenger, turned the radio up and stuck his head out his window. "Fuck yeah!" he yelled.

Ahead, a car was barely troubling the speed limit.

"Let's bully 'em," Mike screamed, grabbing his bat. "Get closer!"

The Porsche pulled up alongside the old woman's car and Mike clubbed it.

But then screamed, as she drew a sawn-off, blasting him. The Porsche wobbled, overturned, and the engine caught fire and detonated.

VHS: The Future of Home Entertainment in the 22nd Century

"Why so cheap?" Peter asked the owner of the Lost Artefacts and Forgotten Worlds shop. The man beckoned him closer. "It's otherworldly…"

He rushed home, unwrapped the VHS player, and connected it. "Finally, I can watch them in all their glory!" Peter said, eyeing his video nasties collection.

Peter laughed and inserted Hellraiser into the player. "Such sights to show you," a staticky voice said. Peter screamed, flesh burning, as he was sucked into the VHS, transported to a world filled with masked killers, perverts, window-lickers, chainsaw hookers, murderous puppets and other horrors and hauntings that *would* drive him mad…

Inheritance

Jimmy exited his father's mansion and walked towards the tool shed where the man had been cornered and killed by the police.

"The Murderous Millionaire", the media had dubbed him. Most of the victims had been killed by a chainsaw, their bodies scattered across these woods. A shiver tore through him as memories of playing amongst the trees as a child came to him.

When he entered the shed, something unseen pushed into his mouth, flowing down into his guts.

"Like father, like son, boy," he heard his dad say internally.

Jimmy's eyes settled on the blood-spattered chainsaw before him.

Timothy Button:
The Vampire

I t came from the darkness and clacked along its tracks. Timothy Button, wide-eyed and grinning, boarded the famed rollercoaster. *What if there're real ghouls*? he thought, giggling.

"Vampire, take flight!" the operator screeched with laughter.

The ride reached its zenith, zoomed down the other side, thundering into its corkscrews and loops with menace. As the carriages rounded the final bend back to the station, Timothy saw a swarm of creatures descend upon the Vampire, blanketing it, the screams around him blood-freezing and real.

When he alighted, seeing fewer riders than boarded, he knew he'd never forget what he saw tonight…

The Runner

It came from the darkness and gave chase along the woodland path. Timothy Button, knowing he'd disturbed *that* spot, looked over his shoulder and saw it lumbering towards him out of the misty morning; its leafy arm was outstretched, its twig fingers reaching.

"Take up an activity?" the doctor suggested. "Exercise your demons; go back to where it began!"

The woods, he thought. Being touched... The man and his purple root.

Timothy couldn't face away. "Fuck off!" he said, tripping and sprawling along the floor. Before he could get back up, the demon grabbed him, dragging him into the woods.

Death in Paradise

It came from the darkness and swallowed him forever. His laughter was profound, his mind a melting pot of guilt and unravelling thoughts of the life, wife and children that he'd left behind; suicide beckoned from the fringes of reality in this lonely, lovely sanctuary.

"Run, but no hide," he jabbered, rocking on his heels. "Your problems are your luggage."

The sun outside his veranda window winked off the razor he held. Timothy gargled his prayers, his blood spraying, as he tried to flee to another land of hope and peace.

This time, he thought, *the pain will go away…*

***

Donor

It came from the darkness of the corridor and eased the door open. Terry, bent over the provided skin mag, wanking, looked up at the stockinged legs before him and smiled.

Finally! he thought. *With all the times I've been coming here to donate my love-muck, leaving the door unlatched, a nurse walks in and makes my day!* Pre-come dribbled out of his dick, his eyes climbing the slender, uniformed-wrapped body.

Terry's cock shrivelled, his eyes latching onto a gaping mouth filled with razors. "Blood giver too!" it screeched, ripping his prick off and placing a beaker to the fountain.

Preaching the Perverted

It came from the darkness of Carla's mind and stirred a heat in her. Her sex dripped, gluing her knickers to her, as she watched the choir girls sing, hips sashaying.

Young bitches! she thought, sweat beading her flushed face. *They know what I did, and they mean to out me as a pervert!*

Carla shook her head, giving in to their subtle lip-licks and winks. She stepped from behind her pulpit, undoing her clergy robe, exposing her bare tits and diddling fingers. "Oh God," she gasped, climaxing, her flock wailing, the girls giggling and pointing.

The Lord's work done.

Outnumbered

with Natasha Sinclair

"There's too many," Lisa wailed. "The cabin's surrounded!"

"Nail the fucking door closed!" Tim said, securing planks to a window and dropping nails as rotted hands punched through the glass.

"Urrrrgh!" groaning outside, the undead huddled six deep, their weight pressing against the thin walls.

Lisa gripped the hammer and rammed the claw into Tim's skull; it stuck in the bone. Unable to release it, she grabbed the tool from his limp hand and tore into his soft belly, smearing herself generously in his warm gore.

They were getting in; the least she could do was try to blend in.

Eaten Alive
with Natasha Sinclair

Sat at a table in his tattered brown suit, manners departed, he scooped up handfuls of pulpy flesh on the plate before him and stuffed it into his slack mouth. As he chewed, blood oozed out of the holes in his cheeks and throat, his worm-riddled hands returned for more.

The dining room door swung open, breaking through the squelching of meat grinding against dead meat, "I told you that, I'd never let you go." His wife's sister placed a severed leg onto the plate of innards. "She always thought she had better legs than me. Eat up." Vicky winked.

The Last Freakshow on Earth Presents: Diablo (The Dagger) Dynamo

with Natasha Sinclair

After Diablo's glamourous assistant secured the female audience member to his wooden, spinning Wheel of Death, which sported a trillion knife holes and scuff marks, he donned his blindfold and unsheathed his famous Flying Daggers. With the-hand-is-quicker-than-the-eye movements, Diablo tossed all nine of his blades, one after the other.

With meticulous methodical precision, the daggers each strike their mark; five around the woman, each 72° apart. One in each of her eyeballs to unlock her sight to the dark, the sixth piercing her womb for she may bare seed of the despicable underworld demons, and finally her barely beating heart.

Unsuspecting Victim

Vincent floated towards her bedroom window and looked in, his fangs growing. "My love," he said, his eyes coursing the contours of her sleeping body. "We'll reign in blood, my queen!" With ease, he rolled the window skywards and slipped inside, her smells entering his pores. "Such beauty."

He pulled her duvet back, exposing her neck, and a clicking sound ensued. Something pressed against his balls, and when he looked, he saw a pistol there. "Huh?" he gasped.

"Thought that might get your attention," she said, her other arm bursting from beneath the covers, plunging a stake into Vincent's chest.

World War Three

Pritchard was on site with his workmen and bulldozers—clearing the land he'd bought through the courts—to make sure the protestors behaved. "Bloody rabble," he said, watching the mob with placards behind the fences encircling his property. "Historical ground my arse…"

"Argh!" someone said.

Pritchard looked, his cigar falling from his mouth, spotting zombified, World War One soldiers rise up out of the ground; earth and beasties tumbled off their muddy-green uniforms and gas masks. Some of the troops affixed bayonets to their rifles, while others picked up dropped workmen's tools, and laid siege to those who'd disturbed them…

The Stick Up

Roxanne watched from behind black shades, the descending sun at her back, as the last blood donor of the day exited the clinic. This is my chance, she thought, removing the sawn-off shotgun from under her raincoat and entering the building.

"Hands in the air, bitch!" Roxanne said.

The nurses nodded and cried. "What do you want?!"

"Blood! Now take me to it! Move!"

Her raid done, a month's supply of blood hers, Roxanne ducked down an alley and devoured some of the life source. "Being a vampire that's allergic to skin isn't so bad," she laughed, quaffing more blood.

Assassins

"You think you can come here and steal my creation?!" Daniels laughed, turning to see the door to his laboratory rattle in its frame. "My serum of life!" he continued, inoculating the six dead warriors on his work slabs. "Arise!"

As the half a dozen, once slashed-to-death ninjas twitched, jerked and arose from Daniel's test stations, the lab's door burst open. "Give it up, Daniels!" a gun-brandishing goon said.

"Never!" Daniels said, standing behind his combatants, as they unscabbarded their swords, unsheathed their daggers and sprang into action.

The room filled with the sound of gunfire and steel on bone.

The Last Freakshow on Earth
Presents: The Ventriloquist

"Here's our chance to impress, Harry, as they'll be watching!" Crystal said, looking at her gangster dressed dummy. "Let's do this!"

She entered the stage and sat on the stool at the stage's centre, eyeing the circus' visitors sat in the VIP box before her. There they are, she thought, placing Harry on her lap, starting her series of filthy sketches.

At the end of her routine, Harry's mouth opened, and a hail of bullets spewed forth, riddling the VIPs.

"Bravo!" someone called from the balcony, the ringmaster showing himself. "A splendid display," he continued, laughing and clapping. "You're hired!"

The Last Freakshow on Earth
Presents: Balloon Man

"Kiddos, gather around, for I am going to show you magic the likes of which has never been seen by a living soul!"

"What about people at the fair before us?"

Balloon Man smiled, his garish, cracked make-up flaking. "Such a perceptive child," he said, grabbing the boy by his cheeks. "I said living…" With bellowing laugher, Balloon Man slipped a balloon from his hip pouch and blew it up. "Who'd like to see a rhino?!"

"Me!" came a chorus of voices.

Balloon Man, producing the rubber animal, set it free and watched as it stampeded and crushed the children.

The Last Freakshow on Earth
Presents: Alligator Alice

"**R**oll up, roll up… Step inside and feast your eyes on the most vicious gator to have ever walked Earth!" the freakshow announcer said, holding a flap open to his tent. "See Alice, the ginormous reptile, found thousands of years ago in Brazil, now frozen in time for your viewing pleasure…"

Customers poured into the marquee, eager to see the bizarre wonder, not realising the tent was sealed at their backs. Screams ensued, as Alice, half-woman half-alligator, trudged out of her swamp-like enclosure and snapped her massive jaws.

"Let us out!" the people screamed, crying, only to be swallowed whole…

The Invitation
with Natasha Sinclair

Claire reread the email's subject. "You are cordially invited to a masquerade at my castle in the woods… Who'd invite me, the ugly duckling, to a fancy party? More to the point, a castle? In the woods? It's got to be a joke!" Her curiosity bettered her good judgement.

From the surrounding darkness and foreboding silence of the monolithic building — a cloaked swarm swooped upon her. Like a wake of vultures driven by a unified mind; feed, satiate the hunger. Her clothes were torn from her young body, a myriad frenzy of fangs pierced virgin skin. She was their swan.

Out of Body, Out of Mind
with Natasha Sinclair

Every tooth had been yanked from Ken's bloody mouth, the tips of five fingers gruesomely severed with rusty bolt cutters.

"Just tell us where the money is!!" the gangster screamed for the countless time.

Ken's mind had been swinging between broken and some out-of-body euphoria. Surely it would soon end.

"This arsehole isn't talking, Vinnie," the second thug said, unholstering his snub-nosed .44. "See ya, prick!"

"Wh-who are you?" Ken choked, eyes popping, seeing a cloaked figure floating his way. In its unseen hands, it held a swinging billhook, which swiped at his face as hot lead ripped into him.

Death of Paradise

Death removed his surfer shades, placed them in the top pocket of his 'gnarly dude' shirt and laughed at the racy postcards he'd bought. "He's stealing her bra," he chuckled, pointing at a lewd image, slapping his knee.

"Wish you were here," he scribbled it on the reverse of a card. "How's my apprentice—" A message pinged through on his mobile, disrupting him. With a huff, knowing it was the Big Cheese, he read the alert.

Carnage in Tampa Bay, FL. Do you mind? I know you're holidaying there…

"Who'd be me?" he said, slipping his robe on, leaving.

Gambling with Death

An "Ooh" rippled through the crowd as the gun's hammer fell on an empty chamber, the pistol slammed down on the table and thrust towards Mikey. "Your play, gringo!" the fat Spaniard said, smiling; sweat beaded his brow.

Mikey placed a trembling hand on the gun, nestled between stacks of blood-coated currency, and lifted it to his open mouth. This was a mistake, he thought, cocking the firearm, feeling cool metal against his teeth.

Fire, fire, fire! the crowd chanted.

Mikey squeezed the trigger. "Jesus!" he gasped, Death forming in the revolver's smoke, the back of his head tearing open.

Furloughed

"Goddamn pandemic," Death said, throwing peanuts at the TV, swigging on his eighth beer as he watched the hockey. "Come on, ref! Game's fixed!" He was close to lobbing his bottle at the screen, restraining himself, as he dug his bony fingers into the pull-out sofa bed.

It was great when the flu hit, killing people in their droves, but now…he thought. "Shit, there's no souls left to collect! Population has been reduced to the young and healthy; God knows when the Big Cheese will call me back to work… Still, at least the wife's working. Small mercies," he huffed.

Flesh-Eaters

When Raven returned home from Glaring Graffiti, she stripped off and got into the shower. She then unwrapped her new thigh tattoo, tossed the bloody bandages aside, and started the water. Wails

"Fucking sick!" she said, looking at the creation, as excess blood and ink sluiced off her, revealing a huge, black and white, Hammer Horror-esque, graveyard scene filled with mist and zombies.

With gentle ease, Raven soaped the gruesome artwork. "Can't wait—Argh!" she said, as the rotten faces on her limb rippled and came to live, chewing into her leg and through her pussy, burrowing up into her guts…"

Flat Mate

The olde-worlde apartment, with its old-fashioned fittings, seafront view and modern exterior upgrades, had come cheap. "Fools," Greg laughed, thinking about the sweet deal, chiselling at the walls as he renovated the inside. "Still, I'll spend thousands…" he trailed off, unearthing a bricked-up door.

Greg twisted the rusted doorknob, yanking the portal open, which gave way with an aged groan and splinters of wood. "Where's my—Argh!" he said, as a pair of flesh-eaten hands clamped down on his shoulders, fingers digging, followed by a mouth filled with broken, discoloured teeth that latched onto his face and ripped it off.

Fight or Flight

He kicked open the doors to the disused cinema, fixed his crooked dog's collar, and cocked his modified crossbow capable of firing fifty stakes. "Come get some, you blood-sucking hell beasts!" he said. "I'm here to kick arse for my Lord!"

Vampire bats swooped, avoiding shafts of daylight coming in through the doors, as he opened fire. "Argghh!" he said, his bolts spearing creatures. "I'll return you to Lucifer!"

When his crossbow ran dry, he tossed holy water hand grenades, but their number were too great, and they fell on him, wrapping him in a black, screeching blanket of hades…

Drawing Blood

with Natasha Sinclair

inc tossed back the warm shot of pig's blood — the closest thing to human that was legal. He felt the faintest ghost of a pulse restart. Scanning the dark, his eyes darted between shapes cavorting between the pulsing strobe-lighting. The pheromones electrified his dead skin, arousing the need for more.

His sharpening eyesight locked onto a woman sat in an inky corner, his knowing now intense. A virgin, he thought. Going to her and shrouding her in his cloak, about to sink his fangs, she stabbed him with a stake. "For my mother," she said, as he crumbled into dust.

The Last Freakshow on Earth
Presents: Pestilence Boy
with Natasha Sinclair

"They say he's walked every realm known to man since the dark ages. Used as a cure, sucking disease and poison from every royal, affluent person and folk with money to burn," the circus hand said, introducing his audience to the green-complexioned boy housed in a large jar.

The ghoulish imp-boy stood, head poking from the top. With eyes closed, he drew in air, puffing out his feeble chest, holding it for the longest minute. When he opened them, his laser-like eyes began burning the humanity from the audience; screaming and chaos ensued — from those who weren't burned to cinders.

Miss Pestilence 2021
with Natasha Sinclair

Tina looked in the mirror and wept, her mascara cutting dirty tracks down her cheeks, as she watched her hair fall out around her lopsided tiara. Behind her, on the TV in her house, the news played: "…Believed that the deadly strain erupted at the Miss Globe…" the anchor droned.

She gnawed the leg as she stared at the screen; blood spurted into her eyes — giving everything a scarlet hue. Consumerism was the problem; consume or be consumed… Her daughter's chubby limb tasted like chicken. Tina wept for the workout she'd have to slam to work off the baby fat.

Choice Cuts

For Mam and Dad

"Eat Some More (Taste The Pain)."
– Alice Cooper

Bank Holiday

The spot was perfect - the sun slashed down through the thinly scattered clouds and the sky was an incredible blue. Miniscule ripples danced on the water's surface which gave off sloshing sounds that were rhythmic and soothing. Tree branches drooped over the river - their leaves just about able to feel the surface. The verge to the waterway was pebbled with a few grassy patches to sit on; it was a great place for a day's sunbathing and reading, or even a picnic with a lover. The foliage worked well with the sun and water; it cast off a bright glint that lit up the area with immense rays of colour.

The entry to the broken track that led to the retreat was obstructed by overgrown trees and undergrowth; it lurked in the shadows of the green. Ystrad's train station and football field harboured the nearby area of the camouflaged path. Jane could not believe that she had walked this way home from work countless times and had never once spotted it.

The sports ground was full today: Bank Holiday Monday. The kids were off from school and out playing football, rugby and Frisbee. Dogs chased tennis balls and sniffed other mutts, as their owners stood sharing their gossip from the week gone by. A man wearing a plain, white t-shirt and red running shorts made laps of the grassland, whilst couples sunbathed on blankets and other groups drank in the sun.

Jane considered coming to the sports park for the Monday, but she knew it would be full. So, when she had happened upon a particular spot amongst the trees and shrubbery, she had planned to come here for the day to just relax and forget.

She had left her house around eleven o'clock wearing blue jeans and a flowery, flimsy top, with a shoulder bag containing things that she would need throughout the day: book, suntan lotion, sandwiches (that she had made this morning – the bread laced with fresh ham and Coleman's English Mustard), sunglasses and a blanket to lie on. Jane had stripped to her bikini hidden underneath her clothes, and had then spread her big, tartan blanket over a patch of grass that was close to the river and pebbles.

Now in amongst nature and the intense sun, she didn't have a worry in the world. The hot rays battered her half naked body and massaged her into a relaxed state of mind, as she lay there on her stomach reading a paperback by Jack Ketchum. Her shoulder length hair blew in the sultry wind. The delicate straps to her bikini top had been undone and left to dangle as the midday breeze tickled her bare shoulders. Jane kicked her legs and wriggled her toes in the air as she read her book, just like when she was a child, lying on her bed. She could hear the kids on the field playing their games, the yelp of dogs, and the odd train whooshed passed beyond her safe haven. She wondered if that fella still made his laps around the field.

After reading enough of Red by Ketchum (because her mind had suddenly flicked to the runner) she sat up, placed the book down by her side, and did up her straps. From her bag she pulled out a green box holding her lunch and a small bottle of water. The food was wrapped in foil and the water still had a slight chill to it. She plucked a sandwich from the wrapper and began to nibble away at it as she looked out at the water. Birds had landed on the iridescent surface to drink and eat the crusts that Jane threw to them.

As she tossed her scraps to the ducks, the glare of the sun became too much for her eyes, so she dug out the shades she had packed and slipped them on. She again began to throw the bread to the birds. One duck out in the middle caught her attention. It had not come with the others to feed – just stayed out in the middle of the river.

Jane took a closer look at the single duck out in the centre. She noticed that it seemed to be struggling, as though it was caught on something out there. Jane began to get up, to move closer. She put on her sandals and eased closer to the water's edge - the bird was definitely in some kind of trouble. It started to beat its wings frantically now, and began to let out awful screeching sounds, as it was pulled under the water.

Startled by the disappearing animal, Jane moved backward over stones which penetrated her sandals and dug into her soles. She removed her glasses and got a better view at what was going on out there. The other ducks by now had sensed the commotion and began to swim away; their eyes held a glaze that was haunting – surreal even.

Feathers gargled up from the depths and floated off downstream. Jane turned back to her things and decided that maybe this was not such a hot idea in the first place.

She pulled her clothes out of the shoulder bag and slammed items back in as a jolting spasm of fear slithered down her spine. It gave off a sudden urge to turn around and look back at the water, but her mind was rushing with questions, and pushed out any thoughts of looking behind her.

Jane slipped her jeans on, and once finished – she began to pull her top down over her head. As she did so, she caught a glimpse of something up in the trees, far off to her left side, but the garment blocked her view, as it was pulled over her face.

Quickly tugging the item of clothing fully down, she looked back up to her left. Her jaw loosened and swung on its hinges. Jane thought her eyes deceived her – how the hell had she not noticed this before?

A beach towel hung from the higher limbs of a tree. Articles of swim gear could also be seen higher up. Her eyes scanned the rest of the area now. Some clothes were caught on driftwood and stuck-out from branches of bending trees a bit further down. Just off to the right, a pair of trainers could be seen by the water's edge. Jane noted that she was shaking and frozen to the spot.

All of a sudden, the water crashed upwards into a mushroom cloud of silver. Jane let out a pitiful whimper. Out in the centre of the water stood a pale figure of a man wearing nothing but black trunks with a small, green tick on their side. His body was peppered with bite marks and missing clumps of flesh – the right eye half closed, and the left a bloodshot mess. His cheeks looked as though they had been chewed through – maybe the fish had been at him, or perhaps they had been dissolved by the water. The lower half of his teeth could be seen in the gaps. As he walked out of the river, he left behind him a trail of grey, flaking skin; a sight that made Jane want to gag. When his distance narrowed, Jane spotted a rather large sized object in his left hand. She wanted to turn and run, but she could not move. She waited with bated breath as he moved in on her, his face motionless.

When the tops of his legs emerged, Jane could see that his whole right thigh was missing – eaten to the bone. The skeletal joints powered onwards as though still being driven by a living person. The closer he came, the clearer the object in his hand became; It was a massive stone.

The sight of the rock jump started her into life – she could finally move. Jane dumped her bag to the floor and turned to run away, but just before she could make it to the shrubbery, something hard and heavy pounded her back – just in-between the shoulder blades, and sent her to the ground, winded. Jane tried to shake the haze from her eyes, but it was an effort. He was on top of her before she could regroup. The thing turned her over – his left, bloodshot eye scanned her all over. His teeth bit into her left breast, piercing the thin fabric. Before she could scream, a handful of pebbles were rammed into her open mouth, making her gag on small bits of chipped ivory and grit.

Jane tried to spit out the stones, but only blood managed to find its way out of her mouth. He pinned her arms down by her side, and head butted her into a state of semi-consciousness. He got off her, caught her by the ankles and began to drag her toward the river. Her head moved from side-to-side; her eyes rolled around inside like marbles.

Her mind screamed do something! Snap out of it! Fight back! But she felt beaten by this man. How could such a thing happen with so many people just off in the distance playing and having fun in the sun, and the birds in the trees singing with such joyfulness?

Her ears picked up the sound of voices approaching from the trees – more people. Jane pushed at the granite in her mouth with her tongue and managed to get some of it out. She got her voice ready to yell. Jane made her move, and freeing her mouth fully, she called out, but it must have only sounded like a whisper - her throat was dry from the mouthful of gravel – which did not allow her to muster enough power to scream for her life. She was about to try again, but a blow to her gut cut off any further chance and she was dragged under the water.

Her mouth worked again as she opened up and let out a massive, gargled scream. The water underneath was a murky grey, leaving her visibility slightly less than perfect, but enough to see the bed littered with half chewed up bodies, bones and articles of clothing. The corpses could not rise to the surface because large stones had replaced the area where their guts had once been. Ribs and other parts of their skeletons had also been fastened to the seabed – the creature had stabbed them into the sand. Her lungs began to fill with the jade liquid as she managed to break out of the thing's grasp once more, getting a hand above the water, before going back under.

***

Tony and Angie stood in front of the rusted, red sign. Just under the moss, a message could be seen, and Angie voiced her disappointment.

"I told you that we wouldn't be able to come here and fool about, didn't I?"

"Why'd you have to go and spot the damn thing for, Angie? The thing is most probably decades old anyway. Come on, it will be fun. Nobody's down there, it'll just be you and me."

She did not seem convinced but knew how much Tony wanted to hang out at the spot since he discovered it two days ago. She caught hold of his free hand and said in a voice that almost convinced her.

"Come on, love. Let's get down there."

They walked down the path, kicking up dust and laughing as they left behind the ancient and crooked sign that read: "Keep out! No swimming, fishing or any other activity."

One More Night

She'd call them tomorrow definitely – just one more night, that's all she needed to help her go through with it, was one more night. This was running through her mind as she looked at the clock stationed above the TV. It read eleven-forty-five, well past her usual ten o'clock bedtime.

For the best part of a week now, Abigail couldn't bring herself to go up to that cold, old bed anymore – not since James had died. They had been married for ten years, most of them good. Every night they would watch TV from six o'clock onwards, then depart for bed at ten sharp, as James had to work early in the mornings. Maybe it was for this reason that Abi never truly went to bed at ten anymore; after all, James wasn't around for work in the mornings these days.

However, it was time now she thought: her eyes had started to close, plus the detective show she'd been watching was poor. Forcing herself up from her comfy chair in the living room, she ambled over to the telly and switched it off. In the blankness of the screen, she saw James, sitting in his rocker behind her. She smiled softly whilst holding her crossed arms at the elbows to keep the chill back. Abigail could hear the soft creaking motion of his chair and spoke gently. "When are you going to fix that, dear?"

She turned smoothly, her smile diminishing at the sight of the empty seat. There was a faint hint of his tobacco in the air. God, how he had loved his pipe. It lay cold now on the small table that stood by his chair - the last of the tobacco long burnt out.

Abigail pulled at her nightgown's lapels and shuddered. She would have to throw out the pipe and sell the chair, for she couldn't bear to look at them anymore. Moving passed the rocker, she made her way into the kitchen to fix a mug of hot chocolate for herself; it helped her to sleep at night.

Passing back through the kitchen with her drink in hand, she knocked the lights off as she went. Then, there in the darkness at the foot of the staircase, it crossed her mind again – just one more night, that's all. Just the one more night, then she would get it done. The strong aroma of the milky drink stuffed up her nostrils as she climbed the wooden hill – a term her father used to use when putting Abigail to bed at night. The yielding carpet underneath her fluffy slippers made soft, swishing sounds as she went. Halfway up she began thinking about not having to get up early in the mornings anymore. That was the only good thing about being passed the age of retirement.

At the top of the stairs, she made straight for her bedroom, leaving the landing light on, as she always did these days. Her room was shrouded in blackness which gave Abigail a slight start – then she scolded herself for being so silly. There was nothing in there that was going to hurt her. Easing the door open fully, she shuffled in, being careful not to slop her drink and burn her frail hand. Getting to her usual side of the bed, Abigail switched on the bedside lamp, then placed her mug down onto the table that supported the light.

She threw back the covers, and the smell brought back a memory of wet sand, frying onions, candyfloss, and other sweet aromas that fused with teenagers' shouts of excitement and fear of being spun and whooshed about on thrill rides. James had bought them both small tubs of seafood from one of the stalls over by the Big Wheel. It was one of her favourite foods to buy at the fair; that and toffee apples. The man selling them had told James that the fish had been caught fresh from the sea that morning.

"How did you know that the way to my heart was through prawns in a tiny plastic pot?"

"To be quite frank, my beaut', when I look into them bountiful, green eyes of yours, I see everything there is to know about you." He smiled at her, pleased at they way he managed to come across all snooty in his mock, posh voice, and how his tacky line almost sounded good.

"Aww, James. You're sweet." Her face kept its serious tone as she spoke again. "Do you think two people of our age can find true love? I'd like to think they can."

"I don't know what you're talking about, love, I'm only in it for the sex." He almost managed to contain his laughter, but it slipped out as he cheekily pinched her bum.

Abigail looked at him and playfully slapped his chest. "Mr. Hooker, I can see I'm going to have to keep my eye on you."

"The left or the right one?"

"Tut, I hope your jokes improve. A smutty man I can put up with, but a shoddy comedian I can't."

She wrinkled her nose as the memory was lost and thought that the smell coming from inside her bed was getting worse. Yes, she thought, it would have to be tomorrow, no putting it off anymore. Before getting in, she looked at his grey corpse – it had once been so vibrant and healthy. He had been such a strong man, but now all that remained was a body that was oozing fluids disposed of by the innards that slowly soaked into the mattress. The heat burnt out, leaving a cold, harsh shell, with flesh rotting and becoming mushy as the days went on. Some of his bones had dissolved, and bits of James were starting to loosen. Abigail had awakened the previous morning having to pry her face off his chest. The skin pulled away like thick strands of chewing gum.

She could have sworn that he had a wry little smile on his face. She'd left him how she had found him a week ago on a summer's day; it must have been a heart attack.

Abigail had failed to accept that her beloved James had passed away in his sleep just like that. He had been so fit and healthy; they had made love that very night. Now, small tears welled at the corners of her eyes as she clung onto those fleeting memories.

"Aw, James," she said in a loving tone, whilst climbing into bed beside his cold naked body. Snuggling up close to the mushy remains, she whispered into its ear, "We only have tonight my love, because tomorrow I shall have to call the doctor."

Term Break

Kylie writhed at the sound of her own voice on the six LCD TVs that were scattered around the Student Union bar, but the sound is down low. The clock behind Phil, beats thunder strokes and the clack from off pool balls fill the empty void. Some students are outside smoking – four of them in fact, Phil thought; he had counted them in his boredom. A further three stand around the pool table – two playing, whilst the third feeds pounds into the House of the Dead game, which stands by the side of the table sporting green baize. Two girls are docked in one of the booths to the left of the bar, their pint glasses almost empty. He knew neither of them, leading him to believe that they're third year students: Phil practically knew everyone in his year, and most from the first, as he parties hard every weekend like a good student should do, in his eyes.

Phil turned from facing the two girls nursing their dying pints and looked up at the thunder storm behind him - half-an-hour in, and four and a quarter hours to go until the end of his shift…

***

Lisa made her way from D block to the Student Union bar to tell Carl that it was over, that she would not be going with him to his parents house this weekend to meet his family, that she would be going home to see her own Mum and Dad. God, she was dreading having to tell him that it was finished between the pair of them, but she had a nagging feeling inside her that he already knew their relationship was on the rocks and coming toward an end. He'd been avoiding her and not answering her calls for the past few days, leading her to believe this, but there was only one way to find out. They had planned to meet at the Union tonight at five-thirty to talk about their plans to go to his parents' home this weekend, where they would have spent half-term, and then returned to university together. But she couldn't. She'd just simply fallen out of love with him over the past few weeks, and, if truth be told, someone else on campus had stolen her heart a while back.

Her mind raced with words of sorrow, of regret, which tugged at her heart. She spoke aloud as she passed the library that was shrouded in Winter's darkness, practicing what she would say to him when she got there. The whole Glamorgan campus looked bleak, with the odd light here and there drenching the grounds with an orange burn. The floor shone from the light soaking it had taken earlier in the day from a flimsy shower. A fresh smell of rain and grass was in the air. The odd student could be seen walking from their last lecture of the day and making their way home; wherever home was.

Lisa passed Bill Chalker, whom she knew from one of her modules last year. He flashed a warm smile and a slight nod of his head, but uttered nothing, as he hurried past, more than likely rushing to catch his train up the valleys, she thought.

After the brief encounter with Bill, Lisa was stopped just outside the closed campus shop by a student that she did not know.

"Got a light?" he belched. His lager stained breath wafted in her face as he got closer. "Wan' to light me ciggie, see."

"Err, I…I…don't, sorry," she retorted with a beam, and clutched her books closer to her chest. "I don't smoke." Again, with the weak smile on her face.

"Aww, like tha' is it. Never mind 'en, love."

He hiccupped his way by, leaving Lisa slightly startled by the way he had burst out of the night. Her eyes were drawn to the doorway of the shop that was in blackness. She was sure that a pair of feet that had been protruding in the light had shuffled back into the shadows.

"Hello?" she called. "Is that you, Carl?" She looked about. The drunk was gone and nobody else was about. The only thing audible was the rustle of nearby trees and shrubbery. Lisa gulped and neared the shop, "Carl if that's you hiding…I won't be happy." Nothing but the greenery answered back. "Carl!" she snapped. "This is not funny."

She broached the shuffling feet that hid in the gloom, bending over somewhat as though it may help her to see beyond the shade, and glimpse the smirking face.

"Come out, you bastard. I know it's you. I know your snigger, Carl."

On reaching the doorway, she felt like a child, standing there clutched in Winter's icy claw, for in the entrance, was nothing more than debris blowing wild in the wind, scratching the walls and the glass of the shop door. A child-like giggle escaped her as she staggered backward. Lisa covered her mouth with one hand, while cradling her books with the other. She tried to muffle the laugh, but she needn't have worried, because there was nobody around to hear her.

"What a silly girl I am," she said aloud, going toward the doorway again. "Fancy being sca…"

A robust hand closed around her mouth, and she was yanked backward. Lisa's muffled squeal was short-lived as her jaw disconnected. She was pulled, then thrust into the darkness she had once feared, and pressed against the wall.

"Move once more you fucking bitch and I'll be forced to rape the living shit out of you so hard you'll be begging for a quick, painless end."

Her jaw was in fierce agony and her mind was awash - Lisa's bladder burst, and the air suddenly had a salty-vinegary smell. She couldn't even manage a pathetic plea of leniency, even if she had wanted. Her eyes bulged, as she felt the coldness of teeny, metallic teeth push against the tender flesh of her neck…the attacker began to saw…

***

Carl Fletcher entered the Union Bar at around a quarter to six. He'd half expected Lisa to be there waiting for him, but she was not. Phillip Carlson was behind the bar looking bored and stupid, he thought. Phil was the sports guy that all the girls seemed to flock to – but he also had brains and talent, because, just like Carl, he is a second year student taking a BA in Creative Writing. He had it all and Carl hated him for it. He smiled and walked up to the bar, nevertheless, adjusting his rucksack as he did so - he felt the weight inside shift from side to side, and that made him smile.

On approaching the bar, he pulled out a stool, put his bag down gently by his side on the floor and spoke to Phillip.

"Hey Phil, can I have a bottle of Beck's, please?"

"Do you know, Carl, that's only the third alcoholic drink I have served since my shift started?" He turned to the chiller behind him and took out an icy bottle of lager, popped the cap off with a bottle opener that dangled by his side on a chain, and served it to Carl before keying the purchase in to the till and taking the money for it. "It's been dead in here. Mark said his shift had been quiet too, before I took over from him."

"Well, would be wouldn't it, what with reading week next week. The whole of the Humanities Department will be off." He took down a good swallow of his beer, placed the bottle back on a Fosters' coaster that had been placed there for him, and continued to speak. "When you off home then, tonight or tomorrow?"

Carl was not sure where exactly Phil hailed from, but he was sure it was in the South Wales area; not quite a local boy.

"To be perfectly honest with you, Carl, I was thinking of hanging around this reading week, hitting the books and maybe getting some writing done. You going to enter that writing competition in Bristol? I thought of sending something to them myself."

"Not sure. It has a thousand word limit, hasn't it? Not my type of competition, I prefer to go in for the longer ones, like the ones they run in that Writer's Forum magazine. They have a two-thousand-five hundred word limit – much more room for really opening a story out, if you ask me.

"I guess so, but I do like flash-fiction. It's a good challenge."

"Hmm, if you say so, Phil. So, what's the reason for hanging around here over reading week, can't get the same amount done at home?"

A slight smile appeared on Phil's face. "Yeah, something like that."

"Who are those two foxes sitting back there?" Carl tilted his head back sharply, referring to the two girls sitting at the booth behind him. "I haven't seen them around campus before. Freshers?"

"Not sure. I know a lot of girls from the first year and they don't seem to ring any bells. Third year, my guess was, when I served them earlier. I wouldn't mind getting the blonde one between the sheets, dude. So, what brings you in here at this hour? Not seeing Lisa tonight?"

"Yeah, she was meant to meet me here at five-thirty, ain't seen her, have you?"

"No, man. She hasn't been in here, not to my knowledge, anyway."

God, he fucking hated Phil calling people man, and dude. It sounded so American and idiotic. Phil really was nothing more than a pleb in Carl's eyes.

"I thought you guys were on the rocks anyway?"

"You guys," Carl thought, "You guys?" Another fucking horrible saying. God, how he would love to cut out his tongue. Maybe I should? Carl had to repress the smile that threatened to come, just in case the big, strong jock should see, and decide to hammer him into the ground like a tent peg. I'd love to see him try!

"No," he said, defensively. "In fact, I'm taking her home with me this weekend so she can meet my parents." Carl drowned the last of his beer and looked at his watch. Where the hell is she? He turned to face the doors as they opened, and thought it was Lisa he saw stepping through them. Nope, it was a girl by the name of Amanda James. "It's not like Lisa to be late."

"I might as well come clean with you, Carl. I cannot keep this pretence up any longer. See, the thing is, Lisa and I had a bit of a fling a few weeks back. We were going to tell you, but Lisa broke it off with me and begged me not to tell you." He saw Carl's face tighten, and his fist clench the bottle so tightly that he thought it might disintegrate under the pressure. "I couldn't take the thought of her leaving me for a little pussy like you, so I took steps." He stepped back from the bar and bent down. "She wanted me to give you this, and to say sorry, that she would not be going with you this weekend."

Carl's face turned from stone to sheer horror, as he saw a severed head being toted in front of him by Phil. He had hold of Lisa's long, brunette hair that was wrapped around his hand, and let it dangle. Crimson fluid spattered the floor and bar top. The mane was stained with rust-coloured flecks of blood. Her nose had two dried tracks of crusting liquid, the mouth set in a twisted, grizzled smirk. Cords and bone jutted from the stump, and Carl could see that Phil was smirking at him from behind the head.

"If I can't have her, dude, then nobody can."

A shriek from behind Carl brought him out of his frozen state of mind, but he was too slow to avoid the slashing corkscrew that sliced through his throat.

The Guardian

"I just put him down, if you'd like to go up and read to him, Gary. I'm off downstairs for a good long soak - work's been a living nightmare today."

Cathy shrugged her shoulders as she brushed past him and headed for the bathroom in the lower half of the house. He watched her go, sneaking a look at her rear as she did so. He told her that he would be down in a bit to rub her shoulders and to wash her back, after he had been up to see their newborn.

When she was out of the room, he took off his work jacket, hung it on one of the hooks behind the front door, and headed for the lounge to remove his boots. He looked up at the ceiling as he did so. Not a sound came from his son's nursery, and he smiled, happy in the knowledge that his ten-month old boy was all snuggled up in the warmth.

After getting out of his boots and stepping into his slippers, Gary headed to the stairs that led to the third floor and began to climb. He was about to do the same ritual he did every night since his son was born – read to him.

He knew James was by far too young to understand anything that he had to say to him, but Gary felt that it was a good thing to do, that it would stimulate the baby's mind. At the very beginning, he used to tell nursery rhymes to James, but now read short tales to the infant out of a jumbo book of bedtime tales.

On reaching his son's room, he placed his right hand to the handle of the closed door, and was about to enter, when he heard a small, scratchy noise coming from the other side. Bemused by the sound, he put his ear to the door and listened closer. A fat quiver rolled down his back as he made out that the rough sound was a whispery voice – someone was in there, talking to his son, and it could not be his wife, as she was in the lower half of the house.

He swallowed hard, stood back from the door and thought about going in again. He decided against it and peeked through the slender crack in the wood instead. Gary could see the glow coming from the nightlight, but nothing else. Then he glimpsed a moving shape, and shadow play on one of the walls - someone was definitely in there with his boy.

Gary took a deep breath, threw open the door, and stepped into the room. His feet sank two to three inches on the marshy flooring that was once the carpet; his face getting enveloped in webbing like that belonging to a spider. He clawed at his cheeks, brow and covered eyes with fierce panic to try and clear his blurred vision. He pulled his feet out of the boggy ground that slurped and gargled on doing so, and tried to find solid ground, but to no avail. Both his slippers had been consumed by the quicksand-like floor. Gary's heart rate began to thrash wildly as he managed to free his sight and saw that the whole room had changed – if you could now call it a room. A thick wall of trees stretched as far as the eye could see, with hanging limbs of weeds and vines. Vast and dense colours of greens and browns enclosed Gary and felt suffocating. The once aqua/green walls of the nursery, with a jungle theme border, were now replaced with the real thing.

Gary turned to leave, but the door had gone. So had the cot bed, the chest of drawers and a wooden tier that had held soft cuddle toys of a jungle theme, rattles, baby monitor, teething rings and various other bits and pieces. Alice the alligator, the guardian of the room, had disappeared along with the rest of the stuffed animals. He had named the gator protector of the nursery out of jest and had told his sleeping son on many occasions that Alice, named after Gary's favourite rock star, would always be here to look out for James as he slept at night.

He edged forward - "James," he called. "James." His voice wobbled and cracked, and tears burst from the corners of his eyes, but the sound of his sobs were blocked out by the jungle's inhabitants. Natives could be heard off in the distance screaming their war cries, and light rain pattered the gigantic leaves and wild flowers. Birds screeched overhead, and Gary's feet submerged with every step he took, which he then had to fight to draw out again. "Where the hell are you, son?"

Out of the impenetrable olive of the jungle, came a long mouth, filled with chalk white teeth. They held a look of immense sharpness about them. In the middle of the mouth and just above the forked tongue, were brown straps that led out of the open, snapping mouth and around to its back. They appeared to be reins. A guttural hiss/growl escaped the colossal alligator's mouth. Gary could do nothing but back away from the huge lizard and watch, as its robust, cracked, green body kept appearing from the deep. Its beady, black eyes sparkled at Gary, and strings of saliva held a philosophy of eating him whole. The brown straps in its mouth were indeed reins, and the rider of the primeval creature came into view. It was his son, James.

His eyes were rolled back in his head, his body naked except for a nappy. He seemed to know his dad was standing in front of him, for he yanked on the straps which brought his snarling ride to a halt.

"Don't be scared daddy, Alice won't hurt you, she likes you and mummy."

Gary was jolted from his slumber, and the book of tales fell to the floor. He'd fallen asleep in the rocker in the nursery. A small laughed escaped him as he remembered reading to his son. I must have dozed off halfway through, he thought to himself. He rotated his head, clicking his aching neck. As he was about to pull himself from the seat, he noticed the stuffed gator standing on the chest of drawers looking at him; the eyes white and watching…

Date Night

He'd tried it all – speed dating, blind dating, online dating, and he'd come up empty every single time. Six years of trying. Not one decent woman out there. And now at the age of fifty-four, Vincent thought he was doomed to be single for the rest of his life. A sad, little man, whose mam lives with him. That's a woman repellent right there, he thought. He was sure they could smell it on him – a mammy's boy.

But what was a man supposed to do? When Vincent's father had passed away, God rest his soul, he couldn't bear the fact that his mother would live life on her own, and in such a large house. After all, a mother is a boy's best friend. And so, he moved her in with him.

Then, just like that, he'd met Judith – a woman who had been right under his nose at his workplace – a single, good-looking forty-something woman. Vincent had managed to persuade her into a date. She'd looked beyond the fact that his mother lived with him, finding it charming; a little helpless.

He'd spoilt her with lavish dinners and fine wines. Of course, being as single as long as Vincent had, he'd managed to build up a pretty nice bundle of cash in his savings account. And, having mam live with him, who helped pay some of the bills, he could afford to spoil his goddess, as he liked to call her.

Looking up from the paperwork in front of him, Vincent glanced at the small box on his desk. It was time, he thought, time to take the relationship to the next level. He would propose to his love tonight over dinner.

The clock came up on the five-to-seven mark, so Vincent started packing away his work for the day. He was meant to be taking Judith out at eight, to be seated for dinner by eight-thirty.

"Damn it, I'll never make it home for a shower now. Bloody work and time have got the better of me again," he said out loud. "Never mind," he muttered, slamming the drawer he'd put his work into shut. "I'll just get ready here."

His office was well equipped for such a thing, with a private room out the back which he'd turned into a bathroom and kitchenette. Vincent had required planning permission for the add-on to his office, as he liked to call it, knowing that keeping odd hours and working lots of overtime, he wouldn't have to rush from his work.

His mother liked him to be home for tea at nights, but he couldn't always keep that arrangement with her. Duty calls, he often told her. And, just like tonight, paperwork had kept him busy; derailed his thoughts, slightly. If he didn't hurry, he'd be late for Judith.

Getting up from his desk, he went out to the bathroom, and started to fill the bath with hot water. He shaved in front of the sink as the tub filled. Hot steam engulfed the box room and started to mist the glass, forcing Vincent to open the single window, which was also beginning to fog.

He started to whistle, "Always look on the bright side of life," as he worked at his face. "She'll say yes, I know she will," he said, smiling at himself in the mirror. "My lovely Judith. I'll make her a queen." He resumed whistling.

She was the first woman he'd been close to in almost twenty years, apart from his mother. He felt good. Content. It was meant to be, and this would be their fifth date. "I hope the sight of the ring doesn't put her off." No, he told himself. Judith is looking for love, too. She told me over a candlelit dinner the other night.

She understood him; would cherish him.

Finished shaving, he put the cutthroat razor back on the sink next to his lather brush and flannel and started to strip. He knocked the hot water off, and began to pour the cold in, dipping his toes in to make sure it was cool enough to step into. Satisfied, he lowered into the bath.

"Ahh," he said, as the water enclosed all around him, soothing his back and aching muscles. He removed his glasses, and started to whistle again, as he poured water all over the top half of his body with the aid of a plastic jug, he kept by the bath for such a job.

After washing his body and face, he leaned back, and slipped down into the water. "Ten minutes rest isn't going to harm," he said aloud, and closed his eyes as the water slopped and sloshed about him, causing him to drift off. It had been a busy day today, he thought, as he tried to think back to what he had actually done. Strange, he thought, I can't seem to remember much, just that damned paperwork. It seems to have zapped all my energy and thoughts.

"Oh well, I'm sure I did lots," he said, letting out more "Oos" and "Ahs," at the touch of the heated water. "Just five more minutes here and I'll get out."

He woke up startled by the coldness of the water, his skin wrinkled. "Damn it, I fell asleep!" he shouted, as he jumped up and out of the bath, throwing water everywhere. He ran into the kitchenette where his mobile phone was. Picking it up, he saw that it was just after eight. "Bloody hell."

He dialled Judith's number.

It didn't ring. Just went straight to answer phone.

He left a message.

"Hi Judith, it's Vincent. Sorry I'm not there yet, but I'm running late. I'll be there as fast as I can. Love you."

Cancelling the call, Vincent ran back into the bathroom, towelled himself down, and applied spray to his underarms and aftershave to his cheeks and neck, before dashing back to the kitchenette where he had a fresh suit hanging up.

"Can't believe I'm late. Dash it. And she's not answering her phone. She's probably mad at me now. Perhaps I should leave the proposing for another night. No. Go ahead with it," he argued with himself.

After getting into his shirt, bow tie, trousers and jacket, he picked his phone back up, and started to ring Judith's number again, and again, got the answer phone. He didn't bother with a second message.

Vincent turned off all the lights to the back rooms as he made his way back out to his office. Once there, he switched the lights off and went through to the next room where he did all the "hands-on" work.

As he stepped through the door, his phone almost fell out of his hand at the sight of a woman sitting at the dressed table in the room. The small, lit lamp in the corner cast her in a half-shadow. The air inside the room was putrid. Damp, almost.

"Judith?" Vincent whispered. "What are you…?"

Most of the room and its contents couldn't be seen due to the poor lighting. They hid in the dark recesses. His insides felt cold. Goose pimples climbed his arms. He tried to remember but couldn't. Had I told her to… "Judith?" he tried again. She sat still, her back to him. Her hair hung down, reaching the top of the chair.

He walked up to her slowly, and a floorboard creaked. "Hello, my dear."

From the side view, he saw two lit candles on the table, two plates set for dinner, with cutlery, and a wine bucket, with a bottle in it. He still couldn't see her face, but he could see the tight, flowery, summer dress she wore, and the necklace of pearly-white beads around her throat.

"You look a picture of beauty," he told her.

She didn't look at him.

One of her arms rested on the tabletop – the skin a blue, grey colour.

"Radiant, too," he said, as he made for the chair opposite her, and pulled it from the table. From where he sat, he could see the open coffin behind the door he'd walked through and smiled. It had been her place of rest since he'd collected her from her grieving husband three weeks ago.

"And they thought you were dead, remember? That silly husband of yours. Well, one man's loss, is another man's gain," he smiled.

A coffin had been buried with a body, but not Judith's, he remembered. Oh, no. It had been his dead mother's carcass that had gone into the ground instead of the lovely Judith, who'd not been dead at all, just sleeping. The inadequate doctor that had examined her had been wrong, he thought. Wrong, wrong, wrong. And so, she was mine. And who would suspect an undertaker of swapping bodies? Not that anyone checked, of course.

It had been sad, saying goodbye to his mother, but now he had a new woman in his life.

He took her cold, dead hand in his, and looked her in her eyes. Her pupils were

white, and her mouth, throat, and chest were all sewn shut from the post-mortem, and his botched preserving skills. Taxidermy had never been a hobby or an interest to Vincent. Freckles of sawdust lined her upper lip and chin, her cheeks somewhat sunken and wrinkled, like a dried-out peach.

"You remind me so much of my mother," he told her. "We'll be so happy together." He kissed the back of her leathery hand, and produced the small box from his jacket pocket, flipping open the lid and revealing a gleaming ring.

"It was my mother's," he said. "Would you do me the honour of taking my hand in marriage?" he asked, whilst slipping the ring onto her finger.

"A perfect fit," he whispered.

Brain Decay

Trix lay there motionless. The dream machine on her chest rose and fell slowly with her rhythmic breathing. She'd bought the thing second-hand at a flea market for a hundred-and-fifty quid. When they'd first come out, the asking price had been too far from her reach, with her being a student and only having a part-time job as a barmaid.

Lying there now, with the small plastic box attached to her arms via wires, and a plastic tube up her nose which monitored her breathing, she tried taking herself to a new place, and not another hell that she had visited so many times in the past. Unfortunately, it was too late trying to go to good places with her dreams – she'd decayed her brain a long time ago.

But this did not stop her from having a go. Besides, from what she had read, if she started to go into a nightmare, the machine would stop her. She waited for her breathing to hit twenty-one breaths a minute. Once this was achieved, Trix knew that the rapid eye movements would start, letting her know that she was beginning to dream. This would activate a small alarm on the machine which would then allow her to start to control the dream that she was starting to slip into

Beep, beep, beep…twenty-one breaths a minute had been reached – try to think happy, Trix, try to think happy for the love of God…

***

The dream machine was created by a Dr. Keith Hearne, which, over a period of time, allowed Trix and others who bought the machine to be able to control their dreams, roam wherever the heart desired. This gave her a chance to be able to play out her sick fantasies, to spy on the dying or visit the insane at mental homes, even see the hanging or electrocution of a convict. She could see anything her depraved mind wanted. She also tried to imagine that she was the pain the people felt in her dreams. Just like her favourite rock star had once sung about.

Once out of the dream, she'd write them down, remembering the vivid images and unholy screams so she could go back there again and again whenever she wanted. Trix had taken herself to a hospital delivery room on the last occasion, only to see the mother die whilst giving birth to a stillborn baby. She pictured that it was her younger sibling, Grace. Oh, how she had spoilt everything between me and dad when she came along, Trix thought. He didn't want to know me then. No, it was all about that little bitch, Grace.

The smell of the blood and solutions in the box room was pungent, so real that she could taste them; the shouting and screaming so loud that she could hear them even after she had woken up, safe in her bedroom with her posters on the walls of death metal gods watching over her.

The first time she'd managed to start controlling her dreams, going to places and scenarios that she wanted, had scared the hell out of her. She could still remember that first dream now. The smell of wet earth and the feel of the bombarding rain hitting her. Trix's heavily made-up face of blacks and purples, which sat on top of a thick foundation, were a running mess. The small gathering of people dressed in black; their grey faces veiled. And of course, the lowering of the coffin into the six-foot, muddy hole – all so very lucid. She could even remember the name of the man being sunk into the ground, and so she should, because it had been her own father. She'd wished him dead ever since she'd been a little girl and his touching had started. She had been sworn to secrecy by him. At that age, she hadn't known any different.

After that first experiment, the creation of her father's funeral, Trix had gone on to bigger and better scenarios. When she had learned of her dad's death inside prison, she'd taken herself there. She didn't know how he had died, she'd just made that part up. It was a favourite of hers, one she went back to countless times.

He's in his little cell, and in they come. Three brutes built for just kicking the shit out of kiddie fiddling scumbags. The first one is holding a bowlful of boiling hot water with sugar, that's thrown over her dad's face – the hot sugary substance glues itself to his skin, making him howl in pain. Then the other two move in, raining kicks and punches onto him whilst he lies curled in a ball, calling for the guards. But they never come – only death does, as one of them always ends the dream by slitting his throat open with a large shard of glass that was exchanged for a packet of cigarettes.

Maybe it was the visiting of this dream which had caused it? It couldn't have been healthy for her, seeing a man viciously killed almost every night of the week; or maybe it was her grave robbing expeditions; or the digging up of the dead for pure fun; or maybe it was the burning down of a church, whilst the people inside sung the praise of our Lord? Whatever it was, something had snapped her in the end…

***

She woke up screaming, the machine flung from her. It had failed to let her know she'd slipped into a nightmare. It was used to her depraved thoughts. Trix thrashed and wriggled on the bed, unable to flay her arms about wildly due to the white, straight vest they made her wear these days. Her body was strapped to the bed. The only movement possible was to wriggle, making her resemble a fish out of water.

She raised her head up off the stone-like pillow, which was cold as well as hard. Trix's hair had lost its raven colour – it was now white from the years of tortured dreams that had been inflicted on her.

She saw them all looking back at her, while Dr. Rees circled the bed like a vulture, with a clipboard in his hands. Trix screamed until her lungs burned. Standing directly behind the stout doctor was the dead mother from her dreams, nursing her lifeless child – her white nightgown blood-soaked and clinging to the lower half of her body. Crimson liquid trickled down her legs and formed a pool on the floor which Rees walked through, leaving bloody shoe prints behind him.

Standing by the mother cradling her child is her father. He lifts one of his bony fingers and points at her. When he smiles, his throat seeps blood, adding to the pool that was fast becoming bigger and bigger. He turns to the woman bearing the dead child and takes it into his own arms. Trix begins to weep at the sight of it. Others were standing behind and around 'the parents'. There are burnt churchgoers with their skin flaking to the ground; their bones crunch when limbs are moved; their sex, too difficult to make out. Skeletal corpses shuffle around the room. Some look freshly dug up from their resting place, others appear decrepit. Many others stand looking on, smiling. Her screaming reaches a new height as her mind plays tricks with her.

"Settle down, Miss Jones," Dr. Rees says, whilst shaking her wildly by the shoulders. She snaps at his fingers with her teeth. Rabid-like spittle flies from her mouth.

He slaps her, and beckons Trix to be still, but she keeps on thrashing until he is forced to jab a needle into her neck and pump her full of methadone.

As she gradually settles back down, he tears the readout from a little machine by her bedside. He studies it while rubbing at his imaginary beard. "Hmm, very interesting. Yes, very."

Her love for ghastly fantasies had become too much for her mind to take. She'd been committed by her mother some time ago. Now she was just a guinea pig for the professionals at Castell Hirwaun – a home for the mentally ill.

Homes from Hell

He parked his Audi opposite number one of Ynys Park Cottages, Ton-Pentre, and looked out of the passenger's window. He wrinkled his nose at the sight of the rented accommodation, at the windowsills with flaking paintwork, and front door that looked as though it needed a good scrub.

He huffed, looked at his watch, and noted it was ten-thirty. Taking his clipboard off the passenger's seat, which lay next to his heavy, aluminium briefcase, he set it on the steering wheel. Drawing his ballpoint pen out of the top pocket of his shirt, he proceeded to write the time down on a 'Home Inspection Sheet'.

"What treasure troves of terrors will I find at this home, I wonder?!" he said aloud, huffing again, as he clicked the nib home and re-holstered it. "Some people," he muttered.

Before getting out of his car, he bared his perfectly polished teeth in the rear-view mirror, and inspected his neatly combed hair, which was raked back. His face, which had been scrubbed, had a healthy glow to it. He didn't look his twenty-seven years. Fixing his nametag, which read

Archie, he got out of the car with his clipboard tucked under his arm. He then leaned back in to grab his case.

"Almost forgot you," Archie said, smiling.

Unbending, case at his side, he took in a deep breath, filling his lungs with the clean, morning air. He felt good; had a lot to smile about. He was a man who loved his job; took pride in it. His CV was immaculate. Chink free. Bullet-proof, even.

Having worked for three housing agencies, Archie had built up an impressive résumé and accolades alike, having won Employee of the Month many times at all three previous workplaces. He was an employer's wet dream.

It was his job to go into rented homes and inspect them for any damage or negligence, so that the rightful owner could take action in removing the tenants and find more appropriate occupants. It was Archie's job to weed out the bad, and by the looks of the outside of this one, he thought, giving number one the once over again, these people would have to go. It made his blood boil at how people mistreated things that didn't belong to them.

Smoothing his expensive suit jacket, and fixing his crooked red tie, Archie made sure there were no cars coming before stepping off the curb, his military style, polished shoes just avoiding a puddle under foot. He hummed as he walked up to the door, noticing that there was only a handful of vehicles here and there. The street was graveyard silent.

Facing the PVC door, he ran a finger through the inch thick dirt that graced it. "Piglets," he said, giving the tip of his finger a disdained look, before putting his case on the floor by his side, and removing the clipboard from under his arm. He made a note of the state the door was in, before moving over to the windowsill.

"Good, God!" he blurted, prodding at the peeling paint with the edge of his board. The crumbly, white paint rained to the floor, and lay scattered on the paving stones. "Unacceptable behaviour from someone renting a home," he said, and clacked his tongue like a chicken.

Archie made another note – The outside of the house is in total decline, and is in much need of 'sprucing up'… An empty crisp wrapper that had blown its way onto the doorstep angered him more. Further still, the occupants of number one, Ynys Park Cottages, have failed to maintain a decent standard of their rented accommodation, and are also letting the street slip with their littering habits.

He put his pen away.

For now.

Going to the corner of the street, Archie peered down the side, and noticed there was a back entrance to the property. He headed for the backdoor, and found the old, wooden door to be unlocked. His pen made a return to the Home Inspection Sheet.

Note: The occupants of number one, Ynys Park Cottages have also failed to keep the home safe from intruders, due to their negligence of keeping the property fully locked down whilst away from the house.

Walking back to the front door, he removed a spare key from his trouser pocket, and inserted the Yale key into the snug lock. A voice boomed up the street, addressing him.

"They're not home, lovely."

Stepping back from the door and displaying his best smile, Archie looked down the street at the young mother, who was two houses down. She had a small child about her legs.

"Mammy, Mammy, Mammy," the child yelled over and over again. It sounded like a girl to Archie. Her bare, lower half exposed her nappy-clad bottom. She had a small, yellow, plastic bowl in her hand, which she drummed with a green plastic spoon.

"Shush, Rachel," the mother instructed. "Mammy is trying to talk to the nice man." The smile returned to her face when she looked at Archie. "Sorry," she said.

"Not to worry, my dear," Archie said, smiling. "I'm not looking for the occupants as such. I'm with their letting agency."

She looked at him vaguely, head slightly bent to one side.

He produced a card from his top pocket and walked down to her with it.

"It's just a routine check-up of the property. We do it every so often just to make sure things are in order."

"Oh, I see," she said, handing the card back to him.

"Hello," Archie said to the child. She eyed him and moved behind her mother's legs.

"Say hello to the nice man, Rachel."

Rachel shook her head and poked her tongue out at Archie. He smiled.

"Kids," the mother said, flicking her head back and rolling her eyes. She fluttered her eyelashes at him.

"Well, best get to the job at hand," he told her.

"Huh? Oh yeah, right, of course. Bye," she said, but he had his card back in his shirt pocket and was already heading back to number one.

"Bye," he called over his shoulder, hearing her door close. "Now, where was I?" he muttered, casting his eye over the key still cosy in the lock, "Ah yes, of course," he said, going to it and turning it. He heard the locks snick-snack.

Pushing the light, PVC door wide and picking up his case, Archie moved through the doorway. Once in the passageway, he shut and locked the door. The waft of white musk filled his nostrils, and he took it down, as he walked through another door. It led him into a large living room.

"Incense," he said, matter-of-factly, putting his case on top of the glass table in the room. He was still antsy from the neglect to the outside of the property, and he clicked his neck by giving his head sharp, left and right movements.

He looked around the room, with its clean white walls, and shag pile to match. A large mirror hung above the open fireplace, and a nest of oak tables sat at the side of a beige sofa, with two matching chairs. The TV donned the corner of the room, seated on top of a wooden cabinet that matched the tables. The place was well presented. Homely. Trinkets and photos lined the mantle above the fire, and a bookcase stood against the wall behind the settee. American Psycho jumped out at him.

"A good read, surely," he said, catching himself smiling as he looked in the mirror. "Hmm, well, this is a surprise," he said, excitement evident in his voice.

Going to his case, he popped one clasp at a time, click, "Still, it's no excuse for keeping a shoddy outside," click. Archie lifted the lid of the case and drew out a pair of latex gloves. He pulled them on slowly, smiling all the while.

Next, he withdrew his mp3 player, and popped the earphones in. He hit play as he dug a claw hammer out of the aluminium holding, clutching it good and tight in his right hand.

Walking over to the closed and solid wooden door to the kitchen, Archie placed his free hand against it, and chuckled as he thought about Ms Braid, the rightful owner of the property, who'd told Archie's boss all about the new doors she'd installed in the property, and how it had cost a "Pretty penny".

"Oh well, if you will let trash rent your home, Ms Braid," he said, as "Psycho Killer" kicked in on the music player, "Then you can expect a few breakages. You stupid whore!"

The claw end of the hammer pounded its way through the heart of the door, time and again, until an impressive split raced up the centre, and a chunk came free, falling to the floor.

"Delicious," he whispered over the music, as he swept some stray splinters from his jacket. He placed the free piece of timber in his case, and took out his camera, snapping off a few shots of the damage. "These people will have to go. Bloody ragtag so-and-sos," Archie said, raising his voice because of the music.

Putting his camera back in the case, he walked into the kitchen, and closed his eyes. He let the music empower him, as he stood there for a while, savouring the moment. Opening his eyes and rotating the DIY implant in his hand, Archie eyed the cabinets, skirting and paintjob.

Letting out a sigh at spotting cobwebs in all four corners of the ceiling, he hit the flathead of the hammering tool at the door of the closest cupboard drawer and shivered, as the hefty steel just punched straight through the wood.

Before leaving the kitchen, he took more photos, wrote another paragraph on his sheet, and made his way back into the living room. Here, he had to fight the urge not to sweep all the photos off the mantle and put the hammer through the DVD and CD player.

So, instead, he took a fat cigar out of his case, lit it, and took a few drags. He then started burning holes in the carpet here and there, before putting out the fat Cuban on a wall close by.

He took photos.

Wrote his report.

Smiled.

"They must be happy as pigs in shit here," he said, not amused in the slightest, just sickened by the tenants' total disregard for the owner's property. He felt ill by it all. But this was not the first pigpen he'd come across in all his immaculate years of home inspecting. Oh, no.

Closing the lid to his case, Archie made his way upstairs with it, and into the master bedroom. A huge, king-size bed filled the room, along with a massive wardrobe and chest of drawers, complete with a vanity mirror sitting on top of it. The room smelled of cheap perfume and was too pink for Archie's liking.

He tore the head off the pink, stuffed, bunny rabbit that sat by the pillows. Then he took to the floorboards, pulling a few free with the claw hammer, so that he could spill a container full of cockroaches into the recesses. He took a few quick snaps, noting on his sheet that there was an infestation in the property, due to the uncleanliness of the property.

This led him to take two packets of dog faeces out of his case, which he proceeded to tread in, and march through the upstairs of the house, driving it deep into a white shag. He giggled all the while as he did, then reamed off more photos, as "Psycho Killer" came to an end.

He started the song again.

As Archie went about his work, going into the spare bedroom, he smashed holes in the walls, exposing electrical wires and burst a water pipe, which sprayed. The carpet was quickly sodden, which would soon soak through to the boards.

Archie let out a "Tut-tut," as he left the room to fetch his camera.

More photos.

More reports.

More laughter.

More, "They'll have to go's!"

Happy with seeing enough of the upstairs, he made his way out to the back of the property, finding it spotless. "Well, this won't do," he muttered, finding the rubbish bags close to the door. He ripped through them all, until the contents were scattered all over the area.

Archie went back to his case again, and set free some rats into the rubbish, snapping off shots of them scurrying among the debris, before writing up more reports, his smile remaining as he did so. "Ms Braid will be mortified at who she has renting her "Beloved" home."

After watching the rats for the best part of five minutes, he went back inside, unplugged his earphones, took off his gloves, and packed them all away in his case along with his hammer.

As he made for the front door, he stopped and listened. He could hear the pipe upstairs still spitting water. A brown patch was becoming visible in the ceiling. "Bloody wasters," he said, looking about him at the carnage and disrupt. "They will most definitely have to go."

As Archie was locking the front door, the voice from down the street came again.

"How's the house looking, then?" she asked.

"Disgraceful," he answered, filling his tone with disgust.

"That doesn't surprise me," she said.

"Oh?" Archie said, genuinely shocked.

"Nah, they play their music pretty loud at nights, and it keeps my Rachel awake. New neighbours would be nice."

The smile came, and he found it hard to contain. "Not to worry, my dear. These people won't be at this property for much longer, not after what I have discovered."

As she drawled on, he wrote a new note – I've just been informed by a neighbour that the occupants of number one keep raucous parties going until all hours, all week, which has started affecting others around them with their noise pollution.

"…and they"

"Thanks, my dear," he said, cutting her dead, flashing his trademark grin.

"Er, em…Bye," she called after him.

"Bye," he answered, getting into his car. Then he was off, driving to his next inspection, the next – home from hell.

Hello, you're Through to Charlie...

"Can I take your account number, please?"

"I want to speak to your fucking manager. Now!

Great. A shouter, Charlie thought. He looked at his watch, noting that it was just off the stroke of 9.00 a.m. He sighed. Barely two hours into my shift, and already I've got a dumb shit shouting and swearing at me.

"That's fine, sir, but I'm going to have to get into your account before..."

"Your fucking company is thieving me blind, and I'm pissed off with having to call in all the goddamn time..."

Charlie let the man rant on and faded out. This crap was starting to take its toll on him. And, to top it off, he had a meeting scheduled with his team manager at the end of the day. Of course, he knew what it meant. The end of his job, career and life, with a long term behind bars to look forward to.

But surely, they would have cornered him before the start of his shift? Wouldn't something as important as firing Charlie and handing him over to the police come before letting him do his job? What? And cost the company money by being a man down? Not a chance in hell. These fuckers are sneaky, he thought, as the banshee continued to molest his ears.

They're leading me up the garden path, he thought, lulling me into a false sense of security, hoping I won't cotton onto them trying to flush me down the toilet. Fuck 'em. I ain't running. I'll sit here and keep on smiling, and they'll say – "Why, he wouldn't even harm a fly. Look at him. He's cherubic."

"Yes, sir, I fully understand, but I will have to access your…"

"Fucking monkeys like you do nothing but nibble at the banana. I want to speak to the big chimp. The one who runs the show. The wheel greaser, sonny…"

What the fuck is this douche going on about? There isn't a shovel in the world big enough to scoop up the crap he's spewing, Charlie thought. Thieving from him? What a piss take. He's more than likely run up a bill he cannot cope with, and, now that he's fallen into debt, he's blaming us.

It's the same, violin playing story he heard all the time. Dicks, he thought.

"So, what are you going to do about it, boy?" the man spat. "Are you even listening to me? Are you awake on that end, even?"

Charlie could feel his blood boil, a tick developing at the side of his neck. "Yes, sir. And, as I have already informed you, I have to access your account…"

The disgruntled customer was off again, cutting Charlie dead before he could get the rest of his sentence out.

"Oh, account, account, account. That's all you people want is numbers and money! I want to…"

Again, Charlie faded out and waited for the next outburst to come to an end. It was never meant to play out like this. The job had meant to be a stepping stone to something bigger and better. It was a means to an end while he paid his way through university. But the shit hit the fan with the economy, and businesses started falling through. Nothing was available out in the big wide world. Times were tough, and work dried up. A stop gap became a permanent one. Charlie got comfortable, and one year turned into six, all dreams and prospects down the drain.

In the beginning, it saddened him, not to the point of suicide, but to the point of wanting to run away. To become a slip-off-the-grid kind of guy. But, as time passed, he worked with it.

His good looks and shaggy blond hair got him into the females' good books, especially the good books of the older ladies – the ones who lead the teams and held higher positions. He had worked it to his advantage and flattered them with sweet remarks and innocent flirtation.

Especially his own, 'TM', who thought the sun shone out of his chiseled, Welsh arse. Gloria, who was currently dieting, was putty in his hands. His arse-grovelling comments of "Oo, have you lost more weight?" and, "Wow, that dress looks great on you. Look at your bum!" had propelled his job status into an indestructible one.

He couldn't very well tell her she looked like someone had draped fabric over cow. Ugh. On many occasions he'd caught her checking his arse out, which he would then play on.

He smiled a giddy smile at that one.

"And another thing, lad…"

Hasn't this guy finished ranting yet? Charlie looked at the little clock above his phone – the call had been running close to five minutes with no end, or beginning for that matter, in sight.

The TMs love me, he thought. He couldn't see Gloria handing him over to the police. He looked over at her now, giving her one of his best smiles. He noticed she was wearing her tights again – showing off those God-awful cankles. She smiled back, as always, putting his fears to rest. Well, somewhat, anyway.

"Hey? Hello…" the guy was saying on the other end of the phone.

This meeting has got to be about my behaviour, Charlie thought. They're trying to play me for an idiot. I'm surprised it's taken them so long to finally catch onto it all. I mean, there's been so much in the papers, too. The police will burst through those doors any second…

Hey! Jesus Christ," the guy muttered to himself on the other end of the phone. "If he's hung up on me, I swear…Hello?!"

Charlie faded back in, totally unaware that the guy had finished speaking, and was waiting for a reply. What the hell had he been asking? What was his enquiry? Something about us robbing the seat from under his stupid arse, I think, Charlie mused, and almost burst out laughing.

"Oi?! the man yelled, causing Charlie to remove his headset briskly, the piercing yell hurting his eardrums.

That was the final straw.

He didn't care if he was going to go back on his promise of not being nice.

The AA classes he'd been attending to try and help give up the badness was for nothing at current. This dickhead needed putting in his place.

He hadn't accessed the man's account, which meant the call could not be traced.

"Hey, little dick," Charlie said. "I've got your phone number in front of me, and I can easily access your account from just that, which in turn, would give me all your details – E-mail, home address, postcode, the whole nine yards. And, by the sounds of that accent of yours, I'd say you are pretty close to me."

"You…you…you…"

Charlie smiled. "What? Can't speak to you like that? Think again, fuck face. I'll pour petrol down your fucking throat as you sleep."

When they started to stutter, he knew he had them on the ropes.

"Walk away now, and I'll promise not to cut you apart as you lay in bed with your wife, then burn the place to the fucking ground," Charlie spat, making every whispered word count.

Charlie made sure to keep his voice low. But even this outburst rattled him, because he'd never gone this far with a customer on the phone before.

The line went dead.

Charlie's smile grew as he removed his headset, making sure he'd put himself on hold so that another call wouldn't come straight through.

"Morning, Gloria. You're looking as ravishing as ever," he said, giving her a wink and a flash of his pearly whites. His rage receding like a tide.

She tittered like a nervous schoolgirl.

How very fucking unattractive, he thought. He just about managed to keep the look of disdain off his face, as he turned back to his screen. Taking a swig of tea, he hovered the cursor over the hold button on his screen. Nah, not yet; I'll burn a bit of my hold time today. Sod it, he thought.

He leaned back in his chair and tried to remember when it had started – when his patience had finally worn thin. When had it snapped, and thrown him into Norman Bates mode?

He started shaking his head, thinking it wouldn't come to him. After all, so much had happened between then and now. But then, it finally washed over him. Miss Rosie Grandford, the Swansea whore. Ah, yes, he remembered it now.

It must have been the Summer before last. No, wait, it was the Summer before that, even. God, how long does my depravity go back? Charlie thought, letting a giggle slip as he blew on his tea.

Love it.

"Something amusing, Charlie?" Gloria asked, looking over at him with a warm smile on her face.

"No, not really," Charlie said, unfazed by being caught chuckling to himself.

Now, where was I, Charlie thought. Oh, yes, Miss Grandford. She saw off the old Charlie and breathed fresh life into me. She was the gateway to enjoying the job, something I thought would never happen. She had such a sweet voice. Innocent, almost.

Of course, Charlie had fantasised about doing it many times in the past, especially with the young customers. But Grandford, she was a totally different story – they'd flirted on the phone. Only mildly though, as it would have been against company regulations, and he didn't want her complaining. Not that she was. She was enticing, and she finally gave him the courage he needed to push the boundary.

To turn dreams into realities.

Going off her account information after the call had ended, it took him less than five minutes to get her phone number, E-mail and home address.

That's the beauty of working in a call centre – you have access to all your customers' information, he thought. These pricks really should think of adjusting their attitudes on the phone. After all, they don't know what type of person they're speaking to.

He beamed at this.

He'd started off slow with Grandford, sending her random text messages, proclaiming he had the wrong number.

But she answered back.

"That's OK."

So, Charlie replied, excited about the whole situation, hoping he could keep the game going. And keep going it did, as she again replied back, and again, and again, and again.

Before he knew it, he had her engaged in a long chat, which lead to phone calls and E-mails later on down the line. On days off, he went to her house. Spied on her. Crept in her shadows. He found out all kinds of personal information about her, from her parents' address; who her friends were, and what her pet Rottweiler was called.

Bozo.

Who the fuck calls a killer mutt Bozo?! he thought. His jaws could have made a Hammerhead blush, for Christ's sake. When it drooled, it looked as though it had swallowed a shoe, and the laces hung from either side of his mouth.

The creeping around Grandford went on for weeks; months even. The joy of it all made work fly for Charlie, as he kept himself entertained with thoughts of her. Then she asked to meet up, and maybe get it on. That's when Charlie backed down. It was getting too heavy.

He cut her out of his life, changed his phone number and thought no more of her. He swore he'd never toy with his job or life in such a fashion again. That was until Jayne Silver came through to him on the phone one evening.

She lived just round the corner from him. The temptation had been too strong, and he'd acted on it. After all, he'd already done it once. Spying on Jayne had been a great kick. She was a supple and very sexy eighteen-year-old. Not quite as sexy as Grandford, but pretty Goddamn hot.

It ended with blood on Charlie's hands.

She'd caught him sneaking around outside her house one night, and, as though she had an elephant's, recognised his voice.

Without thinking, he'd picked up the closest thing to him, a flowerpot, which he used to cave the top of her skull in with. She'd collapsed backward, falling through her open doorway, her gushing blood absorbed by her cotton pyjamas and soft shag.

The feeling which pounded in Charlie's chest had felt like no other, as he watched her gargle and choke on her own blood and vomit. Her piss-stained PJ bottoms had given him an erection like no other. Semen had trickled out of him.

With it being so quiet that evening, he'd gone undetected. This allowed him time to be able to 'fool' with the cooling body and bury it in a shallow grave out back.

Charlie never knew such a deep and dark side existed within him, and it rattled him. It rattled him beyond belief, but he couldn't help himself.

It had taken a little over three weeks for Jayne's body to surface. The time had been a very unpleasant one for him. He feared prison, and the thought of it played on his mind until the heat died down.

Then it came that the police had no leads.

No clues.

No witnesses.

No Charlie behind bars.

This act had given him a good scare, as he tried to ignore what had happened – to move beyond it and get on with his job; to focus on moving up the corporate ladder and getting on with life again. After all, he had a marvellous record at work – no sick, late or any other kind of bum excuses for taking a day off.

He was conscientious in that respect.

It wasn't long before the cracks started to appear once again. The walls of reality came crashing down around Charlie four months after the murder of Jayne Silver.

He went back to his old tricks after a very silly thing pushed him over the edge, making Charlie totally flip off the deep end.

A male customer – Mr. Lewis – had come through to him in a complete rage about the loss of money from his account one evening. The call had ended with the man bleating like a sheep down the phone to Charlie.

Mr. Lewis was dead before sun-up the following day.

Charlie had driven to 174, Oxfordshire Rd, Delta Av, Oxfordshire, after his shift. He'd then proceeded to butcher Mr. and Mrs. Lewis in their bed as they slept soundly.

Whenever Charlie tried to recall the events of that night, all that came to mind was blind rage, and the wet soggy sounds the hammer made.

It took him a while to stop hitting.

It had sounded like a meat mallet pounding away at raw cutlets.

Blood had spewed up the walls, as their pet Beagle cowered and whined at the bottom of the bed. The stench of their demise and his fear and excitement had stayed with him for a long time.

When he'd finally stopped bludgeoning their limp bodies, Charlie had stood breathless in the moon glow which shone through the huge bedroom windows. He'd taken the Beagle and burned the house to the ground, leaving his clothes and hammer in there, and making his escape in Mr. Lewis' clothes.

Two more murders followed – A Miss Perk, whose name matched the person, and an old cunt by the name of Mrs Sparks. That old bitch had kept him on the phone for well over two hours one afternoon, as she ranted on and on and on about claim fees the company had slapped onto her account.

The insults and bad language she had come out with for a lady of her grand age of eighty-eight was beyond him. She'd died a slow and agonising death a few days after the call.

Charlie had spent four days holiday making her suffer.

He'd practiced his 'organ extracting' skills on her.

After the killing of three students a few months later, Charlie had planned to call an end to it all and sought help from attending AA meetings. Even thought it was a group for drunks, talking about 'having a problem', helped Charlie control his urges, and he soon had his temper under control on the phones over the coming months. He started leading a 'normal' life again. He even job hunted and met someone.

Holly.

She also helped keep him on the straight-and-narrow.

Even though the papers continued to print the stories of the unusual murders, which police didn't think were connected, the heat remained off Charlie.

Until now, it would seem…

"Charlie? Charlie?!"

"Huh, what?!" he said, surprise and shock in his voice, thinking for one moment he had fallen asleep at his desk.

"Charlie, Charlie! For Pete's sake, wake up, will you," Gloria said. "You've been on hold for the past twelve minutes!"

"Shit, have I?" he said, giving her a flash of his lashes, but it didn't work. Her face was set as she looked at him.

"Put yourself into Consultation. We've brought your meeting forward to now, which means we won't need you to stay after your shift."

Sweat began to pour out of him. His breathing became irregular. He kept his eyes on the door, excepting to be rushed by police at any given moment.

"Come on, Charlie. We haven't got all day, you know," Gloria said.

"I…I…I need to go home," he blurted, grabbing his jacket off his seat. "I'm not feeling too good. That's…"

"Oh, Charlie," she said, smiling all the while. She came up on his side and whispered in his ear. "We thought you would have liked the idea of promotion? We're promoting you to section manager at the end of the month."

The giddiness left his head. His vision cleared. A smile spread across his face. The thought of more power enthralled him.

"Is that what the meeting is all about?"

Gloria smiled as she nodded – "Don't think for one moment all your hard work and graft hasn't been noted around here.

Well, well, well…Looks like things are looking up for good ol' Charlie boy after all, he thought, managing to keep the giggles suppressed as Gloria led him to the office to get the paperwork signed.

Diet

He looked at her from across his side of the table and felt relieved that Gloria had nothing hefty at her side to throw at him. Between them lay the usual things, mixed with breakfast items: salt and pepper, sugar bowl, jug of milk and his Weetabix – which he was shovelling down in great spoonfuls. Pausing, he tried to coax a smile from her with a bright one of his own. He was pleased with himself, and why shouldn't he be?

She glowered at him from over the rim of her glass which contained a Slim-Fast shake. As she drew on the straw, the thick liquid was hauled up the beaker. He produced another synthetic smile for her and thought to himself: this is for your own good, you fat pig. Greg wanted his fit, slender wife back, the one he had married five years ago. The go-getter, ballsy-bitch that could spit venom into a person's eye from six-hundred yards – her works persona. At home, she had been the opposite.

"Can you pass the milk over, my love?" She gave him a crazed-look of passion as she spoke to him. "Please."

He could feel the passion start to rise in him and he tried to hide it. Those walnut brown eyes of hers flashed at him in a certain way which drove him wild, and she knew it. No point in trying to hide it, he thought – she was wild for it.

"Sure thing."

He handed the milk-jug over to her, trying to avoid that lingering look. He pushed his fishbowl-like glasses back up the bridge of his nose, trying not to leer at her, but she could read his mind.

"Maybe we should just sweep this lot off the table, Greg, and get it on right here?" The naughty glint was fierce in her eyes as he looked up. She had her pencil-thin lips poked out in an enticing manner. She laughed cheekily and said, "What you think about that then, handsome?"

He blushed, broke her stare and gazed into his cereal that was disintegrating into a mushy mess.

"Stop it, Gloria. You know I don't like that kind of talk in the mornings. Anyway, I have to go early today – Ethel Watkins is coming in to pick up her diuretic drugs. Poor woman has awful problems with her waterworks."

He picked his wiry frame up from his chair, muttered, "Really, Gloria," and frogmarched his bowl of pulp to the sink, where he rinsed it, and placed in on the draining board. She kept on grinning all the while.

The first few years had been like that, great, but then she lost her job and Gloria began to spiral out of control, becoming a full-time couch potato. Her tough working attitude began to dwindle and the fire in her look became nothing more than a shaking flicker of light. She'd been laid off due to the credit crunch. The bank she had managed was tightening their belts by streamlining their staff.

"I'm going to write a letter to head office. They can't just sack me like that; the amount of time and efficiency I have given them over the years." The letter never materialized.

Oh, how they had spoken about it plenty of times – about how Gloria would start to pull her act together again and get back out there, to find that spark of hers. But talk was cheap, and as the months and conversations passed, the pounds kept piling on. Six months and three stone later, Greg had finally had enough. It was time to take steps before the hopes of having an offspring one day were gone along with the old Gloria.

He was sick of the Atkins diet this and counting calories that, with no signs of improvement in Gloria's shape and health.

He was willing to bet the tubby cow was just sitting there in front of the idiot box scooping handfuls of crap down her gullet all day while he was at the chemist. Well, not anymore, he felt like saying out loud as their looks clashed and fused again.

Ah yes, this would definitely be for her own good. In a few weeks or so she would be starting to look like her old self again. Panic washed over him. Had he hidden all the sharp, cutting objects? He must have, he was sure of it. He had used the time she was unconscious to search and clear the house of such things. Plus, she never had guests around or stepped foot out the door because of her shape, so he was okay there too.

Nobody will ever find out. A wry smile pulled his lips tight and made his cheeks ache slightly.

He finished the rest of his cereal, pushed the bowl to one side and got up to leave for work. I will check the house once again tonight, just to make sure, he thought to himself, while straightening his tie.

By now he could see tears in the corners of his wife's eyes; the centres glassing over with a watery sheen. He went to her, making sure she didn't have anything sharp in her hand, bent over and kissed her on the forehead. She just sat there transfixed on Greg's vacated chair; the straw to her thick drink still pursed between her lips – the glass empty.

"I've got to go now honey. Please take care of yourself and drink your milkshakes when you're supposed to. Don't worry, this will all be over before long, and you will be as right as rain again."

He spoke to her like a father would a child, raking his fingers through her knotted, greasy hair.

She turned to him, tears now spilling down her face as she tried to say something, but bile leapt up in her throat.

"Shhh," he said soothingly, whilst placing a hand under her wobbly chin and turning her face toward him. "Don't say anything. You may do damage to your pretty, little lips, and you wouldn't want that now, would you?" Before letting her face go again, he ran his thumb over her mouth, feeling the strimmer twine he had used to stitch her jaws together while she lay unconscious in their bed – drugged of course.

Greg had made chloroform from bleach, ice and pure acetone to knock her out. He could have got hold of the stuff from a friend, but he didn't like to lie to people. Making it was easier – he had all the ingredients in his shop.

He'd waited until she'd fallen asleep in their bed and gone in there in a swift attack, pinning her down, and pressing a rag soaked in chloroform over her mouth. Gloria had awoken with a muffled scream. She'd torn at his hands at first with her bitten down nails, then gone for the eyes, but it had been no good. The stuff had taken an almost instant affect. He had then gone about sewing her mouth shut with a needle from his shop. It was a standard suture needle. It had punctured Gloria's lips with a bit of effort. A thin stream of blood had escaped the ruptured flesh as she lay there dead to the world. In time, he was sure that she would thank him...

Remembrance

She'd love him forever, Kathrin thought, as she gazed out the kitchen window. Her eyes settled on her roses, which bloomed and shone in the late, summer evening. He'd been an exceptional lover – kind, passionate, romantic, caring, loving, funny…everything a woman could ever ask for in a man. Things had been perfect.

Until she'd come along.

He'd tried telling her that it was all in her mind.

That losing the baby had messed with her head.

That stress was causing a strain on her.

Cracks started to appear in the relationship's foundation. Arguments, backbiting,

sly digs, jibes, slaps, shoves…

It tore us apart, she thought, filling the kettle and putting it on its pod to boil.

She could tell something was wrong when he started staying away from home until all hours – beers down the pub with the boys, late working hours, overtime, visits to his mother, etc…

It spiralled out of control. The relationship passed its use-by-date.

But Kathrin failed to accept it, even when he came out and told her it was finished. Kathrin's face burned as she remembered her outburst in the garden.

***

"I'm leaving you, Kathrin. I can't stand it any longer. Your moods. Your temper. It's not healthy. The baby was nobody's…"

She struck him across the face – her studded wedding ring cutting a gash across his cheek. Some of his blood found its way into her mouth. The salty taste almost made her gag. Droplets of blood splashed the garden's paving stones, grass and soil.

"You…you…"

"You what? You pathetic little shit," she snarled.

"Pft," he scoffed, wiping at the blood on his face, all the while eyeing her with a look of disdain. "You're not worth it," he said, turning his back.

"Don't you walk away from me," she screamed, following him while raining blows down on his back. "Bastard!" she snarled.

Turning, he caught one of her hands in mid-swipe. Twisting it, he made Kathrin yelp. "I'll snap it off," he warned.

"Argh, get off – you're hurting me!" she pleaded.

This had been the only time he'd raised his hand to her, even in defence. Never had he struck her.

"Then leave me alone, Kathrin. It's over. Please."

"Okay, I'll drop it," she said, wincing. "I'm sorry. The whole mis…" she just couldn't bring herself to say it. Tears formed at the corners of her eyes. "Don't leave me, John. Please. I can't bear the thought of losing you, too," she begged, her tone close to hysteria. "I don't know what I'd do."

John managed to swallow with some difficulty, before speaking again. "I'm sorry. It's over. Things haven't been right between us for a long time, Kathrin, and I'm starting to fear for my health with you," he said gently, letting go of her arm. He turned and started walking away again.

"But you can't just leave, John," she pleaded.

"I'm moving away, Kathrin," he told her. "I need a change of scenery. I've left my job, and…"

"You what?" she barked.

"Please, don't make this any harder. It'll be best if I leave now," he told her, not turning to face her. "I think that'll be best for both of us…"

His sentence trailed off, as pain tore through his body and exploded in his stomach. Knees buckling, John placed his hands on his midriff, seeking out the source of agony.

As his fingers touched the red metal prongs that jutted out of his guts, he whimpered. Blood spilled out of his mouth and dribbled down his chin. More drizzled out the left side of his trouser leg, forming a neat pool around him.

Crimson bubbles formed and popped at his lips as he tried to speak. "B…b…b…" John slobbered thick strands of dark red saliva, which looked more like ropes of liquorice. Finally collapsing to his knees, he heard Kathrin at his ear, catching only half of the whispered sentence.

"…nobody shall have you!"

"But there isn't anyone else…" he managed.

Then he felt the blades twist in his guts, as she tried rotating the gardening implement. He felt his veins knot. Putting a knee to his back, Kathrin drove John forward, pulling the mini fork free of his torso, bringing with it chunks of flesh and gratuitous sounds of slurping and sucking.

Laying on his back, gargling on his own blood and clinging to life, John held out a pleading hand. "Help…" he managed to whisper.

Throwing the fork to one side, she picked up a pair of snips used to de-stem flowers and bent down close to his ear again.

"Maybe I should emasculate you?" she said, working the scissor-like tool in front of his rapidly blinking eyes.

"Urgh…argh," John agonised. "No…"

She rammed the tip of the sheers into his throat and twisted, ensuring the main artery was severed. The pulsing veins spat at her face and top.

"Goodnight, my love," Kathrin said, stroking John's forehead, as his life drained away.

When he finally stopped bucking, she started to cry over his cooling body, until there was nothing left to give. Tugging the clippers out of his jugular, she started digging a hole where John had intended to plant his beloved roses. It took her close to two hours to dig a hole and to roll his stiff corpse into the worm-infested ground. The snips and fork had gone in with him.

***

That had been a year to date, Kathrin thought, pouring her tea. Finishing with the kettle, she returned her gaze to the roses once again. They hadn't taken long to blossom, she recalled, covering the whole, ungodly area and filling it with vibrant colour. The flowers hid her secret deep beneath their colourful presence.

Sipping at the cooling tea, she thought back to how there was no suspicion. No acquisitions. No pressure. No black looks. No sneers. No eyes on her. Not even a call from the police. Everyone thought he'd left her. His employer certainly knew he was going.

Not even his fancy woman had come looking for him.

"What a heartless bitch," Kathrin said, a giggle escaping her.

Draining the last of the tepid liquid, Kathrin rinsed the mug and set it on the draining board. Glancing at the clock, she found it to be just after nine. Leaving the kitchen, she made her way into the living room and sat in her big, single chair.

Picking up the book on the table, she smiled, and began to read, but soon gave up on it due to heavy eyes. Putting the book down, she turned the TV on, noting it was almost midnight. "Not much on at this hour," she muttered, eagerly flicking from one channel to the next. She finally settled on an old horror movie – Day of the Dead. "God, I remember me and John seeing this in the cinema," she said aloud, shaking her head with a slight smile on her face. "It seems like a lifetime ago now."

Looking over at the mantelpiece, Kathrin spied their wedding photo. "You looked so handsome there," she whispered. "I miss you," she told the captured image of John, her head pulling to one side, as she drifted off to sleep.

The sound was faint, but it had been enough to disrupt her from a deep slumber. Lifting her head to focus on the screen of the TV, while blinking the sleep from her eyes, Kathrin saw that some late-night game show was on. A game she'd never seen before.

More noise.

The sound of splintering glass, which was followed by the sound of it showering the floor as it gave out.

Now she was fully awake.

Slowing creeping through the dark living room, Kathrin opened the door to the passageway as quietly and as stealthily as possible. If some little bugger thinks he can break in here…I'll catch him in the act, she thought.

When it was open wide enough for her to poke her head around, she viewed the front door. "Damn it," she mouthed. The glass there was intact, which meant the intruder was trying to force entry at the back of the house.

She grabbed the letter opener off the phone stand in the passageway, turned with cat-like speed, and screamed.

The silhouette of a large figure standing in the kitchen almost stopped her heart.

It was holding a shovel, the handle across its chest, the dirty tip pointed skyward, as though ready to be brought down on someone's skull.

Her skull.

"Get out!" she screamed. "I have a knife. I'll bury it in your chest," she threatened.

The figure moved forward, getting closer to the only light in the house, which was being cast by the TV.

There was an awful noise as the dark shape moved. It sounded like dry kindling, snapping.

A sliver of light found the bottom of the intruder's legs, exposing muddy trainers and filthy jeans, which looked scuffed and bloody. Soon the T-shirt-covered-torso appeared. That too was blood encrusted.

"J…J…"

She couldn't bring herself to say it; to form the word.

An awful sound of breaking bones grew louder in her ears.

Louder still.

"No. It can't be."

"You're dead!" she yelled, until her own voice rang in her ears.

As his face came in to view, Kathrin threw up at the sight in front of her. She emptied her guts all over her favourite nightgown – a birthday present from John.

Most of the right side of his once, handsome face had been eaten away, exposing his chattering teeth and worms which were sliding and slithering around inside his mouth. Maggots and God knows what else rolled off his body, leaving a path behind him.

His white, dead eyes kept staring at her. Unblinking. John's nose, what was left of it, twitched – keeping in sync with his sneering half-lip. She could see his tongue, all withered and partly eaten.

He was almost on her when she finally finished gagging. Turning, she gripped the door handle to the passageway, plunged it downward, and prepared to open the door to make her escape. As she did, her hair was clutched, and she was pulled backwards. Torrid pain ripped through her scalp.

Kathrin let out an ear-shredding screech, and writhed in her dead husband's grip, refusing to let go of the handle. Clumps of her hair tore loose, freeing her, allowing her to turn and plunge the knife deep into his chest, driving him back.

Ignoring the attack, he gripped her throat and squeezed. Vessels burst in her nose, and leaked blood. Her eyes bulged as he dragged her toward him, but once again she managed to break his grip.

"This can't be. You're dead!" she screamed in the thing's face, before a powerful blow to her head from his shovel rendered her unconscious.

A rupture of applause burst from the TV, as the game show kicked on, and Kathrin was dragged from the living room, facedown, into the kitchen. He hauled her across the glass covered floor, and shards nicked her face, sliced her lip, scratched her cheek, and slashed her clothes.

Rose petals fell from his decayed body, leaving behind a sombre trail.

Slowly coming around, Kathrin was conscious of the glass all around her, managing to pick up a lethal looking shaft of splintered pane, as she was pulled through the debris. She slipped the weapon up her sleeve and waited for her next opportunity.

When he had her at the open back door, he ripped her up and off the floor with one rotten hand, and threw her limp body over his grotesque shoulder, which was sodden, and stunk of wet earth. Worms and maggots now slithered over Kathrin's body, but she didn't whimper, just closed her eyes as tight as she could, and managed to keep the vomit down.

He slammed her down onto the garden bed so hard, that she rebounded off the grass and into the air. Kathrin managed to keep her composure, even though the wind had been slightly knocked from her and took her opportunity when his back was turned.

Getting into a sitting position as fast as she could, Kathrin thrust the piece of glass deep into the back of John's knee, and ripped it down to his Achilles' heel, making him howl.

"Bastard!" she yelled up at him, tugging the glass free and stabbing at him again and again, covering her face and clothes with blood until she was breathless.

He turned on her rapidly and caught the side of her face with his shovel. The tip sliced through her cheek, which exited her mouth, severing her tongue and uprooting teeth in the process. The ivory ricocheted off the garden walls and conservatory, as her scream tore the night apart.

She rolled about on the floor, holding the flaps of ripped skin together, that was once her cheek. John pounded away at her ribcage, breaking at least four bones, before kicking her body with vehemence into the hole from which he'd come.

Dirt filled her mouth, which smothered her screams, as John buried her alive.

Inch.

By.

Inch.

Signed, Sealed and Delivered

"House Inspector Under Inspection."

Jimmy read, as he glanced over the newspaper on his boss' desk. The guy's name was Archie. There was a photo. Jimmy knew him; had delivered to him. A right creep. A creep who had seemed a bit screwy to Jimmy. He ordered copious amounts of the same shit – pens, pencils, paper, paperclips, envelopes, etc. Jimmy should know – he'd opened the man's parcels every single time, before resealing and delivering.

Maybe Archie was trying to corner the stationery market – undermine Staples? Take them down a notch or two?

Jimmy smiled.

Had he not been in company, he probably would have let a right rip-roaring laugh free. Shattered windows with it. Instead, he took a drink of coffee from his mug – 'Delivery Men Do It on Your Doorstep' was etched into the plastic. His #1 Sex Machine mug was in the wash.

Looking back at the photo, which was situated under an advertisement for a ventriloquist by the name of Crystal,

Jimmy read the caption – 'House inspector Archie Dreadbank was this morning being questioned for the morose murder of his employer…'

"Jimmy?!" Mr. Clyde said, raising his voice in annoyance, "Could you please answer the question?"

"Huh?" Jimmy said, totally unaware a question had even been asked.

"Jimmy, please. These are very serious accusations which have been pressed against you," Mr. Clyde said, stroking his moustache. "You're one of my most loyal, dedicated and trusted members of staff. I don't want to see you get the chop, my boy."

"Thank you, sir," Jimmy said, looking glum.

Mr. Clyde was a well-liked man…slightly feared, but well-liked and respected. He'd built his parcel company up from the ground floor, with little financial help. The company was now in its fortieth year, with no cracks appearing whatsoever. Where other such companies had collapsed due to market crashes, Parcel Brigade U.K, kept on pushing.

Mr. Clyde was proud of this fact, and why shouldn't he be?

He drove a Jag and holidayed three times a year; he still glowed from his latest trek to Quebec. The same could be said for Mr. Flowers, who sat next to Mr. Clyde. He, in turn, was Jimmy's supervisor and second in command at Parcel Brigade U.K. His tan was equally impressive – a three week break in India would do that for you.

Oh, how the rich live, Jimmy thought, smiling, inwardly. When Clyde and Flowers were both away, another kept an eye on things. 'Administrated'. A Spaniard by the name of Romeo. Hell, you couldn't write that shit, Jimmy thought. Luckily for me, he's gone back to his motherland for a fortnight.

"Well?" Flowers pressed.

He was getting impatient, Jimmy thought. Good. I've never liked you, you weaselly fuck. Sweat, you bastard. "I'm not sure what you're asking?" Jimmy said, playing the 'I'm-as-thick-as-pig-shit, boss' – please spoon-feed me your questions.

"The parcel, Jimmy. From yesterday – did you tamper with it?!" Mr. Clyde asked.

"Parcel?" Jimmy said, looking confused.

"Yes! Parcel," Mr. Clyde said, raising his voice.

Jimmy liked this game.

"…The one you delivered to a Mr…"

Best of luck pronouncing it, dickhead, Jimmy thought.

"Mr…erm…Mr. Nd…ik…um…ana…Ndikumana…"

Taking another sip from his mug, Jimmy shook his head. "Mr. Clyde, with all due respect, sir, I've worked for this company for years – man and boy – and not once have I ever, ever tampered with a parcel. Good, God!" he said, putting on his most horrified face. Eat it up, chumps, he thought.

"Are you trying to tell us, that Mr…" Flowers started, but mumbled the customer's name. "…is lying to us? Why? Why would he do that?"

Because he's a football hooligan, Jimmy thought. A fucking Zulu, to boot. More of a Wolves man, myself. "I have no idea, sir. We have these kind of complaints on a regular basis, and ninety-five percent of them turn out bogus."

"Yes, agreed," Mr. Flowers said. "Parcels do go 'missing' and turn up tampered with, and yes, a large percentage of the complaints are 'bogus'. The customers like to blame the carrier, etc, so they can wangle a discount."

"Exactly," Jimmy said, almost letting a smile slip. He knew this investigation was a load of crap. They had nothing to go on, apart from a wrecked football jersey, which the customer could have done himself.

Oh, how Jimmy had enjoyed cutting the crests and logos off the expensive Birmingham City top, before delivering it to the customer in an immaculate package.

"But still, we can't let this matter lie, not until there's been a full investigation," Mr. Clyde said. "The customer's playing hell, Jimmy. Claims you've been harassing him."

"Excuse me, sir? Harassing?" Jimmy said, slightly shocked. What else do they know?

"Yes, harassing," Flowers chirped in as he fixed his cheap taupe and tie to match.

"Apparently, one of the customer advisors at our Cardiff contact centre rang you last week?" Mr. Clyde asked.

"Yes, possibly," Jimmy said.

"He was asking the whereabouts of Mr. Ndikumana's package – I believe it was a set of pans this time? This was…erm…" Mr Clyde said, consulting his notes. "…last week?"

"Maybe," Jimmy said. "I receive lots of calls," he lied. He remembered the call all right. The guy from the contact centre was a right little jumped up shit. What was his name? Charles? No. Charlie? Yes, Charlie. He must have put a driver's complaint in about me. Fuck!

"Well, this advisor says he spoke to you, Jimmy. Said you hung up on him when he started asking you questions. Is this true?" Mr. Clyde asked.

"I'm sure it's not, sir. I wouldn't do that. I have a duty to my customers. After all, Jim'll Fix It!" he said, pointing at the badge he had pinned to his chest.

"Yes," Flowers said. "I don't think that's appropriate, do you?"

"Why?" asked Jimmy, knowing full well why it wasn't appropriate.

"Never mind that," Mr. Clyde broke in. "It's not just about the pans and ripped up jersey. The man says you've thrown numerous parcels over his fence, posted them through open windows, and lobbed them into his pond at the front of his house. Is this true?!"

"Definitely not!" Jimmy said, standing up. "I demand an apology!" He was hoping the dramatics would work.

"Jimmy, please," Mr. Clyde said. "We're not here to crucify you. We have procedures to run. To check. To follow up any complaints the company receives."

"Mr. Clyde is right, Jimmy. We just want to hear your side of things, that's all. You of all people should know that."

Jimmy sat down. He didn't want to overdo it. He kept the sullen look on his face, though.

"Victor says you've been acting odd, too," Mr. Flowers said.

"Odd?" Jimmy asked.

"Yes. That you've been missing calls from him. The com guys need to know the whereabouts of our drivers at all times."

"Oh, come on, Mr. Flowers. We've all heard the rumours about that Yankee. Loves his whiskey!"

"Jimmy!" Mr. Clyde blurted. "Saying such things, especially in the presence of your superiors, is a sackable offence!"

"Sorry, sir."

"You will be, if you carry on, Jimmy. These are serious accusations against you."

I'm sure you'd be sorry, Mr. Flowers, if I told you I was fucking your wife, Julia, and daughter, November, on a regular, ménage à trois basis. Still, perks of the job, I guess. Do you know how much your wife spends, I wonder? Did you authorise her cracking boob job? How I love motor boating those things! Your credit card must be melting in your pocket as we speak.

"I have no idea where these claims have come from. I've done nothing but do a good job for this company for thirty years. I've given it my all!" Jimmy said. My all!"

Looking at Jimmy, Mr. Clyde couldn't help but feel sorry for the man. He was slumped in his chair like a naughty schoolboy, the yellow jacket which made up his uniform was rucked up. Unkempt. He looked worried, as he fidgeted with his salt and pepper hair.

Mr. Clyde was pretty sure the claims against his man were false. Complete and utter hogwash; but he had to make sure. The last thing he wanted, was to give Jimmy the push. The driver had nothing, apart from this job, which meant the world to him.

"Maybe you need a break, Jimmy. Take some time away? You have plenty saved up…" Mr. Clyde said, treading carefully. He knew Jimmy had no real family either. Nobody to spend quality time with.

"No, I couldn't do that. Not now, sir," Jimmy said.

"Why?" Flowers pressed.

"It's peak, sirs. No, the show must go on!" Jimmy insisted.

"Fine. But we'll have to suspend you, while this case goes on," Mr. Clyde said. "I don't want a company scandal on my hands. Mr. Ndikumana wants you sacked, but I held him off at a suspension."

"But I've done nothing wrong, sir! I've given my life to this company," Jimmy said.

"I know, and I'm sure these allegations are bunkum. But still, as I've said, I have to follow up on any complaints, you know that," Mr. Clyde said. "You'll be on paid suspension."

To be fair, I hope you give me the push, you bastard, Jimmy thought. I've never liked it here. Disgruntled customers and arse-wipes for co-workers. Stick it where the mice won't get at it, you bald-headed bastard! I just don't want the law on my back, which will happen, if I don't wriggle out of this mess. If the Zulu presses charges, then they'll dig, dig and dig, until they find out about all the other things I've done, too…Now, that would be embarrassing.

As Mr. Clyde ruffled his paperwork and filled out the suspension form, Mr. Flowers filled the minutes.

This gave Jimmy time to think, to reflect on all the other naughty incidents which had taken place over the course of his career at Parcel Brigade U.K.

TVs pinched, along with other expensive electrical equipment, such as PlayStation's, DVD/Blu-ray players, stereo systems, sound bars, sub-woofers, microwaves, toasters…You name it and he'd steal it and sell it on. Christmas time was a goldmine. The losses were always blamed on the hundreds of new drivers brought in for the festival period. Poor Polish bastards, Jimmy thought, sniggering inwardly.

And look at these two dildos in front of me. Clyde and Flowers, who think butter wouldn't melt in my mouth…well, Clyde thinks that – Fucktard Flowers has always had it against me. How can such a loser have such a nice wife? Hell of a set of twins on her. Pussy, too. Tight. Tight, and always wet and welcoming.

For me, anyway.

Of course, it was as big a thrill for her, too. She loved the thought of fucking one of her husband's co-workers. Getting her teenaged daughter to join in had even been her idea. Dirty bitch.

Down, boy. Jimmy though, putting his hands over his crotch.

"Say it. Say it!" she'd demand. "Say it!"

"Jim'll fix it! Jim'll fix it!" he'd be forced to shout, as he screwed her doggie style in her marital bed.

Great afternoons, he thought, smiling, but sadly, they'll have to come to an end. I need to start being a good little boy. This is too close to a prison cell for my liking.

All the products he'd tampered with over the years had never led back to him. He'd been crafty. Sneaky. There was always someone else to blame. Forms to lie on. His favourite kind of parcels were parcels which contained liquids – oh, how he loved to fuck with those products. Especially if the people they were going to were douchebags or pretty women who rejected his advances.

Harmful solutions can be easily disguised in fluids.

Such as acid.

Poison.

Ink.

Anti-freeze.

Bleach.

Anything you can think of, really.

It all depended on just how cruel you wanted to be.

Ever seen a pretty girl trying to wash her hair in acid? Jimmy thought. They ain't so fucking pretty afterward, I can tell you.

What about a guy choking to his death on poison or Anti-freeze? It's a blast, especially if the guy has shooed you from his doorstep with foul language and the threat of violence.

How many have I killed? Not sure, but many have been maimed. Hundreds, even.

It's fun.

Mixes things up.

I may abhor the job, but I'd hate to be without it. I'd miss Mrs. Flowers and her peachy daughter. I'd miss fucking with all those retards and their parcels. Now that's job satisfaction! Jimmy thought.

Who'd fix it, if good ol' Jimmy wasn't about?!

"Sign here, please," Mr. Clyde asked Jimmy. "It's just to say that you understand why you're being suspended.

"Okay," Jimmy said, cooperating. One does not want to protest too much.

"You seem rather blasé," Mr. Flowers said.

"There's no point in fighting it," Jimmy said. "I have nothing to prove."

"Good man," Mr. Clyde said. "I know deep down that this will all lead to nothing. Of that, I am sure."

"Yes," Mr. Flowers concurred. "We see this kind of thing on a daily basis, and rarely is the driver at fault."

Jimmy signed his name. "Am I allowed to leave?" he asked.

"Of course, Jimmy," Mr. Clyde said.

"Can I finish my shift?" Jimmy asked.

"I'm not sure that would be wise," Mr. Flowers said. "Just in case, you understand?"

"Perfectly, sir." Both Mr. Clyde and Mr. Flowers nodded. "I'll make my way home," Jimmy concluded.

"It's a three week suspension, Jimmy," Mr. Clyde said. "Why don't you take my advice, and go away for a break?"

"Oh, I'll do just that sir. I've heard France is nice this time of year."

"Good. Good!" Mr. Clyde said.

"It'll act as the perfect alibi..." Jimmy said under his breath... "After I off the Zulu..."

"Pardon?" Mr. Flowers said.

"Nothing," Jimmy said, turning to smile at both men.

"I'll be in touch," Mr. Clyde said.

"Great, I'll look forward to coming back to work after my break," Jimmy said, closing the office door behind him.

Level 13A

"Ugh," she groaned, as she sat up straight. She immediately placed her hands to her head, as a headache began form behind her eyes. "Jesus! How much did I have to drink?!" she moaned.

Sweeping strands of her lengthy, black hair out of her face, she tried to focus her eyes on her surroundings, but couldn't understand where she was. "What the…? From where Millie-Jane sat, the city was splayed out in front of her. Lights twinkled out of office windows from miles away, and car horns blared from the streets below.

Moving to her right, she looked down, and saw that she was mounted on her bike. The Harley had been a gift from her boyfriend, Bill, last year after she got her big promotion.

Dismounting, she staggered to one side and almost went down. The drink had turned her legs to pillars of jelly. Her body ached and cried out for sleep. She needed to get home; to get to bed. She looked at her watch, the face was cracked, but the hands were still ticking.

01.05.

"Shit! Panic woke her up, as she turned on her heel. The rooftop to the concrete car park was empty. Deserted. Bits of rubbish blew around the place, which reminded her of an abandoned, old western town; all that was missing was the rolling weed.

The whipping wind lashed at the backs of her legs, which were covered in tights. The Doc Martins that graced her feet made crunching sounds as she walked over to the edge of the rooftop. She peered over the side and looked down. Even the streets were empty, apart from a few moving cars.

"Right, Mill. Let's haul arse, girl."

For the first time, she noticed that the barriers to the exit and entrance ramps were down.

She was going nowhere.

"Crap. Someone must have noticed me asleep up here, for Christ sake." Digging her phone out of her pocket, she saw there was no reception. "How can that be? I'm standing on a roof!"

Shaking her head, she placed her mobile back in her pocket, and made her way over to the door that led down to the next level.

As she did, she pulled her cut-offs up, which had slipped down her arse revealing a five inch tattoo of the band Whitesnake across her right buttock. The detailed tat showed a snake coiled around the letters of the band, its mouth wide and spitting venom.

When she was at the door, marked 13A in bright white lettering, it opened without a squeak. The lights in the stairwell were out. Below, an azure light blinked on and off, as though the backup system had kicked in due to a power cut.

"Odd," she said aloud, narrowing her eyes to try to penetrate the darkness. "Hello," she bellowed down the steps, which cut a hollow noise through the stillness. "Anyone down there? I think…

Her words derailed on hearing the clanging noise. Metal on metal. It grated on her. It made her teeth grind. The noise was almost unbearable as it grew louder and louder. Clang, clang, clang, clang, clang, clang, clang…

Was it getting louder?

It certainly sounded that way.

Millie-Jane backed up. She beat a hasty retreat up the stairs. Her heart hammered like a Derby winner.

Clang, clang, clang, clang, clang, clang…

It was definitely moving in her direction.

When it seemed closer still, she heard a low, guttural snarl she thought only a wild animal could make, trail up the stairs. A sort of "Ewww-ugghhh…"

In the flickers of light thrown by the ungodly illumination a few levels below, it cast shadows of the hulking mass moving up the steps towards her, the clang-clang following behind, but unseen.

"Wh…wha…No. It can't be! What the fuck is this? Some kind of joke?!"

Then she caught sight of it, but only briefly, as the light splashed across its face. It looked reptilian in the light, but that could not be.

Impossible.

It's the poor light, she argued with herself, before seeing it disappear into a veil of blackness.

The horrendous hissing came again, forcing her to slam the door shut, and run for her bike. Jumping on, she kicked the engine to life, and turned it to face the barriers.

"I'll go through the fucking things if I have to," she yelled, whilst revving the engine.

Kicking the bike's stand up into place, Millie moved the bike forward, just as the door to the rooftop entrance was thrown wide. The man-thing threw a large object at her as she neared the barrier.

She screamed when the decapitated head smacked into her side, causing her to lose control of the bike and go into a slide. The Harley came to a stop when the tyres slammed into a wall, crippling both wheels.

The thing, which was wearing a long, Humphrey Bogart-like trench coat, advanced on her. It was now evident what the scraping sound had been – an axe head – which was attached to a foot-long shaft of wood.

The axe was over its shoulder, ready to be brought down on her.

"Help! Help me!" Millie screamed. "Help, for fuck's sake! Someone! Help!" she continued, whilst desperately trying to drag her left leg from under the motorbike. The engine continued to whine, as the throttle was jammed.

Its eyes were set deep in its grotesquely, misshapen head, which definitely had reptilian features to it. Its ears small and pokey, its nose non-existent under that hard looking skin, which looked tougher than that of a rhino.

It came at her in a hunched position. She saw that its clothes were nothing more than rags, as the tails of its coat blew out behind it like a ship's mast. It licked at its chops and gripped the handle of the axe. The cutting edge of the tool looked freshly used, and somewhat blunt.

Finally, freeing her trapped leg, Millie scooted backwards on her arse as it kept coming. It was taking its time. Playing with her. Toying with her like a cat would a mouse.

Her right hand found something.

A rock?

When she looked down, she noticed that she'd placed her hand on top of the decapitated head; the eyes unblinking and staring straight through her; the mouth twisted into a death scream. Rivers of blood had pumped down the nose, leaving behind slug-like trails, which had dried to crusts.

She couldn't scream.

Vomit filled her throat.

She gagged and closed her eyes; tears running down her cheeks

The engine to the bike finally came to a crescendo and blew. Black smoke billowed out of the ruptured tank, and leaked oil and other fluids onto the concrete floor. The sudden outburst stopped the 'reptilian' in its tracks, the fume-laden smoke making him cough and splutter, giving Mille-Jane the chance to escape down the up ramp, onto level 12 of the car park.

As the black hole of the ramp swallowed her, she darted a glance behind, and found she wasn't being pursued. Once down on level 12, the unholy stench hit her. She couldn't tell whether it was vomit, piss or excrement – or perhaps a ghastly mix of all three bodily fluids.

She contemplated the stink as she stood drenched in the azure/indigo illumination, which lit up level 12. Millie whimpered, looking both right and left. Which way? Which way to flee to? Which way out? Her mind was a runaway train of derailing thoughts.

Her breathing came and went with ragged tears, as she tried to feed her starved lungs. She glanced back again and saw him standing at the top of the ramp, unmoving; the axe held across its chest, as the smoke billowed over it.

"What do you want?!" she screamed up at it, thinking the bike's engine was still alive and kicking but it wasn't. It advanced towards her.

Choosing to go left, she fled screaming and shouting for help, thinking at least one person would hear her. Someone must be here, for Christ sake. Security, at least!

After running as fast as her boots allowed, Millie stopped, scrambling to undo the laces, and tossing the boots to one side. She stole another look back, and saw it advancing, slowly. It was taking its time, its image nothing more than an eerie outline in the poor glow.

Millie took two minutes rest and put her hands on her knees as she bent over. Sucking air in copious amounts, she managed to regain control of her breathing. I need to make it down to the bottom of this concrete prison, she thought. There's bound to be someone down there who can help or let me the fuck out at least.

Unbending, she dashed for the ramp leading down to level 11, which was close by. Her assailant was nowhere to be seen, but it could be heard dragging the axe along the floor.

"What the hell is it doing?" she whispered.

Not stopping to think, Millie made for a bank of elevators at the far end of the abandoned level. Wouldn't they have powered out along with the lights and everything else within the place? she asked herself. No harm in trying. They may run off a different circuit.

Excited, she approached the electrical carriages, which smacked of hope; a flight to safety. Moving closer, she noticed a pair of feet to her right, which jutted out from behind a pillar close to the lifts.

"Hello?" she called, knowing it wasn't her attacker, as its scraping could still be heard from above. "Can you help me, please?" she asked; her voice frantic.

Stepping closer to the feet, the ankles started to come into view, then the thighs, which were covered in filthy blue jeans. What if it's an accomplice? No. Not a chance. If that was the case, they'd have been on me by now.

The person's lap came in to view, and a hand, which was holding a half empty bottle of Gordon's gin. The base of the bottle was snug in the person's crotch, and leaned to one side

"Hey?" she whispered. "Please, I could really do with some help. We both need to get…"

Never, ever had Mille-Jane laid witness to such vile imagery as she discovered the rest of the person which was hidden behind the concrete support beam. She couldn't even muster a yell or a scream, as her body was too weak, and jelly-like; her jaw slack.

She watched as the fat, black rats scurried up the arms and across the shoulders of the homeless man who sat on the floor with his head missing. They clutched at the exposed veins, bones and muscles, which protruded out of the gory stump.

Their disgusting squawks echoed inside her head, as they went about their feast Some of the rodents had congregated in the thick pool of blood which had gathered on the floor, their miniscule muzzles encrusted red. Tiny footprints of blood could be found all about the body.

Turning, Millie gagged, and never saw the man-thing come at her from behind. He shoved her up against the wall close to the fast decaying, and rodent swamped body, and sniggered in her ear as he throttled her.

Her legs flopped and struggled, as he picked her off her feet, and applied more pressure to her throat. Black spots appeared in her vision, as everything started turning dark.

Wheezing, Millie-Jane fought desperately to be free of his ice cool grip. She knew he could rip her head off her shoulders if he wished to do so, and it came as a great shock, and relief, when he threw her to one side, discarding her like a rag doll.

Her tights tore, her knees scuffed, as she rolled along the floor. Her ribs connected with a pillar, bringing her to a gasping stop, as the air was smacked from her.

The thing, which stood hunched over her, played the axe back and forth between its open hands, while letting out a sneering, little, hiss of a laugh. For the first time, she could see that it was naked underneath the trench coat – its body as horribly scaly as its face and hands.

"What are you?" she asked, looking up at it and holding her side at the same time.

It hissed at her, causing the hairs on her arms to prickle. Her blood felt Arctic within her veins. She swallowed a scream, as it placed one of its rough, gigantic hands on her left ankle, and ran it all the way up her leg.

Whimpering, Millie-Jane managed to keep it together, as she clenched her teeth and bladder, but then screamed until her lungs burned, as his hand went from her slender leg to her hair.

Gripping a fistful of hair, he dragged her from the floor, and flung her once again, her body landing close to the bank of elevators.

"Please," she spluttered, clutching the one rib which felt broken, as she dragged herself along the floor, edging herself closer to the elevator it had sprung from – the door still open.

He was back to dragging his axe, as it increased its pace to go after her. It was content playing its game...drawing the kill out.

Millie-Jane made it to the inside on the left and hauled herself up to a standing position. She turned in time to see him standing over her, the axe coming down. She screamed and avoided the blow, by diving through his legs and crawling to safety.

She just had enough time to see it fall inside the lift, its axe bouncing off the back wall. The doors closed on him, as he turned to face and scream at her.

"Fuck you," she said, scooting away from the lift on her arse with the aid of her hands, her palms cut and bloodied.

Managing to get to her feet, she dared not try the lifts again, just in case it should come back up for her. Taking her eyes of the dead man swamped in rats, Millie-Jane hobbled over to the next ramp. She made her way down to level 10, which was desolate, much like the floors above, but this one had a car standing in one of the parking spaces close to her.

Above, she could still hear the rats, as they squeaked with delight at their find.

Making swift, sweeping head movements to her left and right, Millie made sure the coast was clear, and staggered over to the Nissan Micra. The windows appeared to be blacked out, but she told herself it was down to the poor lighting.

Her ribs ached with her movements, but she knew now, that nothing was broken, just badly hurt and probably bruised.

Making it to the car, she collapsed against it. The small car rocked on its chassis to the sudden disturbance. Sweat poured down her face from the exertion, as she tried the handle to the passenger door. Nothing. The door didn't budge. She clobbered the window with her fist and yelled in frustration.

Using the car as support, Millie-Jane circled the small vehicle and stopped at the back window to look in. All she could see was herself staring back, her outline framed in a black/blue colour.

She gave up trying to see inside, and continued to circle the car, like a vulture would its prey. Making it to the driver's side door, she tried that handle. Locked.

"Fuck," she said under her breath, giving the car another rap with her fist. Before turning away from the car, she noticed marks on the bonnet.

"Is that blood?"

Millie-Jane moved closer until the marks were identifiable. It was blood all right. There were also chop marks in the metal, where that freak had undoubtedly attacked this vehicle, and probably its owner.

It was probably the reason why the whole car park was plunged in blue/black darkness.

The elevators pinged to her left, and when she looked, she saw it slink out of the steel box. It headed for her, as she began to hobble off.

Then, she heard a second noise, followed by a plea for help.

"You must…help me…for the love of…"

It was strained and gargled.

She dared a look back and saw the driver of the car hanging out his open door. Blood pelted the concrete, as he fought to keep his guts inside him with one hand. The fat, steaming-hot ropes of his intestines pushed between his fingers. His face was chalk white, as he fell from the car.

"Help," he screamed, his red stained lips pulled back over his teeth, emphasising the agony he was in. She could see that his mouth was full of blood and broken teeth.

She rushed over to him and helped him off the floor. In the process, Millie-Jane spotted his keys dangling from the ignition. "Let's get you in the car," she said. "Quickly."

Wetness trickled out of the sleeve he had over her shoulder and slipped down the front of her top.

"I…I…" he tried, then wet his lips. "I…Aaarghh," he screamed. "The pain…It's too much…" He coughed and spluttered. Red spittle patted the floor at his feet.

She propped him against the car and snatched the keys from the ignition. The thing was just standing by the open elevator, looking at them in amusement.

Millie-Jane rushed around to the other side of the car and unlocked the passenger door, then went back for the wounded businessman.

"Hurry," she said, letting him fall against her.

Getting him halfway around to the open door, the thing started out from the lift. It was whistling, "Whistle While You Work", as it stalked towards them.

"Move!" she told her wounded companion. Her ribs screamed in agony from the pressure resting against them.

As Millie-Jane started to lower the man into the passenger seat, he let out a bellow that tore the night in two. The shriek ripped down her ear, deafening her momentarily, as he was torn from her clutches.

Turning, she saw that the thing had slammed the axe into the businessman's back – the head of the cutting tool was buried to the hilt in the man's back. She could even see a bulge in his chest, where it had almost gone straight through from the force of the blow. His once white shirt was now sodden red.

The one hand which had been holding his torn apart stomach together now flopped at his side, leaving his guts to slide from within him and splash to the concrete.

Millie-Jane turned, and swallowed down the hot, acidic vomit in her mouth. It burned as it slipped back down her throat.

His gargled screams were almost suppressed by the thing's grunts and groans of pleasure, as he dragged the dying man around the open space by the shaft of the axe.

She wasted no time stopping to look and dove into the open door. She scooted over to the driver's seat and turned the key in the ignition. The engine kicked to life.

Throwing the car into gear, she had just enough time to see the businessman come sailing through the air at her, as the car jerked forward. His carcass hit the windscreen full on, breaking it.

Millie-Jane screamed as the glass showered her like silver rain. Hundreds of tiny pieces of the window now sat in her lap. The man's head poked through a huge hole in the window, his tongue lolling. The shards of jagged glass which remained, dug into this neck, ripping his throat wide.

The car swerved and screeched, as she drove blind, hoping to run the fucker down. She heard a hard thump, and what sounded like a body rolling over the top of her.

Looking up, hoping to confirm it, Millie-Jane ploughed the car straight into a concrete pillar, disabling the vehicle. Fluids rushed out from under the car, as the engine hissed and whined.

She could smell petrol.

Scrambling out of the car, she fell to the floor in her panic to be free of the totalled machine and clawed herself away from it as fast as humanly possible. Hearing a whoop, she knew something had happened. A fire had broken out under the engine.

Tears rolled down her eyes at the sting of smoke and fuel battered her. Her nostrils burned. Glancing a look to her left, she saw the thing lying on its back, the axe six to eight feet away from it.

Is it breathing? she thought, still trying to scramble to safety.

Glass popped and broke. The car's metal whined and groaned, as the fire buckled its bodywork. The upholstery from the seats started to burn, and the fresh smells took their place in the atmosphere with the other stinging fumes.

Not long before the fuel tank catches, she thought.

Minutes.

Seconds, even.

Soon, roaring filled her ears, as black plumes of smoke engulfed her.

For fuck's sake, you'd think somebody from outside would notice this, she thought.

The bang shredded her thoughts, as a door was thrown overhead and came to a skidding halt twenty feet away from her. More glass rained down on her, as a mini quake rippled the ground below her.

Looking back, she saw the pillar she'd crashed into, crumple and collapse onto her wreck. It helped dampen the flames. Dust and smoke assaulted her lungs, causing her to cough and wheeze. Torrid tears raced tracks down her cheeks and found their way into her mouth.

Before she knew it, Millie-Jane had crawled almost the length of the level. Looking back again, she could still see it lying on its back. It hadn't moved. Had she killed it with the car? It was possible. She'd been travelling at a fair clip.

Finally managing to get to her knees, Millie-Jane staggered over to the next down ramp and almost fell down it, as her knees buckled under her, sending her into the wall. She put her hands out to stop herself from going down.

Braced by the wall, she got down to the next level unhampered. If he was dead, then she had all the time in the world to get to safety. Stumbling over to the lifts, she decided to ride one to the bottom.

Cracking sounds caused her to look up, and to her soul-numbing fear, she saw the ground above fracture and splinter. White, dusty powder floated down, as chunks of stone started to fall away and land at her feet.

The whole level above seemed to be coming apart, caused by the car explosion. The lift doors pinged behind her and glided apart. Facing the empty carriage, she went to step inside, but a rumble grumbled its way down the shaft from above.

Cables snapped, giving the lift a tilted appearance. She backed away and then hobbled down the next exit ramp to Level 8.

Just keep going, she said to herself, wiping the tears from her eyes and cheeks. She sniffed heavily, trying to dislodge the stink of smoke from her nostrils. I don't need the lifts any…

As though thunder boomed in her ears, Millie-Jane heard what could only be one of the lifts crashing to the bottom of the elevator shaft.

Keep moving.

Ignore it.

But the laughter and jokey sounds she suddenly heard ahead of her made her tense. Three, maybe four people were in the darkness somewhere in front of her. They were close.

The thought of possible help waned. Who are they? Why had they not come at once after hearing the explosion above? A new threat? Still, she had to try. To at least warn them of what was going on.

Maybe it was a couple of security guards, making a sweep of the building? She stood in silence, trying to keep her breathing as calm as she could. She wished Bill was here with her.

She prayed she'd see him again; would make love to him. They'd only been apart once since getting married four years ago, when Bill had flown to New York on business.

Who were these people laughing and joking in the darkness of this death trap? More tramps, perhaps? she thought. They're probably wondering where their friend is.

"Shall we go and check it out?" she heard a female voice say.

"Nah, fuck it," replied a female voice. "It's probably Pete fucking around up there. You know what he's like, Julie. Remember that fucking stunt he pulled last week?!"

"Yeah, like, we could have gotten pinched for that."

Millie-Jayne didn't like the sounds of these people. These women. They were bad news, and it sounded like they had a third in tow in the form of fun-loving criminal, Pete.

"Don't be so hard on Pete..."

A new voice.

Millie-Jayne hunkered down lower in the darkness, scolding herself for being so silly, as she couldn't be seen by people, she couldn't see herself. Just stay still for now. Don't make a move. Just listen. They may move on. Go looking for their friend.

… "He's a good kid."

"Good kid, my fuck," the first female said.

"Ha-ha, you got that right, Jo. He's a fuck up," Julie piped up.

"You dopey cunts," the man said, his voice harsh and rasping, sounding like he'd been smoking forty a day for most of his life. "That kid would get you out of a scrape if…What's that noise?"

The scraping was back.

The horrid sound of metal on concrete.

Millie-Jayne's scalp suddenly felt hot and itchy – prickled by the fear that clawed its way up her back.

"Wha's tha?" the man said.

"Fucking Pete, man," Jo said. "I told you he's…"

It wasn't the scraping that halted Jo's words. It was the intense hissing which now floated over the top of that sound.

"Knock it off, Pete – you're scaring the little cunts down here!" the man yelled, making Millie-Jayne wince. She wanted to tell them all to keep the fucking noise level down.

"Hey! Fuck you, Larry, you fucking arsehole!"

Millie-Jayne couldn't tell who was saying what, as the noise from upstairs had thrown her off-kilter. Her concentration broke.

Then it stopped.

"Hey, guys, listen. It's gone away. Maybe it was Pete after all."

"Of course, it was fucking Pete, Jo! There's no fucker here apart from us and the pigs downstairs."

Pete's dead, you dumb shits, Millie-Jayne thought, and best you get out of here, before you end up like him. Me, too, for that matter. There must be a way around these wastrels, and…

"Well, well, would you look at what we have ourselves here, Larry. Mmm-mmm!" the voice called out from behind Millie-Jayne. Before she could turn to see him, she felt a hand on her right arse cheek, gripping it firmly.

"Get the hell off me!" Millie-Jayne screamed in the guy's face, smacking his hand away.

"Ooh, a feisty one," he said smiling. The blue light gave the features of his face an eerie, disjointed look. He gripped the hand she'd used to swat his. "Be nice, bitch!" Pete said, "Or I'll have to snap the fucker off." His grin widened, revealing a mouth almost devoid of any teeth, his gums a disgusting and decayed yellow colour.

Millie-Jayne almost spewed her guts up and down his throat, as he pressed his chapped and cracked lips up against hers. His breath reeked, as though he'd been power eating dog shit.

She clawed his face, going for his left eyeball.

"Get the fuck…off me!" she screamed, not caring if the freak upstairs should hear, as she struggled with the bedraggled Pete.

Almost freeing herself from the gin-soaked creep, she felt hands slip around her waist, yanking her backwards.

"Let's get her fucking panties off," one of the women said.

"Yeah," Larry said, pulling an object from his pocket.

Millie-Jane heard a click, then a metallic snick-snack sound.

The blue light reflected off the blade Larry held in his right hand.

"Jo, Julie, grab her legs, for fuck sake! Keep 'em still!" Pete said.

"No, please!" Millie-Jane said. "Don't do this. Please! I beg you! We have to get out of here. There's…"

"Put a sock in it, bitch!" one of the girls said, in a grunting way, as she fought to keep one of Millie-Jane's legs still.

Pete took hold of Millie-Jane's arms and pulled them out, allowing Larry to move in with his knife.

"What the fuck do you think you're doing on our turf?" Larry asked, beginning to saw his knife through one side of Millie-Jane's cut-offs.

The blade sliced through the fabric with a lot of difficulty, giving her more time to try and get her legs and arms free.

"You fuckers," Millie-Jane bellowed, almost tearing her voice box apart with the ferocious and frantic cry. "I'll fucking kill you!" One leg slipped free of one of the women, and she lashed out blindly. Her heel connected with something soft, and a cracking sound ensued, like dry branches being snapped.

"Ahh, you fucking pig whore!" one of the women yelped with a half cry. "I think you've broken my jaw."

"Stop pissing about, Jo" Larry said, "And get that leg pinned back down. Now!"

"Fluck ewe Larrwe," she said, unable to form her words. Blood pissed out of her mouth and into her hands, which were cupping her shattered jaw. Teeth surfed out and rained to the floor.

Now she was crying, as Larry took his hands off Millie-Jayne, and grabbed the girl by the hair, pulling her to the floor.

"Do as I say, you fucking whore, or I'll slice your neck open." He shoved Jo back toward the flaying leg with such force, that she fell on it, pinning it to the floor once again. "Stop squirming," he told Millie-Jayne, "Or I'm going to jam this here blade into your eyeball, miss. We wouldn't want to mess up that pretty little face of yours, would we?"

Pete snickered behind her, as he pulled on her arms, making her think they were going to pop at the shoulders.

"No," Millie-Jane whispered, tears spilling down her cheeks. "He's going to kill us all, if we don't get out of here…" she let her words trail off.

"Who the heck are you talking about?" Pete asked.

"The boogieman," Julie said, laughing at her own crap joke.

"Ha!" Pete scoffed, leering down at Millie-Jayne's now exposed lower half, as Larry peeled away the ruined denim shorts.

Larry sniggered and was about to pull Millie-Jane's panties off, when he saw Jo's head go flying off to the left, and thud off a lone car. The bloody stump left a print on the driver's side window, as it ricocheted off the glass, before thumping to the floor.

"What the…?" Julie was about to say, before her words were cut short. Gill-man buried his axe into the woman's chest, right between her breasts. The thing grunted and growled as it tried to free his axe, putting one foot in the woman's guts, and pushing her backward as it pulled.

The axe head came loose of Julie's ribcage and dripped flesh and blood. Julie fell backwards and landed on top of Larry, pinning the guy to the floor and rendering him helpless, but giving Millie-Jane her chance to break free and make a run for it.

She had just enough time to see Pete grab a bottle from the floor and use it as a safeguard against the creature, but his wet sounding screams told Millie-Jane that the man's weapon of choice was no match for the wood splintering tool, and that he'd come off the worst for choosing to arm himself, rather than make a run for it.

The sounds from behind her made her skin crawl, as she neared the ramp down to level seven. Her feet began to burn and sting, and she suspected that the rough surface and numerous objects that lay hidden on the floor had bitten into the softness of her soles along the way.

But she didn't let that slow her. She needed to get to safety, and fast, and the only place which seemed to offer any form of safety was on the lower level. There had to be a guard station down there somewhere, but first she would need to get down there.

Finding no trouble on the seventh floor, Millie-Jane slowed her run to a hobble, as her knees ached and screamed out for a rest. At the ramp down to level six, she stopped and caught her breath, to figure out her next move. Maybe arming myself would be wise? she thought.

What the hell with, though?

She looked about her and found a stone close to her right foot. She picked it up and found that the rock fit snugly into her palm. Swiping the air with it a few times, Millie-Jane was happy that the thing would brain her attacker enough to cause some serious damage. A hefty blow might not kill it but would be enough to knock him out.

The skin around its face and skull looked so tough, though. What if it can't be killed? What if…

Her thoughts trailed off on hearing that sound once more, the sound of scraping… Of metal against concrete, which came from somewhere above. Above, and close by, all at the same time. It seemed to be all around her. Around her and in the darkness. Where was he?

"Stop it", she told herself aloud. "Scaring myself isn't going to do any good," she scolded herself. Then she saw him.

He stood at the other end of the level she was on, his figure a mere outline. Then he was gone, swallowed by the darkness once again, causing her heart to thunder against her ribs and glue her to the spot.

"Shit."

Then that God-awful snigger-hiss filled her ears, as it reverberated off the walls around her. It teased her brain, which in turn filled her with dread. She shook and gripped the rock tighter.

I'm going to die tonight, she thought.

My body never found.

I'll end up as another missing person, my photo…

Stop it. I can't think like that, she thought.

Running down the ramp to the next level, Millie kept on going, and soon neared the exit to the next level. As she approached it, she was pulled from behind by her hair, causing her to let out a squeal measured by half surprise and half terror.

She dropped the rock, as her body was pulled to the ground.

"Shut up, bitch," the voice rasped. A foul-smelling hand clamped over her mouth. She could smell piss and alcohol on the skin. "What the fuck is that thing?"

The voice was now familiar to her. It was Larry's. She never thought she'd be glad to see the scumbag who tried to rape her, back in her company, but some things were worse than others, and now she at least had him to help her out of this mess.

She ripped his hand away from her mouth, as she drove an elbow into his guts. The man left out an "Oooof," and blew stinking air out of his mouth.

"Touch me again, motherfucker, and I'll rip your balls off," Millie-Jane told him. "I tried to warn you guys about that fucking thing," she said, letting her anger die off when she realised Larry still had his flick-knife.

"Hey, there's no need to hit me," he whispered. "Or threaten…"

Millie-Jane got right into his face, her gums pulled back over her teeth. "You tried to rape me, you dirty fuck. For that, I should feed you to him. But unlike you and your band of fucked up 'tards, I'm not like that. Count yourself lucky, arsehole."

"I…I…"

"Save it, dickhead. Let's just concentrate on getting down to the bottom floor, so we can get the hell out of here."

His eyes lit up. "I can get us down there real fast. Me and Pete have been sleeping rough in this place for years."

"And you've never seen this maniac before tonight?!"

"No. Never."

"Then where the hell has it come from?" Larry just shrugged his shoulders, unable to form an answer for her question. "Just get us down to the bottom level. We can't stand around here gabbing all night.

Finding the rock, Millie-Jane once again filled her palm and let Larry lead the way down to the fifth level. They didn't hear a sound as they entered the next level, until Larry's wheezy voice cracked the silence, like a whip would the air.

"Maybe it's crawled back into the hole it came out of, girlie?"

"Keep your fucking voice down," Millie-Jane snapped. She could just about make out his facial features and see his eyes boring into her from the darkness. Her semi-nakedness didn't bother her right now. Living was more important.

"I was just saying, is all. Fuck me. Who do you think ya are, speaking to King Larry tha' way, bitch? I should gut ya." He prodded her in the shoulder time and again. "Well?"

"I'm not going to argue with you, Larry. Let's just get the hell out of here."

"Huh, you don't want to argue. Cute."

"That's right," she said coldly. Help me escape, and I'll keep your attempt at rape and murder from the police."

"I should have had my way with ya when I had the chance. I should…"

She turned on him fiercely, and grabbed him by the throat, the rock a few inches from his face. She spoke rapidly and low through clenched teeth. "You keep fucking with me, and I'll break you face with this rock, you little prick." For the first time, Millie-Jane saw all the blood that decorated the degenerate's face.

It was the remainder of Jo, Julie and her ol' pal Pete, no doubt.

"I'm sorry," Larry said.

"I was beginning to think a worthless piece of shit such as yourself was incapable of such humanities to apologise, Larry."

"I…" he lowered his head, and Millie-Jane instantly felt sorry for him. Even though he'd tried to do what he had, she could still find room in her heart to forgive this wretch of a man.

"Look," she said, putting a hand to his arm. "Let's just get the hell out of here, okay? We can discuss this at a more convenient time."

He nodded, and they moved on, keeping low as they slunk along the bowels of the building. Soon they were at the ramp down to level four, and all had been silent. No attack seemed to be impending. The low sound of scraping and hissing had even appeared to have ceased.

"Maybe he has given up and crawled back into his hole?" Millie-Jane offered.

"Chance would be a fine thing," Larry said.

"Wait," she said.

"Wha' now?"

"Don't you hear that?"

Larry stood there, his eyes scrunched up as he tried to listen as hard as he could. He shook his head. "Hear what, girlie?"

It was close. Whatever it was, it was on top of them. The noise was like that of a crisp packet being rustled.

"That!" Millie-Jane said.

"I…" Larry started, but soon stopped. He heard the noise Millie-Jane was on about, which was now mixed with a cheery whistle.

"Here," she said in a hushed voice, pulling Larry into the shadows and behind a pillar with her. "When he shows himself, we'll bash his brains in with this," she continued in a whisper, showing Larry the rock.

A beam of light cut through the darkness, making Millie-Jane's gut sink. *He has a light now? How much help in finding me does that fucker want?* she thought. As the light grew stronger, indicating the thing's approach, she got ready to strike out by lifting her rock hand high. *I'll get him to the ground and keep on hitting him.*

Peeking from behind the concrete, Millie-Jane saw not the lizard-thing who had been stalking her behind the flashlight, but a guard. A guard that stood at well over six feet tall; his navy-blue jacket bearing the emblem of the company he worked for. His hat lay slightly crooked on top of his head. The tune he whistled showed him to be in a chipper mood.

Dropping the rock, Millie-Jane showed herself, the light catching her in the face.

"Hey!" the man yelled. "What are you doing up here? You can't be here."

Even though he had his voice raised, he didn't sound angry or threatening. Millie-Jane gasped, and tears spilled down her eye. She rasped, "You have to help us. Please!" Her shoulders jumped as she crumpled and staggered forward into the guard.

"Wow," he said, almost losing his hold on the torch as he caught her. "What the hell is going on here?" he asked, though it was not Millie-Jane who answered, but Larry, as he stepped from the hiding place.

"We got some psycho killer on our hands," he said, trying to keep his voice as low as possible. "We need to get outta here, son, and bloody quick about it, too."

"Who the hell are you?" the guard asked.

"He's with me," Millie-Jane said. "You have to listen to us. We're not lying, damn it. There is a killer loose in this building."

The guard looked down at Millie-Jane and their eyes fused.

"I have been here all night, and I have not heard a single…" he was about to say, but Larry cut him off.

"Well, you ain't got the best set of peepers or ears on ya, son."

"What the hell is that supposed to mean?" the guard snapped, his chiseled face looking hard and pissed off.

"Didn't you hear that explosion on the floor above, hmm? And what about all the screaming and hullabaloo that's been going on – it hasn't actually been like a library around here, son!"

"There's been nothing on my monitors downstairs. We have cameras all over this place. If a rat took a fart, we'd know about it," the guard said. "Now, if you two don't leave quietly, I'm going to be forced to call the police…"

"Good! That's exactly what we want you to do," Millie-Jane said, pushing herself away from the man.

"Look, I've seen no signs of anything going on here tonight. Just you two, who haven't even told me why you're here at this hour – the car park's been closed for hours."

"I woke up here," Millie-Jane confessed. "I fell asleep on the top floor."

"Asleep?" the guard said, sounding disgusted.

"Look, Mike," Millie-Jane said, snapping at the guard and seeing his nametag for the first time. "I don't give a shit what you believe, but if we keep standing around here chit-chatting, we're going to get fucking butchered. Now I say we…"

The scream from behind her almost stopped her heart, and not just her words. Turning, she saw Larry being suspended from the air, his whole body shaking. Blood pissed down his dirty trouser leg and trickled out of the loose cuff. It formed a neat pool below him. His intestines hung from him in fat, bloody ropes. Jutting from his gut was a crimson-coloured axe head.

She yelled until her lungs burned and felt as though they were going to pop within her.

"Holy fuck!" Mike said, as he stepped from behind Millie-Jane, and clubbed the thing which held Larry in the air.

The show of strength by the thing for Millie-Jane was almost, if not the most terrifying, aspect of the whole grizzly display. Staggering backwards, she couldn't take her eyes off the scene which unfolded in front of her.

Mike whacked and whacked at the thing's skull before it finally dropped its axe and Larry along with it. The torch crumpled on the final blow, which plunged the car park back into darkness.

"Run!" Mike screamed. "Get down to the first floor and see my colleagues down there. They will help you."

"Come with me," Millie-Jane protested, as she watched Mike unclip a set of handcuffs from his belt.

Looking down at the unconscious thing, Mike decided to leave well alone. "Okay," he said. Grabbing Millie-Jane by the arm, he turned her around and headed for the ramp down to the next floor. He unclasped his walkie-talkie and started talking rapidly into the device.

"Chris? Chris, do you read me? Chris. Chris, Chris, goddamn it, answer. Chris?!" Devon? Devon, do you read me? Devon?!"

"There's no point," Millie-Jane said, her tone sombre. "They're probably dead, just like everyone else is in this place."

"Hey, don't say shit like that. I've known those guys downstairs for eight years of my life. What the hell is that thing, anyway?"

"I've no idea. I just woke up and found myself trapped in this nightmare, being pursued by something which looks like it belongs on the set of a Boris Karloff film," Millie-Jane said, looking over at Mike, but not seeing his face due to the darkness.

"Let's just get to my guys," he said.

Soon they were at the ramp leading down to level 1. Nothing moved. No cars could be seen. This level was somewhat darker than the previous ones – as though they were in the basement.

"Mike, I'm scared," she said, walking beside the large security guard. She had an urge to lock her arm around his.

"We're almost there, just another floor to drop," he said, unclasping his walkie-talkie once again. "Chris, Devon! Do you read me?" he snapped into the mouthpiece. "Where the fuck are they?" he asked himself.

"Something is seriously wrong, Mike. Where did it come from?"

"I have no idea," he said. "I've been working this lot for ten years, and not once have I seen a bout of trouble, not even from the tramps."

"Can't you raise an S.O.S on your walkie-talkie?" she asked, hopefully.

"No, they're jammed. We can only use them within this building, I'm afraid."

"Damn it!" she said, throwing her arms into the air dramatically.

"I know, the thought had crossed my mind, but then I remembered the jamming."

"Why would your company do that?!"

"Because some dickhead a few years ago tried ordering a pizza through his talkie," he said.

She couldn't tell if he was joking or not, but she didn't find it amusing, one way or the other.

"Fuck's sake," she huffed.

"Chris, Devon?!" Mike continued.

"Look, they're not there, Mike. You're wasting your time, and, not to mention, giving our fucking position away!" she rasped.

"Sorry," he said, his tone hushed.

Since the incident involving Larry a couple of floors up, they hadn't heard or seen anything of the lizard-man, she thought. Where was he lurking? The prospect of him hiding in the shadows ahead made her skin crawl.

Perhaps he's already at the guard station, she continued musing. That's probably why Mike's co-workers are not answering him. They've been taken down! Stop it, she scolded herself. No, but it makes sense. He's not going to allow any of us to leave this place. He's probably loitering close to the entrance.

That's where I would go.

"Are you alright?" he asked her.

"Fine," she said, curtly.

"It's just…"

"What?"

"You went quiet," he said.

"Shh! I was just thinking, that's all," she whispered.

After a few minutes of walking, they were at the next ramp. On that floor, a massive sign with a G on it graced one wall. Again, nothing moved; no cars, no people. The odd scrap of rubbish blew in the wind.

Ahead, a massive office stood before them. It was lit-up like a Christmas tree. A beacon of safety. Before Millie-

Jane could make a bolt for the haven, Mike threw an arm across her chest.

"Wait!" he hissed. "Not so fast. He could be down here, waiting for us."

"But your office is right there, Mike. If we run…"

"No, he could cut us down easily."

"But we'd see him – there isn't many hiding places down here. There's little shadow due to the light coming from your office."

"Yeah, but still," Mike said, turning his head from left to right, right to left. He swept the area, making absolutely sure it was safe to move. "Come on," he told her, leading the way.

With each pillar and shadowed nook they passed, Millie-Jane held her breath, only releasing it when they were clear of danger.

Looking behind her, she saw the path they had travelled was clear. As they got closer to Mike's workstation, sounds could be heard. A TV, or possibly a radio, was playing. It was the first welcoming and friendly sounds she'd heard all night, apart from Mike's appearance.

"Just a few more steps," he said, getting his keys prepared.

"What are you doing?" she asked.

"Making sure I have the door key ready," he said.

"Wouldn't it be open, especially if the other two are inside?" she asked.

"No, by law we have to keep it closed and locked at all times."

As they edged closer, they noticed one of the lifts was active. It was dropping from the third floor.

They watched, as the little, red light above the metal carriage turned from three to two to one…

"It's him!" she said, breaking into a run.

"Wait!" he yelled, giving chase.

She hit the door first, just as the lift reached the bottom floor. Her breath caught in her throat as the doors began to slide open. Slamming her fists against the office door, Millie-Jane screamed. "Let us in, let us in!" she demanded.

As the doors to the elevator opened completely, Mike came to a halt. Looking, he burst into a laugh, which caused Millie-Jane to stop what she was doing. They both looked at the empty carriage.

"What…?" Millie-Jane said, turning to look at Mike.

"I can't believe we thought he…"

"Behind you, Mike!" she yelled.

Turning, Mike had just enough time to dodge the axe. The cutting tool smashed into the concrete. "Bastard!" Mike yelled, giving the thing the hardest punch in the face he could muster.

It was hard enough to send the thing to ground. Its axe crashed to the floor beside it. "Here," Mike called to Millie-Jane, throwing her the keys. "It's the gold one. Get inside and call the…Araagh!" he screamed, as the thing grabbed his calve and squeezed.

Its talons tore through Mike's trouser leg and ripped into his flesh. "Do it!" he managed to bark at her, before turning his attention back to the thing on the floor. Using his free foot, he stamped at the hand around his leg.

"Get. The. Fuck. Off!" she heard Mike yell, as she slammed a key into the lock of the door.

It didn't budge. "It's not fucking working!" she yelled.

"The…gold…one," she heard him struggle.

Had he told me that the first time? she thought. She couldn't remember. Taking the wrong key out of the lock, she went to put the right one in, but dropped them. "Shit!" she yelled. "Fuck, fuck, fuck," she continued, getting to her knees. "Where are they?" she said to herself, as she scrabbled about in the dim light.

"What are you doing!" Mike asked. "Get in there. Now!"

Millie-Jane watched as the thing got to its feet and wrapped its grotesquely huge hands around Mike's thick neck. Before the guard could prise the fingers away, the talons dug deep. Veins popped and burst red. He screamed, which quickly turned to a painful-sounding gargle.

The thing growled and hissed, as it tore its pray apart.

Whimpering, Millie-Jane found the keys and scooped them off the floor.

The right key missed its mark once, twice, three times, before it finally found the snug slit. Turning the key as fast as she could, she shoved the door open with her shoulder, which was a ton weight.

As she closed the door behind her, the thing slammed against the glass. Turning the key in the lock, she screamed at it – "It's fucking shatter-proof, arsehole!" Collapsing to her knees, she started to cry, as the thing continued to pound and pound and pound at the glass.

It even tried to break in by using the axe.

"Ha-ha," she blubbered on hearing it grunt and groan at its failed attempts.

Looking about the office, she found Chris and Devon. One, not knowing which, was sat in a leather chair. His head was missing. A cup of steaming coffee stood in front of him. The walls and cabinets about him dripped red.

The other officer lay in a pool of his own blood. His head was intact, but his back and sides displayed chop wounds. Massive chunks of his flesh were missing, along with an eyeball. His arms were stretched out in front of him. Just beyond his fingertips lay a bunch of keys.

Looking at the phone, Millie-Jane could see the wires had been viciously pulled out of its back.

She continued to sob, as she lay slumped on the floor. "It's over," she murmured to herself. "It's finally over…"

A loud rumble woke her from her sleep. How long have I been out? Was it all just a dream? She asked herself, looking about with bleary eyes. Noticing she was still in the office, she groaned, before getting slowly to her feet.

The grumble she had heard was the main roller door to the car park. It was slowly rising, letting in the brilliance of the sun. "It must be on a timer," she said out loud.

Looking through the glass in the door, she noticed her attacker walking away from her. It was heading up the ramp to level 1A. Breathing a sight of relief, she opened the office door and walked out.

It was whistling, but she couldn't make out the tune. It had its axe in its hand. Before it fully walked out of her life, it gave her a wave.

A chill flashed through her, but she didn't stop it from letting her walk out into the sun.

It's over, she thought. Really over.

"I made it…"

Bad Apple

The Golden Apple Award was going to be John's this year. It was a dead sure winner with his killer recipe. Runner up was no good this time. Top spot was to be his. During a midnight tasting session a week before the contest, John's opponents demanded the secret ingredient. "HOHO, deadly nightshade," he chortled as they fell before him.

Buried Treasure

Martin stopped at the next moss covered stone, his shovel ready, the swag bag full. The grizzled granite bore the name of the person under it, and immediately he began to dig. His spade revealed wood – he dove in – lifting the creaking, putrid lid. The rotting cadaver lunges at him discharging rancid words: "Your money or your life!"

About Your Author

David Owain Hughes is a word-slinger of horror and crime fiction, who grew up on trashy b-movies from the age of five which helped rapidly instil in him a vivid imagination. He's had multiple short stories published in various online magazines and anthologies, along with articles, reviews and interviews. He's written for *This Is Horror*, *Blood Magazine*, and *Horror Geeks Magazine*.

Hughes is the author of six horror novels, four short story collections and a plethora of novellas. Although he predominately writes within the bracket of horror and its multiple sub-genres, he's recently branched out into crime fiction and is slowly carving out a superb series of crime/noir thrillers under the umbrella title of *South Wales*.

https://www.facebook.com/DOHughesAuthor/?ref=hl

http://www.amazon.co.uk/David-Owain-Hughes/e/B00L708P2M/ref=sr_ntt_srch_lnk_3?qid=1458241417&sr=1-3

http://david-owain-hughes.wix.com/horrorwriter

https://www.goodreads.com/author/show/4877205.David_Owain_Hughes

https://twitter.com/DOHUGHES32

Other HellBound Books Titles

Available at: www.hellboundbookspublishing.com

Man Eating F*cks

A dark, incredibly entertaining excursion into the delightfully twisted imagination of David Owain Hughes....

An average teenage girl and her father find themselves caught up in a brutal nightmare at their local recreational centre, when an age-old enemy comes stumbling out of the woods to crash a heavy-metal gig; a gig that has all the promises of being killer. This is one blood-soaked gig you won't want to miss!

Praise for Man-Eating F*cks from Ty Schwamberger (author of The Fields, Deep Dark Woods & The Death of a Horror Writer.) *"Man Eating F*cks is old school horror, but with a new, blood-soaked twist! David Owain Hughes effectively creates enjoyable and lethal characters in this tale that is sure to keep you up at night. This is the type of tale that you need to read with a light on…I'm serious. You better put your seatbelt on 'cause you're in for one helluva ride. Look out, Hughes might very well be headed to the major leagues after this twisted tale! Highly recommended!"*

Man Eating F*ckers

The eagerly awaited sequel to Hughes' critically acclaimed _Man Eating Fks_...**

Two years on from her nightmarish descent into the woods, Storm is piecing her life back together, but trouble is forming...

A new threat is rising - one that promises to grip, shake and spin Storm's world out of control. But that's not all, as a 'friend' and sympathizer also poses a risk from the shadows, combined with a face from the past...

With the cannibals lurking in the background, waiting for an opportunity to deal white-hot vengeance, can father and daughter survive?

**** Features a bonus, previously unpublished short story by David Owain Hughes****

Man-Eating Fucks: The Legacy

Displace everything you thought you knew about the Man-Eating F**ks and get ready for the truth, as the saga goes full circle in this past vs. present tale of blood-dripping carnage.

The cannibals are back, and they're bigger, meaner, stronger, and out for gut-wrenching revenge on the one person who destroyed their family: Storm.

And with the financial backing from a mysterious cult and the devil himself, the F**ks aren't going to let anything, or anyone, get in their way of seeking absolute domination.

Buckle up for some bone-crunching horror, as the stakes just got raised.

Puckered

Percy is kinky.
Percy is perverted.
Percy is a loner.
Percy is sneaky…

…But most of all, Percy wants to be left alone.

Whether it be a nagging mother or something from his past, it feels like he is always trying to escape something. Will he be able to find his own peace, or will the real world catch up to him?

There will be blood.
There will be s**t.
There will be unusual sexual kinks.
But most of all, there will be murder…

Psychological Breakdown

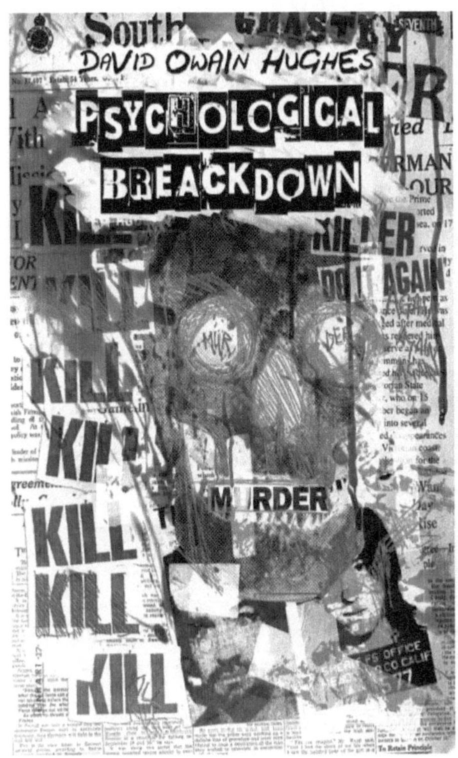

Within this tome lies eighteen tales of mind-bending terror, as Hughes delves into the human psyche and dishes out stories of what becomes of the broken minded, spirited and downright irked.

Part these blood-drenched pages at your own peril, for you will find diseased minds geared towards revenge and bloody chaos, with a few twists, turns and surprises thrown in for good, fucked-up measures.

Keep the lights on!

Cold Cocked

Another exemplary bizarro novella from the great and incredibly disturbed minds behind 'Puckered'!

Betty is sexy. Betty is scarred. Betty is an outsider. Betty is a genius…

…But most of all, Betty wants recognition.

Whether it be a controlling mother or ghosts from her past, it feels like she is always trying to please someone. Will she be able to find her own peace, or will the real world catch up to her?

There will be blood.
There will be j**z.
There will be unusual sexual releases.

But most of all, there will be murder…

A HellBound Books LLC
Publication

http://www.hellboundbookspublishing.com

Printed in the United States of America